THE SILENT SAVANT

D. P. Macbeth

ISBN- 978-0-9911172-4-6

Library of Congress Control Number 2025915704

Cover by: Caligrahics
Printed in the United States of America

ACKNOWLEDGMENT

The author thanks Linda Seibold Macbeth and Heather Wilcauskas for their suggestions.

*In honor of all those who devote their spirit
and their skills to helping others.*

ONE

Archer T. Zane had long anticipated these few private hours in his high rise Manhattan office. He'd been up since five, his customary rising time, showered, shaved, dressed and ready to greet his driver when he arrived to transport him into the city. The Saturday morning traffic was light. Now, just after seven, he removed the jacket of his immaculately tailored gray suit and hung it in a closet. The suit, together with formal white shirt, blue tie, matching handkerchief, 18-karat gold cufflinks and cordovan shoes would be his attire for the wedding.

At noon, Kip Emerson, Zane's protégé, would marry a young woman who, a year earlier, was at the center of a mystery that united a group of previously unconnected people. Zane delighted in Kip's joy, the kind of light-hearted happiness that finding the love of one's life delivers. He often marveled at the events of the past year and the way everything had changed. Rebecca, the bride-to-be, and Edna, Lacey, Dale, Cletus and Sheena were the people who now formed the nucleus of Zane's new endeavors. He had never felt such optimism for his future. The thought of Edna, in particular, brought a smile to his face. They were dating. She would arrive at eleven to accompany him to the wedding. He, a sixty-seven year old divorced workaholic who hadn't thought of romance in twenty years and she, a decade younger. No matter.

He swiveled in his chair to face his computer. After hitting a few keys a file opened. Nothing to see on the screen except volume controls. This file was a recording. He'd planned these hours before the wedding in just this way, to revisit the words of Samuel Jones. He had not listened to them since shortly after the young man passed away. Now, because Samuel was the catalyst for Zane's new life, the lawyer wanted to hear them again.

Apart from preparing complicated wills and trusts for his wealthier clients, Zane had little experience with death. He'd attended plenty of funeral services; relatives, friends, clients, but throughout his life had carefully avoided direct exposure to the dying or the moment of their death. He supposed that many people were like him. The unknown is terrifying. Edna changed his attitude. Through her, he now understood the benefits of hospice and palliative care during the final weeks and days of life. He'd been aware of the terms and vaguely knew their meaning. Still, his aversion to death, his fear of it, kept him at a distance.

Edna was a skilled nurse. When he met her she managed an unusual hospice home in Queens, serving the the indigent and those with no family or friends to care. After his terminal diagnosis, Samuel Jones was brought to that home and through Edna's kind sensitivity and determination, Zane smiled again, the recordings he was about to hear were revealed.

His mind wandered to the meeting he'd hosted ten months earlier. The conference room down the hall had been elegantly set for a luncheon six weeks after Samuel's death. Zane greeted the arriving guests, escorting each to the table with a smile of welcome. Wine was served, selected from Zane's cellar, his very best. Three courses were consumed over an hour's time followed by coffee and tea. Some at the table had not met so introductions were made. The purpose of the meeting, other than to reveal the philanthropic pursuits made possible by Samuel Jones, was anticipated by all. At the right moment Zane stood.

"I will dispense with the reading of Samuel's will. Those of you who are mentioned in its contents have received a copy. Questions have been answered and the details worked out. Also, all of you have received a recording. The voice is Samuel's and, as his attorney, he gave me permission to share his words with you.

"He tells the story of our individual roles in the last twelve years of his life. He is speaking to a young girl he calls Dollface, a woman sitting among us." Zane turned his eyes upon each person, mentioning them by name. "Rebecca Williams, Lacey Williams,

Cletus and Sheena Brown, Crystal Singleton, Dale Messenger, Edna Nieves, Ellis Dorman, myself, we meant something to him. He most certainly means something to us. I am also pleased that His Eminence, Cardinal John Wolfkawitz can be with us today."

A picture of Cletus and Sheena Brown came into Zane's mind. "Sheena was the first to contact me and suggest that we all come together. Then Crystal made a similar request. 'I'd like to say something about him,' she told me. 'To people who knew him and will understand.'

"I, too, want to express my thoughts about this remarkable young man who affected me in ways my legal mind can't quite rationalize. My fellow attorney, Kip Emerson, tells me the same. There is something unusual that has transpired through our mutual associations with Samuel. The whys and hows are mysterious, but it feels fated, new life directions that have come into reality because of him. All of you supported our coming together today. Most of you told me you also had a few words to say. What a testament to this quiet man who, without speaking directly to most of us, touched us so deeply that we must come together to remember him.

"As a prelude, let me describe the endeavors most of us will pursue under the terms of Samuel's will. He left a valuable legacy, financially promising and destined to serve those in our society who need it most. For my part, he has given purpose to my retirement. The formerly uncertain path of my remaining years is now clear and exciting.

Among his wishes," Zane recalled looking at Edna, "is the establishment of a unique non-profit hospice and palliative care enterprise to be designed, supervised and operated by Mrs. Nieves. It will serve those who have no place and no one to care for them during the last weeks and days of their lives. In time, as the promise of Samuel's financial legacy is fulfilled, we will grow this enterprise and make it the best it can be for all who need it. Mrs. Nieves will ensure that it operates with the most sensitive practices so that the final days of all who come under its care are peaceful, as painfree as possible and imbued with compassion.

"Cletus and Sheena Brown," he gestured toward the couple

seated nearest to him, "will establish a foster care program in Chicago. Kip Emerson," he nodded toward Kip sitting next to Rebecca, "will chair its Board of Directors, Chicago business leaders and philanthropists who are all clients of the Zane law firm. They will guarantee the financial security of Mr. and Mrs. Brown's endeavor so it, too, may expand regionally and perhaps more."

Turning to Rebecca and Lacey he announced, "Ms. Williams will open a school dedicated to orphaned children with special needs. She will be joined in its management and administration by her adopted daughter, Lacey, after Lacey has completed her studies at Columbia University. This school is to be funded by my friend and longtime client Ellis Dorman of Blossom Enterprises." He pointed to Dorman who smiled and nodded. "Though private, it will not discriminate. All children in need, no matter their physical, emotional or intellectual challenges will be welcomed. In time, if the instructional concepts developed by Ms. Williams prove to be successful, more schools will be opened as far and wide as financially possible.

"Finally," he turned to Dale Messenger seated next to Edna. "Mr. Messenger has joined with the Archdiocese of New York to establish a center for military veterans devoted to the treatment of Post-Traumatic Stress Disorder. Cardinal Wolfkawitz has endorsed this effort, putting his considerable influence to work, ensuring that it will be on a sound footing with all the resources necessary.

"Our hospice enterprise, Mr. and Mrs. Brown's foster care program, Ms. William's school and the collaboration between Mr. Messenger and the Archdiocese will each bear Samuel's name."

Zane smiled as he remembered Lacey's enthusiastic whoop, clapping her hands and igniting the others. It was followed by raised glasses in toast. He recalled his next words.

"We have come together today to recall our memories of Samuel. We know the quality of his intellect and his character. And, we know he has united us and given clearer meaning to our lives.

"I have rarely dwelt upon the spiritual. I regard myself as a practical man, accepting of the random occurrences of life. Now, I am forced to wonder. The connection we have to one another, through

Samuel, does not appear random." Zane paused and looked at the faces around the table. "There is no format, no special order. I open the floor to anyone who cares to speak."

His mind returned to the present. He looked at the keyboard, pressed enter and adjusted the volume. Then he sat back, closed his eyes and listened.

TWO

Terminally ill patients often devote thought and conversation to an evaluation of the life they've led. I have learned to listen. A lesson in living for me - Edna Nieves

I ain't no idiot. You seen inta me, you heared me an you knowed. An I seen inta you. How long's it bin? You don' know, but I does. Twelve years, seven months an thirteen days, talkin' now. Talkin', that's 'nother 'sprise. Not ta you, but everone else for sure. I quit afta momma don' come home no more. I don' talk ta no one 'cept you.

Know where I be? Layin' on a bed in a ol' house. It ain't far from that residence in Jamaica, Queens where you come readin' ta the little kids. You, I gotta figure, is maybe livin' out where you go afta I don' see you no more, California. Married maybe. I bin thinkin' on that an on you a long time. Comin' ta the end like I'm doin' git me ta wondrin' on maybe all the thinkin' gotta come out. So, if you is married wit kids an all, I ain't tryin' ta git in the way. I jus' wanna talk 'bout my twelve years a thinkin' on you. That's all.

I got a recorder like ya sees in them store windows in the city showin' all kinda 'lectric stuff. Afta I come inta this house I make myself use it like now, layin' in this bed. A course, I ony talk if I 'member stuff good. It git hard afta them seizures. Them times I gotta stop afore I miss out on 'membrin somethin' 'portant. Feelin' okay right now.

I bin here near a week. It ain't no big special place. Jus a ol' house wit peoples like me waitin' on dyin'. I heared the word hospice outta them ladies comin' 'round wit flowers an such. God lovin' man come a coupla times, too. Bein' I don' talk they jus' move stuff 'round,

6

watchin' me layin' here. They ain't mean. Jus' peoples tryin' ta make dyin' good wit flowers an talkin' like they care 'bout me. I hears'em, but I ain't showin' I git what they say. 'Cept for Edna. She a nurse an she do the hard parts them other peoples kin't. I got my ear open for them comin' down the hall. Then I hide this recorder. Talkin' ta you ony be for me.

I heared the word 'obsession' on TV. Some guy followin' a woman an givin'er no peace. I think it fit me, but not in a bad way like that guy. See, you never knowed I bin thinkin' on you all these years. You never seen me agin' afta goin' ta California. So, you ain't never bin put inta no place where you gotta be afeared a me. An I would'na bin like that guy. No way. Not me. So, me bein' like that ain't bad. It coulda gone differnt if we seen each other agin. I tried makin' that happin but Cletus lied ta me. I ain't sure. I mean 'bout me makin' you afeared if I seen you like I tried. Maybe you woulda 'membered me an maybe you woulda liked me cuz a them kisses. 'Member? If not, I woulda knowed an leaved you be.

Nice thing 'bout this room is bein' by myself most a the time. Jus' this bed an me. No sharin' like in the residence over ta Jamaica, Queens afore Cletus an me git outta there. That house them twelve years back where you come readin' ta the little kids in the aftanoon. My sleepin' place in that house was all crowded, crammed inta bunks wit no place ta put clothes an stuff. I was happy ta git outta there, 'specially afta I knowed you ain't never comin' back. 'Cept for Lacey. I'll git ta her.

This ol' house got some kinda steam heat wit a lotta clankin' comin' up the pipe. It git so loud it come onta this recorder. I pay 'tention so it don' mess up the words I wanna say. December an cold outside. Snowed two days back an snowin' agin this mornin'. Christmas comin'. I don' hope I make it ta then, but I wonders on it.

'Course you ain't never gonna hear this. I knows that an I want you ta know I knows. Else you might think I'm crazy. Peoples allays figurin' me for crazy. Maybe you knowed it ain't true, but twelve years kinda git stuff mixed up. I don' know where you is an I don' know who you is no more, married, kids an such an maybe a differnt way a thinkin' an no thinkin' on me t'all. The girl I knowed ain't the one you is no more. So, this jus' be a way a passin' time 'til I don' wake up no more.

We was both seventeen, 'member? You don' know what happin ta make me go livin' in that residence over ta Jamaica, Queens so I gonna start there. Afta I tell you maybe it all come on bein' clear ta me cuz, a course, you ain't gonna hear it so it ain't like it gotta be clear ta you.

My daddy be a boxer once. He talk 'bout it alls a time. He musta bin good wit his fists, but momma say he don' allays win an somethin' got'm kicked outta the ring right afta I got born. I be ten when she din' come home no more. Then it jus' be him an me an we stop bein' happy.

I goes ta school down the street, PS 0875. Most a the time them kids talkin' an foolin' 'round an keepin' the teacher from makin' teachin' work. But it come easy ta me, the learnin' part. I got me a place at the second desk in the second row an no one never try on takin' it 'way from me. I weren't no big kid, but I knowed how ta punch like my daddy show me. An he got a name on the street, too. They all knowed what happin if I git a hard time. They din' need ta know I ain't tellin' daddy nothin'. They din' need ta know it woulda bin worse for me.

I din' learn nothin' inside a PS 0875 'cept how ta git what I wanna know somewheres else. Readin' come first an afta I knowed there be a place wit a lotta books I jus' let the days go by in the second chair a the second row. Then at 2:45 I scat outta that buildin' an down the street, livin' the rest a the day in the public library. I got the letters an how to read'em from Miss Parsons so I gotta be wrong 'bout learnin' nothin' at PS 0875, but that be all.

One book a day, I go readin' an it weren't hard an it weren't somethin' I din' like doin'. At the end, jus afore I quit PS 0875 an daddy git me onta the street wit my own clients... like that? Clients? Nice clean word ta pretty up what we was doin', ...I go readin' a coupla books a day. Anythin' that catch my eye. Library a nice place; quiet, clean an a lotta books. I got me a special place there, too. Second table, second chair from the end aside the big window. I 'member ever word outta ever book I git offa them stacks.

An somethin' else, I gotta be the ony one ever gittin' some a them books down cuz some a them pages ain't cut an I gotta run my knife atween'em ta git'em open so I kin read ever word. Them books be real old an the cover don' tell nothin' 'bout the inside. That be the best part, findin' out.

I din' jus' read make believe stuff, neither. Over t'other side a that library got books wit poems an essays jus' as ol' an jus' as never opened an I like'em cuz a that. Sittin' there quiet, readin', bein' warm, not thinkin' on daddy yellin' an comin' ta hit me – I knowed I be lucky.

Thirteen, I quit on school afta seventh grade. Nothin' differnt over them years, same place everday, library afta. Daddy pushin' me ta git onta the street wit'm. He weren't no businessman, but he got hisself a piece a sidewalk sellin' an he git me ta hep'm git more sidewalk. His way a makin' it happin? A quick punch, knockin' me silly. Like I tol' you, he a boxer an he knowed jus' how ta do it so there weren't no mark. How much punchin' afta momma don' come home no more? Lots an lots. I gotta take it cuz I ain't got no place ta go. He be mad alls a time. I jus' be sad.

Four years, rain, snow, standin' on the sidewalk waitin' on cars ta stop. I got my place near them bodegas. Street corner hustle an a lotta cars comin' ta me. Nice ones, too. Daddy pushin' heroin. He gimme pills, powder an crack. We go sellin' 'til 'round four in the mornin', walk back to our buildin', count the cash, eat somethin' an go ta sleep. Out agin in the aftanoon. I don' know what he done wit all the money. I git a hunnerd ever week on Sunday an he go off ta meet for gittin' next week's supply. He don' make me work them Sundays an he don' come home on them days, neither.

It come apart on a Saturday night two days afta I come on bein' seventeen. Car comin' 'round for a coupla nights, slowin' down an eyein' me on the corner. Six brownies inside an they don' go lookin' away afta I seen'em. Shoulda knowed. I din' tell daddy 'bout'em, neither. I shoulda. 'Bout ten on that Saturday night them brownies stop the car an come out. Ta right now I don' know why I din' run. One of 'em come quick an I pop him like daddy showed me, in the throat an he go down suckin' hard for air. I don' 'member nothin' afta 'til daddy come pickin' me offa the sidewalk, swearin' loud. See, them brownies took my pockets an he git real mad. He shoutin' in my ears an shakin' me 'til he gotta stop cuz peoples comin' outta them bodegas lookin'. So, he carry me inta the alley ahind the Mexican restaurant. I weren't nothin' ta my daddy.

"Where it at?" He yellin', me still seein' lights in my eyes. I don' say nothin' so he git his hands on my shoulders, standin' me on my feet. I sees the look an a fist comin' inta my face.

I wake up on a bed wit other peoples in beds in the same room, Jamaica Hospital. Nurses comin' an goin' an one of'em seen my eyes open. She come over, lookin'.

" How do you feel? What's your name?"

Nothin', I say nothin'. Doctor come afta an aks the same questions. I don' say nothin' an go ta sleep.

When I wake up a man an a woman come git me out, talkin' likes I ain't there.

"He was on the F to Jamaica, unconscious," the man sayin'.

"No ID?" She aks.

"Nothing. The report says he doesn't talk. Maybe there's something wrong with him. You know, mental or something."

I knowed right then daddy put me onta the F so nobody gonna know where I git beat-up an who done it. She come over lookin'.

"Hospital wants the bed. Orders say find a foster home."

"Fat chance," he say. "It would help to know how old he is."

I sees a pen outta her shirt pocket. I git it afore she kin stop my hand an write on my palm 17 an 3 days.

"He wrote seventeen on his hand."

"He won't be going to some family's house."

"No," she say.

"Ask him to write his name."

I write Samuel. They wait on me, but I don write no more an she take back the pen.

"I'll go call the office." She go outta the room, him shakin' his head an lookin' at me.

Afta she come back they make me git my ol' shirt an pants

an go outside inta a white van. They drops me at that residence in Jamaica, Queens an I gotta stay there 'til I make eighteen. Cletus brung me inside.

"Can't talk!" He go yellin' alls a way ta the kitchen.

He make me a peanut butter sandwich an that be how I come on bein' there afore you come readin' ta the little kids.

Maybe fifteen kids livin' in that house. Cletus call it a residence an sometimes a shelter. I be the oldest an git a sleepin' room up a bunch stairs wit three boys runnin' maybe ten ta thirteen. Them boys come an go alot cuz a learnin' how ta do stuff for afta they make eighteen an need somewheres ta go ta work. So, sometimes there ony be me in that room. I ain't talkin' so maybe they ain't lookin' ta teach me nothin' for afta I make eighteen. Alls them others was little kids, more boys than girls. Girls on the first floor an most of'em got stuff wrong wit'em. Cletus run the house an he got three peoples hepin', two ladies an a man. They split up the kids, but Cletus take me cuz a bein' the oldest, killin' time 'til I make eighteen an he kin kick me out.

He knowed I kin hear an I kin unnerstan' cuz a the lady an man who brung me. He make me work. I go washin' dishes afta eatin', cleanin' the kitchen an the big tables in the front room where the residents, we was all called that, go eatin'. Cletus do some cookin', but them two ladies done most a it 'til afta supper an they go home. The other man come at three an go workin' 'til eleven mostly fixin' stuff them little kids go breakin'. Cletus be the ony one livin' in the house alls a time.

You knowed them little kids. I don' need ta talk nothin' more on'em. 'Cept I gotta talk on Lacey cuz she got that doll wit the pretty face, lookin the way you look that first time I seen you readin' in that house. That's why I calls you Dollface. Gotta stop. Edna comin'.

Edna speaks brightly with a tray in her hands. While her patient's appetite had diminished, she noted that he accepted food more readily than others under her care. Yes, he was dying, but the last days' spiral that would smother his desire for food and drink wasn't upon him yet.

"We have chicken soup!" She places the tray on a small table beside the bed. "I have a surprise, too!" She returns to the hallway and drags an upholstered chair through the door. "You don't have to lie in that bed all day. I've found you a nice, soft chair and I'm going to put it by the window." She continues to drag it across the bedroom then settles it into position.

"C'mon now." She helps her patient get out of the bed and holds his arm as he edges to the chair and falls into it. Then she collects the tray from the table and puts it on his lap. "Can I get your robe? I don't want you to get chilled." She knew he wouldn't answer, but he understood. He shook his head and picked up the spoon. "Later, I'll change your sheets and bring you fresh bed clothes. You eat now. I'll be back."

Edna come back maybe a hour afta an I still be sittin' at the window. I gotta talk 'bout'er so you unnerstan' it ain't bad here. Snowin' stop an sun comin'out. I gotta say here Edna know me good even afta ony a coupla days an all the stuff she gotta do. That chair an settin' it up by the window be jus' perfect. She right 'bout the snow bein' pretty an she right 'bout me not wantin' ta lay in this bed alls a time. I love the outside even if I ain't in it. Jus' lookin' an seein' make me happy. I don' know how she know 'bout me, but she do an her hepin' me jus' 'bout the best it kin be if I gotta die.

She git the tray offa my lap an onta the floor. Then she go inta the hall an git stuff for makin' up the bed. She do it everday for me. Best part? Gittin' back onta them clean sheets, cool an good smellin'. I got two pillows an she put'em ahind my head. Then she go slidin' her hand 'cross my face like she checkin' on somethin', but she ain't. Edna jus' a nice lady carin' on me.

I heared it drop onta the floor. We go lookin' an I turn quick back ta the snow shinin' in the sun outside. Alls I hope is she go puttin' my recorder onta the table. She done makin' the bed an git the tray.

"I'll be back in a minute."

I look at the table. Nothin'. It ain't there. She back in a flash an she sit onta the bed.

"Are you ready?" she aks. I jus' worryin' on my recorder, keepin' my eyes lookin' outside. "Shall I call you Samuel, Sam or Sammy? Nod your head when you hear the name you like." She say, "Sam?" I shake an keep shakin'. I got me a name. Then she say it an I nod quick.

She git offa the bed an come over, makin' me look. "All right, from now on I'll call you Samuel. It's a fine name."

She git her hand out for shakin' likes we makin' a deal. I knowed she be wantin' a smile. I ain't doin' it, but I shake. There it be, comin' outta her hand inta mine, my recorder. Not 'nother word.

Edna come wit supper 'round six. I don' want nothin'. It like that, my schedule. At eight she come back an make me go inta the bathroom. No pushin'. Edna ain't that kinda lady. Jus' waitin' on me ta make ready. Afta I git back she got a pill. Maybe ten minutes an I'm floatin' high offa this bed. I ain't, but them pills git me feelin' good. I lose the hurtin' an thinkin' on dyin' an I make my dreamin', cuz that's all it kin ever be, on seein' you.

THREE

"Remember that time?" Patients might speak to me as if I am a part of something they recall – Edna Nieves

Edna Nieves was an attractive, dark-haired, fifty-seven year old widow possessed of a kind heart and nearing the end of her third year caring for the terminally ill. The young man transferred from Jamaica Hospital two days before had a thin file, inoperable brain tumor with three to five weeks to live. It included a narrative describing pain and seizure management options and authorizing liberal judgment. Some brain cancers are less painful than others, but seizures are common. Vigilance was necessary.

Hospice and palliative care, affording comfort and pain management to the dying, almost always took place in a patient's own home or a hospital. There were very few independent facilities like Edna's devoted exclusively to hospice care. She understood the need, however, especially in a densely populated metropolitan area like New York. There are many dying whose loved ones lacked the will or the means to provide end of life care. There are far more homeless, indigent and abandoned. In Edna's world their dying days deserved comfort, too.

Samuel was the youngest among the sixty-three patients she had served thus far. He was slumped in an emergency room chair when a harried triage nurse noticed him. A big male in some sort of green uniform brought him in, literally carrying Samuel to the chair and carefully setting him down. Then he left. CCTV captured it all in blurry black & white, but the NYPD wasn't about to devote resources to identify the mystery Good Samaritan. No crime was committed.

The hospital report listed Samuel as twenty-nine, this based upon one other record of treatment twelve years before. Then he was also found alone and unconscious. Following that treatment he was placed in a home for abandoned children operated by a non-profit called Mission Foundation. There was little else in the file. Just pre-authorization to supplant the pills with a powerful morphine drip when the end neared.

His only form of identification was a passport in his back pocket. Other than that, forty-eight dollars and a small recording device were his only possessions. She alone knew he could talk. Those who entered his room from time to time, the Certified Nursing Assistants, chaplain, and volunteers, never heard him speak. But Edna paid close attention to everyone who came to live their final days under her care, only three in the house at this time. At other times there were more. Finding his recorder under the covers did not tip her off. She'd already heard him mumble several times in his fitful sleep. She also caught an occasional word just before she entered his room in the mornings. She kept his secret.

He bore the pain without complaint, but before long Edna knew the drip would become essential. The instructions from Jamaica Hospital called for a gradual increase. What really kills these poor souls, she worried. Is it the disease or is it the opioids? Is it me? She dared not dwell on the last question, but she prayed for God's forgiveness every Sunday. When the end came she cleaned and dressed the body, uttered her own prayers and consoled any that might be grieving. If there were any, however, they more often showed relief.

Only one other person came to this house all alone like Samuel, a woman with bone cancer. This galled Edna. No one should die alone. No one should be forgotten. The instructions in that case were clear; swift transport to the funeral home down the street, incineration and disposal of the ashes. Not this time. Not Samuel, she decided, for the private reason her tortured emotions harbored. His name would be chiseled on a gravestone. She would purchase it with her own funds. He'll go into the ground near her husband alone no more. That is, if she couldn't track down his family or friends before it was too late. The hospital file had a lead.

He drifted into a semi-conscious state after Edna gave him his pill. Soon he would fall asleep, but in these minutes he could make his mind go wherever he desired. It always went to San Jose, California. He nurtured this final cherished fantasy, setting the stage, willing his imagination to create the make believe scene in which he finds Dollface, unlike the reality of years before when his efforts had been thwarted by tragedy and the subterfuge of Cletus Brown.

The cute sorority girl addresses the crowd.

"Hey everyone, are you ready to party!?!" Whistles and shouts greet her opening.

"I want to party with you!"

She offers a confident smile to the heckler. *"I think I can do better!"* Laughter and hoots. *"Band's ready. Let's rip!!"*

Mornin' an the ladies ain't gonna be comin' 'round for a hour. I got this recorder, sittin' by the window in the chair Edna gimme. I got more. Afta Cletus done makin' me work I read books 'bout romance an mystery an a lotta kid books, too. Maybe a hunnerd in that house on a pile in the front room where we goes eatin' in shifts. I kin give you a line outta all of'em, too. How 'bout this one:

> *'Alice rose from her seat, smiling and clapping, but never taking her eyes from his as each one recognized the meaning of that moment, two people picturing a third absent far away in Vermont, but there with them in their hearts.'*

Chapter Fifty-Four, page 254, last paragraph, final sentence from AT 29 When Saturn Returns by D. P. Macbeth. It take me a a bunch a weeks ta git done wit all them books. Woulda bin faster but Cletus allays makin' me do more stuff 'til I be workin' from afta I git up ta afta the other guy go home at eleven.

January I git'em all done an January you come walkin' inta that residence wit them other two girls. I don' want you thinkin' I seen you at first cuz I din'. I knowed them ladies git the little kids tagether inta three groups, but I ain't payin' no mind cuz a hepin' wit gittin' the supper goin' in the kitchen. Four kids in each group on the floor 'round you girls readin' wit you sittin' on a chair 'cept afta, I seen you go onta the floor wit the kids. They love it. Lacey be one, carryin' that doll.

I come outta the kitchen ta go makin' the tables for supper. What's I hearin'? A happy voice an I gotta stop right there. I bin thinkin' on your voice all these years an, truth be, I ain't never bin able ta 'splain it in words. Jus' lightnin' inta me. Do a person know 'nother jus' by hearin' a voice? Yep.

I go standin' close ta your door. You readin' outta A. A. Milne. I knowed the words an I knowed the page, but it ain't 'portant ta tell it here. You know I kin do it. I ain't hearin' nothin' outta them kids sittin' 'round you an I be afeared a lookin' cuz I knowed it ruin the moment. They was under the spell a your voice like me. So, I jus' stand, takin' it inta my ears 'til Cletus make me go ta the front room. I don' go lookin' inta your room, but it don' matter. Your voice be 'nuff. I never tol' you 'bout that first time.

You do the readin' four days ever week wit them other two girls. I don' know why you don' come on Fridays. The kids alls jumpin' 'round the door at 3:30 waitin'. Me too, standin' a ways back. There be a coupla days a listnin' afore I git up the nerve ta go lookin' inta your room. You be on the floor wit them kids all waitin' on a turn ta git onta your lap. You make it happy in that room an they all want some.

An that be how I come on knowin' you, standin' jus' aside that door watchin', hearin' an sayin' ever word you read outta them books. Them other girls be in other rooms, readin', but I ain't hearin'em. Jus' you. I don' even try stoppin' myself from sayin' the words you gonna read next. I whisper low, thinkin' it ain't bein' heared. I knowed all them words outta all them books cuz I read'em afore an I 'member. Hearin' them words offa your voice be better.

You girls be wearin' the same clothes likes a uniform. Maybe cuz a the school you come outta. I don' know, but it be the finest girl clothes I ever seen. On you for sure. I don' pay no mind ta them two others. You got a white shirt wit buttons open under your chin where daddy show me ta put the first punch. I woulda never done that. It jus' my way a tellin' how that shirt look. An over it you got a a blue vest. You come inta that house wit it buttoned up, but in that room you undoes them buttons quick. Why? I come on thinkin' you din' like that vest much. You got a skirt wit a lotta colors an lines, but mostly blue, green an red an it be short. Afta you goes sittin' on the floor it be hard ta hide your legs up over your knees an you gotta cross your ankles over. Then you lay that colored skirt on top a your knees, hidin' them legs 'til one a them kids git onta your lap. The skirt go up an your knees come out an you don' care.

I kin read fast and I kin see fast. So, that first lookin' be 'nuff ta know you - maybe five feet an six inches, smaller'n me, but not much. You got white skin an yellow hair jus' like Lacey's doll, 'round your head, covrin' ta the back a your neck an sometimes over your ears. Coupla times I seen you move it offa your ears. I come on knowin' that hair afront be called bangs cuz I heared it outta one a the ladies workin' in the house. You got blue eyes, jumpin' when you smile. You smile alls a time. A book woulda called'em expressive eyes. They gotta still be cuz I never seen eyes go changin', old, young, happy, mad, sad. Maybe they got lines an move 'round from mood ta mood, but if ya look hard ya see the peoples ya allays knowed.

Them first weeks it git dark 'round five- thirty an cars come 'round ta git you girls back ta where you 'sposed go. Home I be guessin'. I look outta the front window, watchin' you git inta that shiny car an I seen them peoples drivin', sometimes a man an sometimes a lady, your momma or daddy. You git inta a big white Cadillac, pullin' on the door afore it kin go drivin' away. Hard waitin' 'til I kin see you agin. Thursdays real hard cuz I gotta wait 'til Monday.

I unnerstan' 'bout you comin' an goin'. Jamaica, Queens an some peoples don' know it got two parts. The residence ain't in the good part. Day times ain't bad an you girls kin walk down Midland Parkway an come 'cross 179th onta the block. Dark ain't so good so that big Cadillac gotta be there waitin' on you.

A whole week afore you seen me listnin'. I git ta wantin' you ta see me. Wantin' you ta knows I live in that house like them little kids. You smiled that first time you seen me.

"Come in," you say. An I does cuz I kin stand the watchin' an listnin' jus' so long an I gotta be part a it. I goes sittin' on the floor jus' like them little kids an you. You readin' an I knowed them words 'cept I don' say'em cuz them kids woulda got mad. You? Mad ain't somethin' you got.

"Round 4:30 Cletus come lookin', callin' for Sam. I like my name bein' Samuel like Mark Twain shoulda stayed Samuel Clemens. I knows everthin' he write. Cletus go by the door not lookin' inside, but afta he don' see me in the front room makin' up them tables he come back. He don' even care that he bust in on you readin'.

"Let him stay."

It brung me an them little kids up straight. Cletus musta figured somethin' cuz he don' say nothin' an jus' go walkin' out. You gimme "nother smile an I near shoutin' inside a my head. It be like my momma livin' wit daddy an me afore she don' come home no more. An it ain't cuz I need no momma, neither. It be cuz I got me a friend. I don' never stop comin' inta that room agin, most a them times carryin' Lacey wit'er doll cuz I knowed she be happy hearin' your voice jus' like me. Cletus don' come 'round lookin' for me no more, neither. He knowed I ain't workin' 'til afta you goes outta that door inta that big white Cadillac.

'Member that day you git Lacey offa your lap an stop readin'? They's all good kids an go outta the room, but you tell me ta stay an I watch you button up that blue vest. You git quiet an I come on thinkin' I shouldn' be stayin'. I heared them other girls readin' an I wonder why you stop? Cuz you thinkin' on me? You wanna know me? Is that why you come inta that house? Is that why I come inta that room? Soul talkin'?

"Do you know every book? Every word?" You brung up them smilin' blue eyes, lookin' at me. First talkin' I done afta momma don' come home no more. The book be Stuart Little. I start on page thirty-one an go tellin' the whole page afore you close your mouth cuz a bein' 'sprised. You git the book offa the floor an turn the pages. "Thirty-one," I says. "Afta you stop."

"How..."

But I scat outta there quick ta the kitchen, sweatin' somethin'

19

awful. Cletus go lookin' at me, shakin' like I don' know what.

"Wash up," he say. "You're sweating like a pig."

Everday, that be our time afta the kids go outta the room an you make the Cadillac wait. You button your vest an we talk. I kin 'member everthin' outta books, but I kin never recollect the words we say. All I got afta twelve years be you in that colored skirt an white shirt an blue vest, the yellow hair an blue eyes an happy smile, makin' me feel like never afore an never afta. Ladies comin'.

"Hello, Samuel! How are you feeling today?"

There are two women this morning, each with a small bouquet of flowers in her hand. They cross to where he is sitting by the window and peer down at his face.

"Edna told us you like to be called Samuel. Look, we have fresh flowers for you!"

The one speaking holds them for him to see. The other comes around his chair and collects a vase from the night table. She passes it to her cohort then goes around the bed to the other table and collects another vase.

" I wonder if he hears us."

"Edna says he hears and understands."

"And, how does she know?"

"She's the hospice nurse. She spends the most time with him and the others."

"He doesn't act like he hears."

They arrange the flowers and put the vases back on the tables.

"How much time does he have?"

"Christmas."

"He doesn't seem to be in pain."

"Edna says we have to watch for seizures, call her right away."

"Really? He looks peaceful to me."

Them ladies shouldn' talk like I ain't here cuz Edna git mad if she ever knowed. It ain't nobody's fault 'cept maybe me cuz I ain't talkin' an them other dyin' peoples in this house talkin' more. I like it this way, talkin' ony ta you.

So, that come on how it be atween you an me afore you gotta git inta that Cadillac. Near a hour alone in that room. Forever for me cuz I think on it 'alls a time an not 'nuff cuz I got a lot ta say an there ain't time ta say it. Watchin' your mouth move wit the words, I gotta say I hear'em, but I ain't listnin' for what they mean. I'm listnin' for your soul talkin'. This be the part I most want you ta unnerstan' cuz it ain't never bin 'bout them words an that's why I kin never 'member. You showin' the soul you got. I never knowed nothin' like that afore an nothin afta. Most special happnin' in my whole life. What come outta your soul? I know you! My soul go sayin' I know you back, real happy. An the name come offa my lips, "Dollface", natural like a name I called you in some other time an some other place that ain't Jamaica, Queens. Does ya ever think on that?

Gittin' more powerful, this poundin' in my head. Afore, afta it start whilst livin' wit Dale an workin' on them cars, hurtin' come on slow an don' git real bad 'til afta supper. But it happnin' sooner like Edna say it gonna. I see the clock, four in the aftanoon, same time you done your readin'. I try ta talk through it, but it's gittin' hard. I gotta tell you 'bout Dale, but I got Cletus an Rick first an Archer T. Zane an Crystal. Dollface, our souls talkin'... I feel real bad cuz I'm gonna die an it ain't gonna happin agin like I bin hopin' all these twelve years. That be a worse kinda hurt.

"You know every book by heart," you say. But it be more a question an you come close like no one never come close afore 'cept momma ta hold me an daddy ta hit me. "It's impossible. How?"

I don' have no answer. It happin' afta I read somethin' an see somethin' an hear somethin'.

"In my head," I say.

"Do you realize how special you are?" An you look inta my eyes.

Do you know how beautiful you are? I don' say it an sittin' here in Edna's chair I know I shoulda. What lookin' at you done ta my insides be somethin' I think on. I be too mindful a that ta see what I does ta you. No book ever gimme the way ta git them words out right. I gotta git ta that last day.

Comin' on a bunch a months an gittin' warm. That's when I heared you talkin' ta them two other girls whilst comin' in the door. Jus' like the little kids, I stand waitin' on you.

"I'm moving to California."

One a them girls aks, "Where in California?"

"San Jose."

"Wow!" An the door git shut.

What? I aks myself. Dollface leavin'? Goin' away? An I come on thinkin' it ain't no special soul talkin'. Don' git me wrong. I jus' hurtin' cuz a not knowin' 'nuff 'bout peoples comin' an goin' ta unnerstan'. Now I does, bein' it happin' a lot afta. But it hurt big in that moment.

I talk 'bout Ralph Waldo Emerson an Conduct of Life. All them days I tell you 'bout what he say an you listen whilst makin' the Cadillac wait. Was you learnin' or was you jus' wondrin' on me doin' it? Maybe both. Ony a coupla pages in them minutes so we got time ta do talkin' afore you gotta git inta that Cadillac, but I git it done one day afore I never sees you agin. I wanna aks, afeared cuz a what you gonna say. You musta seen an figured.

"What's wrong?"

"You leavin'?"

"Oh. How do you know?"

"I heared California, San Jose."

Your eyes go lookin' at nothin' an I knowed right then that you don' wanna say no more cuz a knowin' it make me sad. You sit on the chair, tryin' ta make your mind collect the right words. Does we git the meanin' of soul talkin'? Does we git the place we be at in the world? Does we unnerstan' why we come tagether an why we gotta go sepret agin? I come on knowin' it allays gotta happin'cuz a other peoples afta, but you ain't them. You allays bin differnt, Dollface. I din' know then an I don' know now.

"Califa California is far away," you say.

"Why?" Close ta cryin', but I hide it.

"College. San Jose State University. That's where I'll go in September."

But you knowed that ain't the why I'm aksin'. I look outta the window. "Cadillac waitin".

"Let it wait. Come back and talk to me."

I look at your knees an up. You ain't big on top, but you got somethin' cuz you ain't no little girl like Lacey. "When?"

"Graduation is Friday. After that I fly to San Jose for summer session." I kin't hold back no more. I git my hand outta my pocket an wipe my eyes. "Please don''t." You come outta your chair an rub my arm. First time we ever touch. "You mean so much to me."

Cadillac honkin'. "What do I do afta you goes away?" It be a question ta me, not you.

"Find me."

Did you say it? Was them real words comin' outta your mouth? Or was it soul talkin' in that other way that kin ony be heared by us? Ta this very moment I don' know an I sure wanna know 'cuz then I kin go happy ta the next place comin' afta I don' wake up no more.

Next day I'm waitin' wit Lacey in my arms, holdin'er doll an aksin', 'Is she here? Is she here?' She don' know it be the last time. You come in the door an them other two girls git onta their readin' rooms. Lacey holdin' her arms ta you an I give'er over. You smiles a unhappy smile. Maybe cuz that be the kinda look I got on my face, too. You take up the last chapter of Doctor Doolittle an the kids git onta the floor 'cept you keep Lacey on your lap. I stand by the door, lookin' an listnin' and sayin' the words ta myself. Ony you knowed I kin do it. Ony you knowed I kin talk an you keep my secret. I wanna scat outta there an outta that house cuz you goin' away an there ain't gonna be nothin' there for me no more.

Finishin' on that last day take longer an the Cadillac be there afta you stop readin'. I allays wondered why you din' tell them little kids you ain't comin' back. Lacey be the saddest little girl I ever seen for a week afta. It be our talkin' time afore you gotta go. I never bin so heavy crushed afore or afta. I ain't even able ta look at you, but I don' want the time ta end. I don' know how ta make it stop. The Cadillac honk an it be too late. You button up your blue vest for the last time. You ain't lookin' at me. You lookin' at your hands cuz somethin' comin' an we both gotta be ready.

I don' want you thinkin' I planned that kiss cuz I din'. It come outta someplace inside an I done it quick on your cheek. You take it wit no 'sprise, but I be 'sprised an afeared an I turn quick ta the door.

"No!" you say, grabbin' my arm.

That second kiss, your kiss! I kin feel it ta this very moment. Two souls comin' tagether warm an soft like a kiss 'sposed ta be in a book. Poem woulda called it eternal, not jus' part a that moment, but part a ever moment an all time an ever place. An now, in this place, the last place I gonna be, it still be wit me. An I wanna keep it even afta I don' wake up no more.

You wipe my eyes, movin' your fingers 'cross my cheek real soft and slow. Then you walk out. I seen you git inta that Cadillac for the last time an I watch you pull on that heavy door. You look outta the window at me, souls know the truth like all the thinkin' in the whole world kin never figure out. Good-bye.

FOUR

Some linger in pain in order to complete something or see someone before they run out of time – Edna Nieves

Edna sat in a chair opposite the Executive Director at Mission Foundation's College Point headquarters.

"If they are deemed capable of taking care of themselves we release them at age eighteen. You say his name is Samuel Jones?"

"Yes. He came to us with very little information. Just a thin medical diagnosis from Jamaica Hospital."

"Terminal?"

"Yes, brain cancer."

"And, what brings you to Mission Foundation?"

"The Jamaica Hospital file mentions an earlier injury before he turned eighteen, apparently a severe concussion. He was found on a subway train and taken there to be treated. Then he was taken to a home, one of yours. I went by the address, but the house is no longer there. There's a commercial building in its place."

"Yes, I know the one. The house burned down seven years ago. We sold the lot."

"I was hoping you might have some information about him. What became of him after he was released from Mission Foundation's care?"

"Why do you want to know?" It wasn't a suspicious question, curiosity.

"In the time left… well, maybe locate family or friends."

"Obviously, if he came under our care there wasn't any family or none that cared. I have to be candid, Mrs. Nieves, we can't release information without a court order."

"He's about to die."

"Perhaps he has assets that someone with an ulterior motive wants to take."

"Surely…"

"It's simply the law."

"He's liable to be erased from existence. I don't want that to happen."

"What can you do?"

"There must be people who were part of his life. Someone who cared about him. If there were…are, surely they would want to know and perhaps comfort him, be at his side during his last days. He won't be forgotten." The administrator tapped a pencil on her desk. For a few seconds it was the only sound in the room. Edna made another plea. "Please. I'm not interested in taking anything from him. A name, something to go on. Maybe a way to reach the people who knew him before it's too late."

The woman tapped her pencil again, looking at Edna as if trying to decide if she should break the rules. At last, she pushed back from her desk. "I have to go down to the basement files. It may take a few minutes."

When she returned she had a thin manila folder in her hand. She went behind her desk, shaking her head with a disappointed look on her face. "Samuel Jones." She seated herself, put the folder down with the cover open and looked at Edna. "It's not his real name."

"No? How can that be?"

"In those rare cases when we take in a child with no documentation, the house master is instructed to select a name for the file. Just before the resident is released, if no further information can be found, we prepare the necessary forms to make the name legal with the State of New York and various federal agencies. When all is cleared the House Master takes the resident to the nearest Social Security office and registers him or her for a Social Security number."

"But the file from Jamaica Hospital, it predates…"

"Automatic. Legal notice is sent to all known record holders.

Federal law requires name update or correction in the case of a name change, which this comes under by definition."

"Then his legal name is Jones? He chose Samuel, very insistent."

"Yes. What do you mean by chose Samuel."

"I asked him what name he preferred. Not Sam or Sammy. Only Samuel."

"Lucid then. He hears and understands?"

"Yes, of course. Your House Master thought so, too. Otherwise, Mission Foundation would not have released him. Isn't that right?"

"Yes."

"Who is the House Master?"

The woman referred to the file. "Was, he left our employ at the same time Mr. Jones was released. His name was Cletus Brown."

"What happens when you release someone?"

"We find a clean, inexpensive place for them to live, pay the first two months' rent, open a bank account with one thousand dollars in their name and, if possible, find them a job."

"Where did Samuel work?"

The woman scanned the single sheet in her hand. "There's no mention here. No record of employment."

"Where did he live? You gave him money. What bank?"

The administrator shook her head. "I'm afraid that's all I can tell you."

"There isn't more in the file?"

"The House Master," she referred to the file again. "Cletus Brown. He was supposed to provide those details for the file. Apparently, he didn't."

"Are you saying Samuel just vanished?"

"I'm saying his legal name is Jones and he was released from our care upon his eighteenth birthday."

Edna leaned back, frustrated. "What do I do now?" It was a rhetorical question to the room. "Cletus Brown. Do you know how I might contact him?"

"I'm sorry. Unless our former employees keep us informed we

don't keep track."

"Maybe someone inquired about him. You know, a prospective employer?"

The director rose from her chair, shaking her head. "I can't say. It's not that I won't. Please understand I know what you are trying to do for your patient. I respect that. This seems to be all we have on him. As for Mr. Brown, once he left our employ he severed all ties. There isn't any more information."

The stage was hastily put together, a plywood platform, fifteen feet square and raised two feet off the ground. Boys from the next door fraternity house hammered and sawed all afternoon, finishing the task only hours before the band and partygoers began to arrive. That's how he envisioned it in the minutes before the opioid pulled his consciousness away. Not the reality thwarted by Cletus Brown. No, this was an imaginary band for this final fantasy of his life.

He jumped onto the stage and slid behind the keyboards. The audience clapped, whistled and thumped on anything near.Where is she? How will she know it's me? Black sleep engulfs him in its shroud.

Residence got a attic three steps up on the third floor wit a door that got a lock on t'other side. I hides up there for a week, comin' down ony when I hear Cletus callin' loud ta make ready for eaten times. I be real low cuz I knowed I ain't never gonna see you agin. Cletus gimme a look, but aside from sayin', 'Why are you moping around?' he don' push. I don' sleep wit them others, neither. Jus' git my work done an scat back inta that attic, wondrin' why you even happin ta me.

Lotta stuff up there, ol' an layin' 'round an a coupla chairs alls dusty and used up. Cletus never bin up there. Good, I figure, cuz I wanna be alone. I seen a ol' record player an a lotta records jus' as dusty's all that other stuff. I read the covers an if there be more inside I read that too cuz I din' know nothin' 'bout music.

Hot in that attic, real hot cuz a the sun comin' on strong afore summer. I don' care an I don' let me feel bothered by it 'cept it be hot 'nuff ta 'member. Afta readin' them record covers I don' see nothin', feel nothin' or even hear nothin' 'cept what them words tellin'. Music records nobody care nothin' 'bout jus' like them ol' books in the library.

Dollface, I gotta say here that it git me thinkin' on somethin' asides you. I hopes you unnerstan' an I figure you does even if you ain't never gonna hear what I'm sayin'. Music come on bein' the best happnin' in my whole life afta knowin' you. I read ever word on them covers an I take out them records inside an I read them labels. The most 'portant part 'til I heared the music.

The attic got a light hangin' wit a string. T'other side got a socket an that be how I git the record player goin'. Lucky on that. Everthin' work jus' like it 'sposed ta. I ain't gonna talk on all them peoples I heared all them days a listnin'. It don' matter cuz it ony be 'bout the music - ever kind; violins, pianos, guitars, drums takin' center whilst all the sounds come tagether. An the singin'! All them poems I knowed come on soundin'ony half's good afta I heared music ahind them words. I come on thinkin' the differnce atween them ol' days a Ralph Waldo Emerson writin' poems be they ain't got no music ahind'em. Music make poems more perfect. A course, gotta be good soundin' music.

How many records? How many songs? I dunno, but I heared'em all an it lift me up jus' like Edna's pills. It hep me outta goin' wrong afta you close that Cadillac door the last time. I git onta hearin' ever one over an over 'til I knowed the music the way I knowed all them words outta all them books. It ain't hard an I come outta that attic sweaty an itchin' ta make music all my own.

Residence got a piano, maybe ya 'member it, in the front room an never touched by no one in that house far's I knowed. Made outta wood, ol' wood cuz there be cracks comin' outta the paint, or no - maybe jus' some varnish or somethin' brown. At 2:30 in the aftanoon I git onta that piano an make it 'bout forgittin' you cuz you ain't never comin' inta that house agin'. Or, maybe usin' it ta 'member what it be like when a soul go missin' a part. I dunno. It jus' come on bein' what I need 'round then. I lift the mantel, yeah, I looked up that

29

word later cuz I wanna know, an set it back where it 'sposed ta go an see them white and black keys.

I press'em so I kin 'member the sounds. They jus' a little differnt afta I push my feets onta them pedals near the floor an it don' take long ta know what ta do. Findin' the right keys ta make the sounds I 'member outta listnin' in the attic take one whole afternoon afore I gotta go makin' up the tables for supper. An afta the dishes git done an the kitchen all cleaned the way Cletus like I git back onta that ol' piano an play more.

Lacey come lookin', holdin' her doll wit tears comin' offa her cheeks. I knowed why an brung'er onta my lap cuz she missin' you jus' like me. How come Lacey gotta be livin' blind an all alone? I knowed I got it better an I knowed I ain't deservin' cuz I ain't as good as her. I hold'er an she put her face on my shirt an she cry on me wit that doll in her arms.

"Why did she go?"

I turn her little body 'round an make'er touch them keys wit me. Then I git'er safe on my knees an git playin'. Like that everday at 2:30 in the aftanoon, even Friday, Saturday an Sunday. Lacey an me at the piano so's we kin forgit. She do. I don'.

FIVE

The senses diminish one by one, but I am convinced my patients can hear right up to the end – Edna Nieves

Afta you come inta that house for the readin' an you tol'm ta let me stay, Cletus don' show much. It come on bein' differnt afta he heared me playin' that piano wit Lacey on my lap. He done his work an that be it 'til it be time ta go makin' ready for supper. He come inta the front room, seein' some a them kids sittin' an listnin' an he git ta listnin', too.

It be like that all summer an inta the good time a the year afta the air git cool and leaves start fallin'. Lacey go off wit them other kids listnin' ta some new girls readin' like you done. Good cuz she stop thinkin' on you like a little kid otta. I don' play loud cuz I don' want it bein' hard for them ta hear the stories. Sometimes, I stop, knowin' what comin' next an sayin' the words ta myself. Then I play low, makin' music for nobody special 'cept you if you was there, but you ain't. Jus' Cletus, standin' 'gainst the wall an thinkin' I don' know he be there.

I 'member when he brung the guys 'round, the day afta Halloween an I bin thinkin' on gittin' outta that house. Eighteen in three months an it be a question on me, go afore or wait 'til my time. 'Round five an we 'sposed to be makin' ready for supper, three guys walk inta that room, Cletus leadin' and talkin' low jus' ta them. Theys all wearin' black jackets, collars turned up an tryin' ta look the same. Rick be the boss, but I din' know it right then. They go standin' 'gainst the wall, Cletus tellin'em ta listen whilst I keep playin'. They come back the next day and the day afta, but this time they got cases an open'em up, takin' guitars out like they gonna play somethin'. I

31

stop an wait on'em.

"Go on!" Cletus talkin' loud at me ta keep playin'. I look 'round an Rick got a guitar, makin' ready. Them others, too. Dumb drummer come later. "Keep playin'!" Cletus allays pushy if he want somethin'. I git back onta playin', but not cuz a him pushin'. I wanna hear them guitars wit me on that piano. I do a fast run over ever key that piano got. Soon's I hit the end the guitars come in, playin' somethin' them guys knowed, but I din'. Rick lookin' ta see what I gonna do so I jus' keep up by playin' a set a keys over'n over. Rick take over like we bin playin' tagether a long time. Delicious be the ony word tellin' how good that music come out.

"See!" Cletus shoutin' loud an lookin' at them others. "He's a natural!"

Rick run his hands faster over them strings, me followin' wit them other guys atween. It go a while afore the kids come lookin' cuz they bin waitin' in the hall for supper.

Edna sat by the bedside. It was nine p.m. and Mr. Frawley's son still hadn't arrived. The old man went into a coma at six that evening. She knew it was the end and she called his son's cell phone right away. Four calls, hitting voice mail each time. No call back. She emailed Queens County Social Services to announce another imminent death at the hospice house. At nine-thirty his son came through the door, looking impatient. Edna shook her head. A father is about to pass away and his son is annoyed.

"He's in a coma, labored breathing. I'll let you to say good-bye."

"How soon?"

"Any moment. Not more than an hour or two."

"I need to make arrangements."

Edna stands to leave as the young man takes his cell phone from his coat pocket. "There's time for that later," she admonishes, no longer willing to hide her disdain. "He's your father. Sit with him. Hold his hand. Tell him you love him."

His mouth opens in surprise. "You said he's in a coma."

"He'll hear you." She exits and walks down the hall. "God

forgive me," she whispers.

Mornin' an I got more on Rick an the Riders. That be the name a the band an it need a keyboard. Jus' a cover band doin' other peoples' songs. Rick had'em in clubs 'round the city an down the Jersey Shore. I never aks how Cletus come on knowin'em an I don' much care. Time ta git outta that house an I bin thinkin' on a way ta eat. Cletus catch me in the kitchen afore Thanksgivin'.

"I'm leaving and so are you. Rick wants to know if I'll take you on at my place and make you the piano man in his band. I said yes." He make it like I got no part in the decidin' an, a course, I don'. I look at'm, thinkin' on where we gonna sleep. He musta figured that was it cuz he say, "I'll be giving my notice when it's your time to leave and I have a line on a place in Flushing. It's decent and clean. I'll cook, you play." An that be it. Nothin' 'bout money.

Jus' afta New Years we go. I got nothin' an take nothin' 'cept a coupla shirts an pants an stuff. I git Lacey an brung'er ta where no one kin hear an I tol'er I gotta go cuz it be my time jus' like it be her time someday. An, I tol'er it ain't cuz I don' like'er. She need that like she don' git when you go away an like I don' git when my momma don' come home no more. She don' show no 'sprise cuz a me talkin'. She jus' a little kid livin' inside a her world an she don' think nothin' on me not talkin'afore. She cry an I holds'er a whiles. Alls I kin do.

Zane paused the recording. He stood and stretched, then wandered down the hall to the coffee station. As he brewed a double espresso, Lacey, who had been the first to express her memory of Samuel, came into his mind's eye, a pretty, vivacious teen entering her second year at Columbia University. He recalled her words:

"I suppose I'm one of the few who knew he could talk. It didn't come as a surprise to me to hear his voice on the recordings. That was the boy who treated me like his little sister. The big brother I missed for a long time. I was five years old when I knew him at the residence. He talks about my doll, carrying me around on his shoulders, sitting me on his lap while he played songs on the piano. He knew I was heartbroken. It never occurred to me that he was

heartbroken, too.

"Even then, as a little girl, I could feel something special about him. He said he had to go and he was sorry I couldn't go with him. He told me he would miss me and to never forget that I was special. He promised that one day I would have a family. I believed him and lived for that promise. Then one day Rebecca came for me. Somehow, I think Samuel knew."

Cletus git a second floor walkup wit dirty stairs an four rooms. It ain't much, even my daddy an me live better. Neighborhood mostly new peoples comin' outta, I don' know, far away, Koreans mostly. They got their own way a makin' the nighttime safe. We never git bothered in them two years livin' there. An in summer we go down the Jersey Shore, sleepin' in rooms at the club where Rick got a three-month gig. Cletus got the job a watchin' me git onta the piano an makin' sure I don' go makin' trouble somewheres. Look, I allays be playin' dumb. I ain't talkin' an I ain't lookin' like I unnerstan' nothin'. They all figure me for a idiot. Easier by my way a thinkin'.

That winter be the first a the two an a half years playin' wit Rick an the Riders. Doin' covers ain't my thing an I ain't never done none afta. Well, I mean afta I got some solo work. That come later. I gotta say this 'bout Rick, he got a good guitar hand an he mean business when it come ta makin' music. He never say nothin' ta me. Them other three, neither. What ta say? I ain't talkin', but he heared me playin' an I knowed he like it good. Respect be the word.

Rick an the Riders got a circuit from October ta May. Differnt clubs in the Village an Chelsea an offa Prince Street. Cletus an me take the subway an sometimes the bus. Rick allays there afore everbody, no smilin', jus' waitin' on playin'. Rick a quiet man. We play eight ta midnight Tuesdays ta Saturdays. Cold some nights like New York gits. Rick got three sets, allays the same an good them first coupla months, but it git onta bein' borin' an that's why I don' do no covers afta I git my own solos. A course, I gotta make up stuff. I'll git ta that.

We was a band makin' the booze an skirt chasin' go good. Some nights got maybe a hunnerd peoples crammed all tight an makin' noise wit a small dance floor real close ta where Rick go playin'. He git scared a bein' bumped, but it never happin. I be offa the side on a piano cuz Rick like it better than the keyboards his ol' mate leaved ahind. Okay wit me, 'cept I knowed some a them songs coulda bin better usin' keyboards. Rick good on a harmonica, too. He jus' don' play it 'nuff. If I ever talked, an I don', I woulda tol'm ta git onta that harmonica more cuz he make a real good sound. I git'm doin' it jus' the same.

Cletus allays near the bar drinkin' an watchin' women. Atween sets he come 'round, makin' me go ta the side, standin' an waitin' 'til Rick come back an we git playin' agin'. He don' gimme nothin', no water, no beer, nothin' like him an Rick an them others git atween sets. An that be the way wit Cletus. I knowed he go takin' money offa Rick. My money, but I ain't seein' none. An it musta bin okay money cuz I never seen'm git some outta nowheres else. It pay the rent an food bills.

Some nights Cletus git lucky wit a lady an he git Rick ta put me onta a train back uptown. Most times Rick git on wit me cuz he don' figure I kin git off at the right stop. I wonder if he jus' makin' sure for the next gig or he a good person, lookin' afta me. Find out afta it ain't nothin' 'bout bein' good.

We git outta winter and go down the Jersey shore startin' Memorial Day. Differnt from the city, 'cept the covers we allays doin'. First time I ever seen a ocean beach an first time breathin' a differnt kinda air. I likes the Jersey shore alot.

We play two clubs cuz there be peoples alls a time. On Sundays we set up outside by the Tiki bar in the aftanoon, keepin' them peoples spendin' afore gittin' back up the parkway. Half-price drinks three ta nine. Then we pack up. We don' play Sunday nights. Jus' them other six nights. We go inta the smaller club up the boardwalk if 'nother band come 'round wit a bigger followin'. The rest a the time Rick an the Riders headline.

The owner a them two clubs be a hard man allays standin' an watchin' everythin', lookin' mad. Tight, too. Rick on'm for money alls a time, talkin' loud. Rick as tough as he be good on that guitar an he ain't goin' nowheres 'til the money come out. Cletus cruisin' ladies an a lotta times I gotta git food for myself. I don' care. 'Round midnight or afta if I seen Cletus got some woman in my sleepin' place I go onta the beach. Them times cops go roustin' peoples back onta the boardwalk, but I had'em figured afta a coupla nights, knowin' when theys comin' and where theys lookin'. Afta, I jus' go walkin' an puttin' my feets in the water. Moon be some kinda 'mazin! I never seen nothin' like water bein' lit up like that afore. I do a lotta thinkin' on you.

Readin' an stuff, yeah, you figured that for somethin' special 'bout me, the knowin everythin' by heart an recitin' it ta you. I think then an I think even now it woulda bin' better if you knowed my music. Tellin' words ain't the same as hearin' music comin' outta the heart... no, outta the soul, the connectin' part atween you an me. An afta I knowed for sure there weren't no cops lookin' ta roust me offa the sand I come on thinkin' 'bout seein' you agin. I knowed I play good on that piano an I knowed I be gittin' better cuz a playin' ever night. My thinkin' come 'round ta makin' my own music an how it maybe git me ta you. Money hard ta figure. You ways away in California an me walkin' the Jersey Shore wit alls that space atween. I don' care much 'bout Cletus usin' my money, takin' it on me. I knowed it ain't 'nuff an I knowed findin' you gonna need somethin' big like me bein' a star or somethin'.

Rick, maybe, but none a them others got what good music take. Do you git my meanin'? 'Portant ta unnerstan an I don' know how ta talk on what a feelin' down deep kin do. I heared the word passion Them others ain't got it, but Rick do on his guitar an on that harmonica for sure. Doin' covers killin' it. I don' want it killin' me, too. So, that come on bein' my thinkin' whilst walkin' the sand, sometimes 'til the sun come up. I goes deep on music alls my own.

It don' happin' 'til Labor Day. It take that long ta git the piano workin' the notes jus' right. Even Rick gittin' tired a the months a playin'. Afta Labor Day Cletus say how we gonna go back ta the city, take a coupla weeks a doin' nothin' then git back onta the circuit. So, we git onta playin' the last show a the summer for a big drinkin' crowd. Covers the same, but go good cuz it bein' the end give us a bit more ta play for. By the closin' a the first set, maybe ten, theys all greased up, the crowd, dancin', singin' an, like them weekends all summer, lookin' for trouble. Good, this time, for me.

Rick drop it down an we kill the last song for a break. I seen the trouble first cuz, like you knows, I allays seein' an hearin'. Some girl drunk an she drop 'nother girl right onta the floor afta the song stop. All them guidos go in for a look, pushin' an shovin'. My daddy allays say them guidos be tough. It take a lot ta put one of'em down. Now they gits ta fightin'. Cletus, alls a sudden ain't 'round. I figure he scatted outta there cuz, a course, the cops gonna be comin'.

Rick git them other three ta pull the guitars offa the amps an he point ta the back cuz the owner got a office. 'Course, that guy comin' 'round the bar fast, holdin' a phone an talkin' loud. I sees maybe five guidos makin' a mess. Rick gone off wit them other three ta the office. Cops comin' in the doors, lookin' mad. Ony guys I ever seen tougher'n them guidos be Jersey shore cops. They run'em right onta the floor. Cuffs on'em so fast it almost be like nothin' happin. I git it. This got figured out a long time back. Alls 'bout money. Labor Day drinkin' ain't gonna be stopped by a bunch a guys rollin' 'round the dance floor. Coupla extra bucks ta the cops an some extra uniforms standin' close ta make everthin'good agin'. Gone in twenty minutes. An that come on bein' the chance ta make my music. I takes it.

Cuz a the fightin' an cops comin' 'round, the club maybe half full. Most a the peoples gone outside ta the boardwalk, watchin' the guidos gittin'shoved inta police cars. I look 'round an see Rick ain't back, but some peoples drinkin' an standin' an waitin' on the dancin' ta git goin' agin'. I figured Cletus gonna come back. So, time ta git it on.

I gotta talk on Jerry Lee Lewis cuz a his record up in the attic afta you go away. I ain't no expert but he gotta be one a the best guys on a piano ever. There ain't nothin' he ain't doin' an he 'bout the finest sound for what I wanna make come offa my fingers. I ain't never heared'm 'cept them days in that attic an I ain't never seen'm, neither. Don' matter cuz jus' thinkin' on his piano sound show me the way. So, I suck in some air an sit down. I go lookin' one more time at them peoples an none of'em watchin' me. Last time I git no looks that night.

I think on Jerry Lee Lewis an I hit them keys wit everthin' I got an I got alot. It ain't his song, but it coulda bin. He woulda heared hisself an he woulda bin happy. Them peoples sure was. I go long, loud an fast, usin' ever key an pushin' down on them pedals. Alls my own, that playin'. No singin' cuz I din think on no words, but I borrow on the way Jerry Lee Lewis git them piano keys goin' if it be his, but it be mine an I be thinkin' on you.

It don' take long. There ain't no standin' at that bar afore I even git halfway inta doin' my first song. Wit Jerry Lee Lewis it be tempo; fast, fast, fast. I go there an stay there an them peoples git shakin' an jivin' like no time afore all summer. Who lovin' it? Them girls, makin' noise almost as big as me. I hear happy shoutin' an them guidos who din' git rousted afore git onta the floor, chasin' them skirts. That be 'nother part 'bout Jerry Lee Lewis, the part my music gotta do, make peoples happy. I don' stop an afta the first one. I go right inta the next cuz I got ten songs I bin figurin' an knows Rick an Cletus gonna be comin'quick.

Rick come first, movin' fast outta the office wit them other three an tryin' ta see. Them others make ready ta git onta the stage, but Rick hold'em back. He jus' listnin' an lookin'. I knowed cuz I watch'm. I figure on two ways it gotta go down. He be mad at me an mad at Cletus cuz a not bein' there ta stop me. Or, he think on what I kin do an how it work for Rick an the Riders. Them wit passion knows.

Cletus show maybe halfway afore I git finished wit my third song. He come fast onta the side where my piano be an hit my shoulder. I don' even give'm a look cuz I seen Rick comin' an shakin' his head. Then he gimme a nod an push Cletus so he don' come back. I git inta the fourth song an Rick take up his guitar, pointin' ta them others ta git onta the stage. He slides in nice an easy jus' backin' me whilst them others wait on a place ta git in wit'm. Drums come in, screwin' up the beat. Rick give the dumb drummer a hateful stare an I figure on trouble. It don' come cuz the drummer hold his sticks an I git it rollin' agin. Jus' Rick an me an he knowed jus what ta do, follow.

Them other three find a place an git onta followin' Rick like puppy dogs. Good, cuz I got the lead an Rick jus' keepin' his guitar in the right place ta make my piano the ony thing. Now here I gotta say it be the harmonica I want. On that little music makin' piece Rick got all he need ta slip in an take over cuz he be as good on that harmonica as me on that piano.

An it woulda bin the right time cuz ya ain't gonna hold a sound forever. It git atween Rick an me afta. He ain't gonna listen ta me tellin'm what ta do. I jus' a idiot. But, I come on thinkin' Rick ain't gittin' on by havin' that guitar be alls he kin be. Is that what git in the way a peoples bein' the best they kin be? Not knowin' who they wanna be ain't who they kin be an who they kin be is better? I knowed I gotta make'm do it. Ladies comin'.

SIX

Hold a hand, stroke a face. It's important -
Edna Nieves

Edna studied her list, the names she had written down along with the school number, PS 0875. He didn't stir when she placed his recorder back under the covers; Miss Parsons, Cletus Brown, Lacey, Rick and the Riders, Archer T. Zane and two first names, Dale and Crystal. Despite learning little from her visit to Mission Foundation she decided to focus on Cletus Brown. She lifted her eyes to the computer screen and typed his name into the search box. Dozens of matches came up. She cycled through the synopses of the first ten. There was no hint that any could be the man she hoped to find. She clicked on the next page and after four more matches saw the rest dissolve into mere references to either Cletus or Brown, but no more exact Cletus Browns. She went back to the first ten and clicked on the links for each one; social platforms, newspaper stories - all dead-ends.

Her desire to know everything she could about Samuel Jones came on gradually. She knew why, of course, and it pained her to realize that the personal heartbreak she thought was finally dulled could come roaring back at the sight of a dying young man of similar age to her son. He was all alone. That's what bore into her conscience. No one to care other than Edna in this house that had been established for that very purpose. She knew her emotional involvement was unprofessional. She couldn't help it. When a soul struggled against the end she wanted to ease the final steps of the journey. This patient, Samuel Jones, reminded her that she was unable to ease those steps for her most cherished loved one. And, when the end came, after she had devoted all the love she could muster from her broken heart, sat with a physical presence whose spirit fluttered toward another place, held a hand as it gradually became cold, spoke kind words of farewell that she knew were heard despite the apparent coma, she let the mist envelop her eyes. She needed to do these things for her patients. Edna Nieves was also alone. It filled her void.

She fared better when she searched on Rick and the Riders. The band had all manner of social media including an elaborate web site, up to date and loaded with information about the band's current tour, West Coast through February, now playing Seattle. There was a Request for Info link. She clicked on it and filled out the form with her name and return email address. Then she typed her questions with an explanation of her patient's circumstances. The form had a three hundred character limit. It took three attempts to boil it down so the message would be accepted. She clicked send and whispered a prayer.

Archer T. Zane reaped a bonanza. She was thrilled when scores of links appeared on her screen, each referring to the same man, an attorney with some notoriety in a prestigious Manhattan law firm bearing his name. There were dozens of links to newspaper articles. She went directly to the firm's web site, searched on his practice and wrote down the telephone number.

It was time to make her rounds, only two patients remained with no more likely to be admitted in the days before Christmas. Samuel would be finished with his dinner, barely touched. Appetite goes first as the body prepares for shutdown. Families most often find this sign of accelerating decline the hardest to accept. They labor over food, buying and preparing all the favorites their loved ones once enjoyed, believing or hoping it can stave off the inevitable a little longer, assuming it is wanted, ignoring that it is not. Edna made food for Samuel, tiny portions, a different menu each day as she monitored what might interest him. She decided to let him have a few more minutes while she looked in on Mrs. Walker.

Poundin' comin' on strong. Edna be 'round soon an I gotta git a pill. Look, I'm gonna go soon. You wonder how I knows. Me, too, but I do. The body give a message. I got more on what happin atween me an Rick afta the pill run its course.

The nightly routine was completed. Edna lowered the light and turned to the door. Suddenly, his body jerked, legs and arms flailing and twisting as his eyes rapidly opened and closed. Edna didn't panic, but she moved swiftly to his side, reaching down to be sure the pillow was positioned under his head. Then she moved everything that could cause injury to his uncontrolled limbs a safe distance away. All the while she spoke softly, talking him through what was happening and reassuring him that it would soon be over. His head jerked back and forth and his legs twitched, but as the seconds passed his muscles gradually relaxed and his breathing became steady.

The seizure, a side effect of many diseases, but ever present with brain cancer, left both nurse and patient fatigued. When she was sure he had settled, she climbed onto the bed and laid on her back next to him. She stared at the ceiling for a several minutes, seeing the face of her precious son, Eduardo, and feeling guilty tears rise in her eyes. Then she slid from the bed, stood, smoothed her uniform, then reorderd the covers up to his chin and around his shoulders.

She moved toward the door, stopping at the threshhold for a quick look back, making sure, but the thought of Eduardo kept her from leaving. She returned to the bed, settling beside her sleeping patient and taking him into her arms. There she lay, gently holding his head against her shoulder, smoothing his unkempt hair and running her hands over his cheeks. She knew she was breaking all the rules, but she held him for thirty minutes, listening to him breathe, soothing his restless sleep, soothing her aching heart.

In the warmth of a California night, on the lawn of a San Jose State University sorority house, with scores of college students moving to his sound, the last fantasy his mind would ever hold took shape. *It's a party. Play a party song. Make'em dance.*

Just finishing her junior year, a girl from Queens, New York is out of place in California. She barely hears her self-absorbed sorority sisters, chattering, primping and stealing glances at the frat boys all around. It isn't that she dislikes them, they're her friends afterall. She's simply homesick, knowing this lifestyle was not for her. Unlike the others, she pays no attention to the boys ogling her group. Her mind is elsewhere, picturing a small circle of youngsters to whom she is reading. By the door stands a youth. He is whispering each word before she reads it aloud.

The first song comes to a powerful end and the keyboardist moves his lips close to the microphone.

"Tonight is extra special. I've come a long way to see a friend. I'll be playing for you and especially for her, hoping you all like what you hear and hoping she'll know it's me."

'Bout late September we git back doin' them clubs in the city. Rick gimme the eye a lot an I kin tell he bin thinkin' on my Jerry Lee Lewis kinda songs. Come the end a October an he make it so there be a piece a time so I git solos on my piano. Good, cuz in a coupla weeks them clubs git all jammed up wit peoples standin' on the sidewalk waitin' ta git in. Atween, I git ta thinkin' up more songs an I make'em a part a what I do. Come January Rick start keepin' me afta an he tell Cletus ta go on home an he git me back to the walkup later. Okay wit me.

He gimme a look ta git onta the piano an play my songs cuz he wanna figure'em out. I knowed cuz he come right up ahind me an watch. Sometimes, we be at it 'til three in the mornin', him pickin' on his guitar whilst watchin' my hands on them keys. I let'm do it, but it be that harmonica he otta be playin'.

He good ta his word 'bout watchin' over me, not that I need'm. Cletus don' care, 'specially if he git lucky wit some lady at the bar. "He's all yours," he say ta Rick soon's the last set git done. Rick sit wit me on the N train uptown an the 7 Purple ta Flushing. He come up onta the street an walk wit me ta the buildin' an go inside, watchin' from the bottom 'til I gits up them stairs an inta the apartment. Like I bin sayin', no need cuz I knowed them trains better'n him or Cletus. I knowed how ta take a guy down wit one punch an them Korean peoples don' abide no trouble in that neighborhood no how. Rick watchin' jus the same so I let'm.

Memorial Day come an we go back down the Jersey Shore. Rick git on wit the same schedule 'cept now we stayin' afta the show most ever night an he git the others ta stay a coupla nights, too. That come on bein' his plan. I got maybe thirty songs an he make the whole band go through'em one by one wit me losin' the lead an him takin' it up on his guitar. I don' care cuz I got me a plan, too. Rick an the Riders doin' my songs good 'nuff ta git us travelin' an one day I git ta California an find you.

Come on July an we got a real good sound 'cept Rick don' never pick up that harmonica. We don' practice ever night cuz too many women comin' 'round an even Rick gotta look. Gimme my chance ta go off wit his harmonica by myself. It ain't hard, I think. Makin'music come easy to me so I ain't sure. I knowed how I want that sound comin' inta my songs an I make myself figure how ta do it. Pushin' that harmonica on Rick happin in July.

We be at it on a Tuesday, maybe the third week. Rick goin' hard on his guitar an the drummer git clear on the beat. Cletus gone as usual so it jus' be the band. 'Round now Rick take over my parts, leadin' on alls a my songs. Okay, 'cept he ain't gittin' on his harmonica. I knowed I gotta show'm. I stop playin' afta we git ta the second song. Piano be a big part an the song ain't no good witout it. I git up an walk over ta Rick an git the harmonica offa the table on the side. I hold it up an take his hand an put it right there, makin' it so he knowed he gotta play it. Rick lookin' like he ain't gonna do it so I jus' wait. He shake his head an point ta me ta git back on the piano like they ain't my songs no more. Like they be his. Thing 'bout Rick, he don' take no orders from nobody. His band an he be the boss, but he playin' my songs an he gonna do'em my way. I ain't takin' no.

Fearsome look he give. I go thinkin' he ain't gonna wrap his lips 'round that harmonica so I take it back an go ta the piano agin. Soon's I sit Rick stamp his foot an open play. Piano 'sposed to come on top a his guitar in his way a doin' my song, but I ain't touchin' them keys. He go lookin' an I hold that harmonica high an roll it 'round my fingers so he gotta unnerstan'. He shake his head an afta he turn 'round agin I stand wit that harmonica an blow hard. A good sound come out, the right sound, makin' such a good set a notes that the dumb drummer don' know what ta do an he jus' quit. It don' matter cuz I ony care on Rick gittin' my meanin'. My songs, my way.

They all quit playin', lookin' like the first time they git I ain't no idiot. Rick gotta know I'm takin' my songs back 'til he do'em my way. He pay 'tention like that first time he come outta the office an heared'em. See, I don' play that harmonica good as him, but I play it how it kin come inta my songs an cuz he got the passion he unnerstan'. Afta, he go watchin' me take up that harmonica on alls a my songs so he kin hear how I want'm doin' it. That be the breakthrough. He git that harmonica an we go the rest a the summer doin' them songs my way, the right way 'til we goes back ta New York.

I come on knowin' Rick plannin' ta make a record afta he brung me aside one night at the club offa Prince Street. Late October as I think on it now. Soon's me an Cletus git back from the Jersey Shore Rick git onta workin' me agin afta the shows. Rick an the Riders a big draw an lines a peoples waitin' on seein' us so he git the clubs ta give'm more money. 'Bout this Cletus don' miss nothin'. Nose for money he got. Two nights a week jus' Rick an me then alls a sudden as soon as Cletus an them others out the door, most times 'round midnight, a bunch a differnt peoples come in, older guys an a woman on a standup bass. Session players an they be real good. I heared later they cost a lotta money, too. Rick's secret cuz them others playin' in Rick an the Riders good 'nuff for playin' clubs, but they ain't good 'nuff ta make no record. I don' know how he git them session peoples. All I knowed is they be fine musicians an all business jus' like Rick.

We go two times a week for three weeks, Rick waitin' on them others ta git out and tellin' Cletus he git me back ta Flushing afta. Asides that, Rick ain't tellin' nothin', but I heared the woman onta the bass say we gonna go inta a studio come December. Thing 'bout them three weeks? Rick singin' words ta my songs for the first time. He got a okay singin' voice an he knowed what ta do cuz he do most a the singin' parts for Rick an the Riders. Them lyrics jus' no good.

Dollface, I tell you 'bout Ralph Waldo Emerson an them others cuz they come outta times when writin' be the music. There weren't no records or tapes or CDs ta hold the sound, ony words in books that anyone readin' kin say over an over. An cuz a that the words got a rhythm an they fit tagether, makin' a picture jus' like a song otta do now. Rick don' git that. He ain't got the passion for words like he got for notes on that harmonica. I come on knowin' music make the picture better, but ony if the words come out right. Rick's train movin' fast. Ain't nothin' I kin do 'bout fixin' them lyrics.

Second week a them secret sessions an Cletus waitin' on me in the Flushing walkup. He go watchin' outta the window afta I come in the door, makin' sure Rick gone back ta the subway.

"What are you doing with him after the sets?"

Like I'm gonna say somethin' back. I ain't sayin' nothin'. Afta that Cletus don' bother wit the women at the bar no more. He sit right on top a the stage an give Rick a look. He makin' money offa Rick an the Riders, but he smellin' more an he ain't gonna git left out.

Rick onta Cletus an I come on thinkin' it gotta git down ta knowin' if he think he need me doin' the record or he don'. See, Rick figured on takin' my songs for hisself cuz he seen somethin' big for hisself. Them session players real good, but he keep me on the piano. If he keep me on the record do he keep me on a tour? I knowed right then that Cletus gittin' in the way, lookin' ta cash in an makin' Rick think on what he gotta do 'bout'm an, a course, that gotta mean 'bout me, too.

Rick go a week afore he git too itchy ta practice no more. Cletus hangin' back ever night, watchin' an waitin'. Me, too. Them two gotta have it out. Rick go tellin' Cletus ta git on home like them other times afta the last set. Cletus jus' say, "I'll wait."

That be it for Rick. He like bein' the boss. "Get lost!" he say loud.

"Fine!" Cletus come up close on Rick an point ta me. "I'm taking him with me."

"He stays! You go!"

"Why? What are you planning?"

Rick take Cletus by the shirt an push, but Cletus ain't no

pushover. He jus' slide over an take a chair. He shove it ta the stage an say, "Sit down. You want my piano player you get me, too. We're going to work this out right now or you'll be looking for a new man on the keys." Then he grab 'nother chair an sit down, waitin'.

I come on thinkin' I gotta make a decision, too. Them session players come bustin' in them doors an I watch Rick. His face git all red an afta a little while he look ta me. We knowed each other good afta playin' near two years. I ain't never said nothin', but he kin read me good as I kin read everbody else. Cuz a them songs Rick knowed I ain't dumb an that be his edge on Cletus who shoulda knowed. It never bin 'bout what Cletus want. It be 'bout what Rick figure he need an if he need me. He go lookin' long. I holds'm lookin' an I make sure he unnerstan' like afta I makin'm git on that harmonica. No record gonna come out soundin' good if I ain't on them piano keys. No tour gonna happin, neither. Cletus bust inta me an Rick talkin' wit no words.

"What's it going to be? We walk right now or we stay and make some money together."

Rick lookin' at me. He knowed the answer.

"We're making a record. What do you want?"

SEVEN

A patient might complain to God, demanding to know if He exists. Are the promises true? – Edna Nieves

Yolanda Whitely stood in her office at PS 0875, shouting through the door at her assistant principal. "Get on it, now!"

The outer office was a scene of pandemonium, students shouting almost as loud as the harried principal, teachers coming in fast with papers in their hands, brushing past the assistant principal who is struggling to get into the hall and deal with the unknown emergency.

Edna waited in a chair along the side wall with two others seated on her left. The noise and discord were alarming, but she saw no panic on anyone's face. The hallway was full of children and an occasional adult, all going in different directions with shouts and orders bounding off the dirty, graffiti strewn walls. It was the start of a typical public school day in the borough of Queens.

An hour passed and nothing changed. Adults and children wandered in and out of the office, most waylaid by the harried sentries behind the counter, but one or two making it to the Principal's inner office where the door was closed and a serious discussion of some sort took place. Phones rang, some going unanswered. Bells rang, sounding an alert that received no attention. Edna looked at her watch. She stole this time between her early morning responsibilities and lunch so she could inquire about Samuel. She was hoping to find Miss Parsons, a long shot, but the grade school teacher mentioned on Samuel's recording. She had a nine a.m. appointment with Principal, Yolanda Whitely. It was already after ten.

At last, the two people next to Edna are escorted into Whitely's office. As soon as the door closes Edna hears raised voices from within, parents protesting some rule their child had broken. It continues for a minute then the drama dies down. Another ten minutes pass and the door opens again. The parents leave with serious faces while Principal Whitely pulls one of her assistants aside and whispers in her ear. She returns to her office and closes the door. Edna realizes she has been forgotten.

The assistant principal comes back and makes straight for his office, looking to hide. Edna rises and confronts him.

"I'm waiting to see Principal Whitely."

He stops to look at her. "Do you have an appointment?"

"Nine o'clock, but she's gone into her office and closed the door." The bells ring loud and suddenly there is pandemonium in the hallways again. Edna has to raise her voice over the din. "I'm already late for work."

"One moment." He turns to the two women behind the counter. Neither looks up. "This woman says she had a nine o'clock appointment with Yolanda." They nod at the closed door, issuing a silent message, bad day. He steps around the counter, knocks on the office door, turns the knob and enters. A minute later he comes out and beckons Edna inside.

"We have no one named Parsons teaching at PS 0875."

Edna can see that Whitely is distracted, stressed to the point of losing her composure. "She would have been here around twenty years ago."

"Not today? I thought you were looking for someone who is with us now?"

"I was hoping she might still be here."

"Well, if she was here she isn't teaching at PS 0875 now."

"It's about one of her students. I'd like to talk to her about him."

"District office."

"What?"

"You'll have to go to the district office. I'm sorry, but I have a lot to do today." The principal rises from behind her desk.

"He's dying. There isn't much time."

"Dying? Who?"

"The man I need to discuss with Miss Parsons."

Whitely comes around her desk and moves to the door. "Go to the district office. They might have some information." She opens the door. Edna turns in her chair, but does not rise to leave.

"Is there anyone here that might have known her?"

"I wouldn't know. I've only been at PS 0875 for eight months." She nods for Edna to leave. "I have another appointment."

"Mrs. Whitley, a man is dying."

"I'm sorry. I can't help you."

Edna rises, shaking her head. "Where is the District Office?"

"Midland Parkway." Whitely disappears through the door and rushes into the assistant principal's office. Edna leaves via the hallway, passing closed classroom doors that cannot silence the undisciplined noise on the other side.

She walks toward the exit shocked by the disorganization and wondering how any child could possibly learn in such an environment. As she turns the corner she comes upon the last classroom with no apparent confusion emanating from inside. She slows her pace and looks. A pretty young woman is at a white board, speaking calmly, composed and in control. The children are arrayed in an oval around her, seated at desks and paying attention. The woman senses Edna, and looks up with a quick smile. Edna smiles back, staring for a moment as the teacher returns her attention to her class. Then she continues on.

The recordin' be in Jersey. Cletus an me take a train an come out inta a nice town. I wonder on the piano cuz I don' know what ta 'spect. I ain't never done no record afore. There be a lady waitin' on us. Rick an the session peoples waitin', too. I sit ahind a shiny black baby grand. Jus' fine. We do a run afore we git down ta doin' it for real. Lunch brung in an we eat a bunch a stuff I don' know, but it be good. Afta, a guy come inta the studio dressed real fine, wearin' gold chains 'round his neck an the biggest watch I ever seen. Older guy an I knowed he gotta be the boss cuz he do the talkin'. I heared the name Dorman, but pay it no mind cuz it don' mean nothin' ta me. It do afta.

We go three times, doin' sixteen songs an we ain't done 'til it be dark outside. Cletus gone an Rick git me back ta Flushing agin. He talk ta me like the first time ever.

"We're gonna travel," he say. "Cletus will take care of you same as before."

Where? I'm thinkin'. I don' look like I git it, but Rick onta me afta the harmonica fight.

"If the masters are approved Mr. Dorman says he'll give me a contract. Then we pick the best twelve tracks, release an album and hit the road to get some sales. We warm up for a Baltimore group."

Rick an the Riders ain't no random name like some ya hear. He got a motorcycle an the dumb drummer got one too. I gotta figure that be the ony reason Rick keep'm cuz he sure ain't no good on the sticks. We git a bus wit a big picture showin' the new album on the sides, Rick on his bike an them other three ridin' ahind on theirs. I ain't in that picture an I ain't on the CD cover, neither. My songs but nothin' 'bout me. We go ridin' that bus from gig ta gig an sleepin' in hotels long the way.

We warms good crowds for a bunch kids, loud an jus' plain crazy an them crowds love'em at ever stop. Rick got a big motorcycle hauled ahind the bus wherever we go. He git on it for pictures jus' afore we go onta the stage. Sometimes, it ain't 'bout the music.

Loud's them Baltimore boys be they don' allays do the music Rick an the Riders kin do evertime. I sit on the side doin' the piano like allays. I git a light over the keys, but no light shinin' on my place like them others. I write the songs, I make'em do'em good, I make the piano parts deliver so Rick kin sing his lousy lyrics right, but I ain't no part a Rick an the Riders. Evertime we take the stage an he point ta them others an say their names I jus' hit a C ta make it extra special, but he don' point ta me never. The music go real good an them peoples come out for Rick an the Riders.

We ride that bus a long time, all winter and inta the warm air time. Cletus like it a lot cuz a seein' peoples an places he never seen afore, bein' he never got nowhere outta New York. I gotta say them months make a change ta Cletus. He take good care a me, makin' the best food ever an bringin' me bottles a water afore we git ta playin'. An afta the show he be right there waitin' on me an makin' sure I git where I 'sposed ta be next. He go 'round smilin', too. The music. He knowed it be mine.

Near six months an money comin' ta everbody 'cept me. We go back ta New York an Cletus git a nice apartment wit three bedrooms in a nice part a Brooklyn. No need ta be guessin' 'bout it costin' cuz it be a clean brownstone wit nice peoples comin' an goin'. Cletus come up wit a car, too. A shiny Cadillac like the one comin' for you at the residence, but black. He keep it down the street ahind a fence wit peoples in uniforms makin' sure nobody gits in that ain't 'sposed ta git in. Rick gone somewhere for near a month an the Riders don' do nothin' durin' that time. Afta, I heared he got a lady he knowed outta somewhere on the tour. Them other three? I never see'em.

His fantasy, as sleep comes on, does not include the thwarted reality of Rick and the Riders playing a huge concert at San Jose State University. No, that never happened as he'd hoped. Now, years later, he is dying and he wills his mind to a more intimate setting absent Rick or Cletus. His fantasy where he is in control.

"*Beautiful can't be separated into parts like a face or hands or eyes or a smile. Beautiful runs deep, expecting nothing, but giving everything. Are you here?*"

He presses a key and the guitars and drums of his faceless backups come in. The sorority party kicks into full throttle.

Rick an the Riders git called over ta Jersey right afore September. I knowed cuz Cletus near had a fight wit Rick afta he heared an he ain't part a the meetin'. See, the record doin' real good an he figured he bin left outta the plannin' for 'nother tour. Headlinin' this time. Rick an the Riders ain't warmin' for nobody no more. I wonder where I fit, too. Cletus git hisself a meetin' wit Mr.

Ellis Dorman, the man wit the big gold watch I come on knowin' be the boss a the label, Blossom Records. Dollface, that set a songs be mine 'cept them no good lyrics. Cletus wantin' a bigger piece a the action. Me? He don' think on me for nothin', but I do. I got a plan in my head. If a big tour comin' I'm gonna be a part a doin' it an I sure gonna git ta San Jose, California an I sure gonna find you.

Mr. Dorman got a lawyer, Archer T. Zane. I tol' you his name afore if you 'member. He don' see me the first time Cletus go talkin' ta Mr. Dorman cuz I git left out, but them bein' my songs musta come up cuz Cletus come outta that meetin' all riled up an talkin' ta hisself 'bout why he gotta go back wit me. Two days he jus' stay in that nice apartment, not even goin' down ta git inta his Cadillac. All the while walkin' 'round an talkin' loud.

"We need to show Mr. Dorman and that lawyer guy those songs belong to us."

Us? I say ta myself, me! Cletus got nothin' ta do wit my songs. He cook an git a place ta sleep an that be it. 'Cept he pay the bills outta money that otta be in my pockets. Music a cheatin' business if the one makin' it ain't payin' 'tention. Like the business my daddy done on the sidewalk 'cept ya ony feel the hurtin' in ya mind an maybe ya heart if ya got one.

"Mr. Dorman wants to put Rick and the Riders on a national tour. Do you understand what that means? Big money! So, I'll do the talking, but you better show everyone how those songs came to be. Can you do that?"

All this time, him sayin' I don' know nothin'. Now, I gotta show some peoples I do. I ain't talkin' for sure. So, I git ta figurin' how I kin git what I want witout sayin' words. I knowed Mr. Dorman ain't no dummy. He a real good music man. I jus' hopin' Mr. Archer T. Zane be a smart man, too. Yep, I come on knowin' he be the smartest man in the room.

It come tagether in a buildin' on Broadway. It weren't the place Cletus go the first time. That time be ta Archer T. Zane's office in 'nother buildin', Avenue of the Americas, but I tells you 'bout that later. This one on Broadway got all kinda music makin' stuff. Lotta a space an a lotta places ta plug in an crank them amps.

First words outta his mouth show me all I need ta know 'bout Archer T. Zane bein' smart. He lookin' ta call out Rick, but he gotta move Cletus outta the way first.

Mr. Dorman sittin' close ta Archer T. Zane an I wonders on that. See, afore that meetin' I figured he go linin' up on Rick cuz a makin' money offa Rick an the Riders. I seen somethin' differnt this time. It be plain he ony carin' 'bout the truth so he ain't doin' nothin' that ain't right. Rick nervous an lookin' ta me cuz he don' know what I be thinkin'. He got a lawyer, too.

"Idiot," the lawyer say. "I know it's a harsh word, Archer, but there's no better way to say it. He was found passed out on a subway train. Mr. Brown has been taking care of him ever since. There are no records indicating where he came from or who he really is. For our purposes today, we are using the name Mr. Brown gave him, Samuel Jones."

"Yes," Mr. Dorman say. "Idiot, but a terrific piano man." I show'm a hateful look.

"Er... I need to clarify," he say. "Savant. Mr. Jones has unique skill."

Archer T. Zane lookin' ta me, too. I look back whilst he go talkin'.

"To be clear, Samuel Jones is this young man's legal name. Does anyone dispute that?"

Rick lookin' down ta his feet. No one sayin' nothin'.

"All right, then. Our purpose today," Mr. Zane turn ta Rick. "Is to make sure we have the facts concerning these songs so we can form a contract that protects everyone's interests."

"I want to be sure we don't get shortchanged," Cletus butt in.

"You are Mr. Jones' legal guardian?"

"Well, I don't know what legal means. I've been taking care of him since Social Services brought him to the residence."

Zane git a piece a paper offa the table. "That would be Mission Foundation?"

"Yeah, that's right."

"Do you have documents attesting that you are his legal guardian?"

"I guess not."

Mr. Dorman shake his bald head. "He has no standing."

Archer T. Zane keep talkin'. "Are there documents stating that Mr. Jones is incapable of taking care of himself?"

Rick's lawyer say, "We talked about this, Archer. He was released at age eighteen under Mr. Brown's signature."

"Yes," Cletus jump in. "That's right I took him in and I've taken care of him ever since."

Archer T. Zane look ta Cletus an git 'nother piece a paper offa the table. "The Mission Foundation document, signed by you, states that Samuel is released under his own recognizance."

Cletus git edgy. "Huh? I thought we were here to talk about who wrote the music!"

"I wrote those songs!" Rick give a hard look ta Cletus. He don' go lookin' ta me cuz he knowed he be lyin' an he knowed I ain't no idiot. This 'bout money. Archer T. Zane makin' sure.

"We'll make that determination in a few minutes. Right now we have to understand exactly who has standing and who doesn't. In the absence of any documents to the contrary I'm afraid," he look ta Cletus. "Mr. Brown does not."

"What? What are you doing to me?"

"I'm making sure you don't get yourself into trouble by misrepresenting your legal standing in this matter."

Rick give a smile. "We don't need him. We never did. I'll take care of Sam."

"Legally, he doesn't need taking care of by anyone." Archer T. Zane wave the paper. "He has his own standing if it can be proved who wrote these songs."

Rick whisper somethin' inta his lawyer's ear cuz he listen an the lawyer come back ta Cletus. "Are you certain that Samuel Jones is his legal name?"

"Sure. It says so on that piece of paper."

"There are city, state and federal records, and a Social Security number?"

Cletus don' blink. "Absolutely. I took him everywhere he needed to go to make sure."

"All right," Archer T. Zane say. "I'll have my assistant get everything we need. Now, with that settled let's address the issue of who owns the music."

"Blossom Records owns the music," Mr. Dorman say.

"Under certain contractual obligations to Rick and the Riders," Rick's lawyer say.

"Rick didn't write those songs," Cletus say.

Mr. Dorman git edgy. "This gets cleared up today or I'll pull every record from the stores."

Archer T. Zane let'em talk. Rick lookin' ta me. I knowed he wondrin' on how it all gonna play out. A course, the ony way gotta be me showin' them songs be mine. I ain't talkin' cuz even if I do it don' mean nothin' cuz Rick knowed ever beat an ever chord an ever note good as me. An he got somethin' on me, them lousy lyrics.

"Ellis?" Archer T. Zane wave away them doin' the talkin' an go right ta the ony man in that meetin' wit the power. "We could try to fashion some method of proof. Rick could play the songs for us. So could Samuel, but after all this time it's safe to say they both know the music equally well. With no paper trail clearly delineating authorship we could be at a standstill."

Mr. Dorman ain't stupid, neither.

"Now that it's established that Cletus Brown isn't Samuel's legal guardian...," he say.

"Since when? I've been taking care of him for almost three years."

"...and, that he has no standing," Mr. Dorman look ta Archer T. Zane. "It doesn't matter if we can't prove who wrote those songs. I have a contract with Rick and unless someone legally objects," he go lookin' ta me. "Someone with legitimate standing in this matter, I'm beginning to think we don't have a problem."

I come on thinkin' Cletus done me a favor afta all. He don' know it an he ony care 'bout his piece, but Mr. Dorman be smart, too. If Cletus don' make a stink Rick woulda cut me outta his tour an I woulda never got ta California.

"That's true," Archer T. Zane go lookin' ta me. "If, and only if, Mr. Jones is not legally capable of entering a cogent objection on his own. Certainly, he would also need to prove that these songs are authored by him. Or, in the event of a stalemate he and Rick can reach a separate understanding that would not interfere with the contract in place."

"What about me?" Cletus git outta his chair. "I have rights!"

Archer T. Zane don' git riled. "Perhaps, if Samuel and Rick agree to include you in any understanding they might reach. Otherwise, no you don't."

"Lawyers." That be all Cletus kin think on sayin'. He sit back down, shakin' his head.

So, I knowed it jus' be Rick an me. I make my eyes wide, so everone in the room knowed I unnerstan'. See, Dollface, this tour be my chance a findin' you. It come down ta showin' them peoples they be my songs or makin' Rick think he takin' too big a risk tryin' ta push me out. Cletus ain't no part a that, but he good at gittin' out the truth a what Rick be plannin'. I wonder on what kinda piano player he got lined up 'stead a me.

Thing 'bout Rick be nerves. I tol' you 'bout'm havin' a good guitar hand an singin' okay an bein' real good on that harmonica. A course, he ony done covers 'til I go makin' up them songs, but afta we make that record an afta Rick an the Riders done that tour he come on wantin' somethin' so bad it eat at his insides an make'm cheat. Rick wanna be a star. In all the time in that meetin' an not countin' Cletus, Rick the ony one gittin' up a sweat. His nerves kickin' in. He got a chance ta be a star an he afeared a me bein' in the way. But it ain't really me. It's Rick tryin' ta take it all for hisself an knowin' he ain't doin' right by me. Archer T. Zane givin'm a chance ta git me outta the way, but I ain't goin' easy. I looks at'm wit my eyes wide an a shake a my head. I look ta Archer T. Zane, pointin' my hand ta the piano. He knowed then if he din' know afore, I ain't no idiot.

"You want to play the piano?"

I turn ta Mr. Dorman, makin' sure he unnerstan'. I look ta Rick's lawyer, too. But I ain't lookin' ta Rick no more. Let'm git sweated up. Let'm think 'bout what I kin do on them keys. Let'm go wondrin' if it be better'n what he kin do wit my songs.

"Yeah!" Cletus jump in. "Yeah, play them so they know the

songs are yours!"

"It won't prove a thing!" Rick stand up. "He can play them. I can play them. We've been doing them for more than a year."

"Not so fast." Mr. Dorman be onta knowin' the truth. "Let him play if that's what he wants to do."

The piano be 'nother baby grand, black an shiny. It sound true from the first key an I gotta say I likes it better'n them console pianos I bin playin'. I git on the seat an jus' play. None a them songs we bin talkin' on, but a coupla new ones I bin figurin' in my head. I forgit alls them others in the room an go thinkin' on you cuz, a course, it be you I make music for alls that time. Seein' you agin.

I go maybe ten minutes an I ain't lookin' up 'til I git the last one done. Rick gone back ta sittin' an Cletus got a satisfied look wit his arms folded 'cross his chest. It be Mr. Dorman I wanna see cuz I knowed he unnerstan' music makin', what be good an what be mine, not Rick's. An he got that look tellin' me what I wanna be sure he heared. See, all music have a way a sayin' who it come outta. Rick gonna git up an pull on his guitar an he gonna play my songs, but he gonna play'em like Rick. I run them baby grand keys onta new songs he ain't never heared. Them songs got my signature way deep, coupla chords comin' tagether, a key change, even the place where a note git played, it gonna be me comin' inta the air offa his fingers. A music man like Mr. Dorman unnerstan' an he do cuz his face tellin' it.

"Not even the songs we're talking about," Rick say. "I bet he doesn't even understand what's going on."

I go sit on my chair next ta Cletus. He pat my shoulder like we workin' tagether or somethin', but I jus' wait on Mr. Dorman. Archer T. Zane watchin', too. He don' know 'bout music, but he know 'bout peoples. The other lawyer start talkin'.

"Look, I think the issue is moot."

Mr. Dorman shake his head no. He git up an tap Rick on the arm. Rick come 'round an start ta git up like everthin' bin settled. It ain't.

"I'm going back to New Jersey," he say. "The rest of you stay here and come to an agreement."

Rick's face 'bout went red.

"As far as I'm concerned we own the album, but I'm not convinced who wrote the music." He turn an go lookin' ta me. "I won't get behind a national tour until all parties in this room, except Mr. Brown who has no standing, have signed an agreement. Bring it to New Jersey tomorrow and if I like it, I'll sign and we'll go on from there. If I don't," here be the whens I be sure he onto   Rick lyin', "somebody gets sued."

"But…" Rick's lawyer say.

"But…" Rick say.

"But…" Cletus say.

Mr. Dorman move out the door. Rick sweatin' an talkin' loud ta his lawyer whilst Cletus tryin' ta git Archer T. Zane ta splain legal standin'. I watch'em, knowin' all the mad gotta git outta that room afore we kin work somethin' out. Archer T. Zane musta bin thinkin' it too cuz he nod ta me sometimes an his lips make a funny look like he wanna smile 'cept them others woulda got mad even more. I ain't gonna smile neither cuz, a course, I 'sposed ta be a idiot.

"Gentleman," Archer T. Zane finally make'em stop. "Before we go any further, we need to establish representation for Mr. Jones."

"Archer…" the other lawyer try ta speak.

"He has standing. There is legal documentation stating that Mr. Jones is of sound mind and is capable of taking care of himself. You can fight that, but your client needs to understand it will be a long, expensive battle."

"What about me?" Cletus ain't nothin' if he ain't pushin' alls a time. "You say he can take care of himself? I'll throw him out! See what happens to him. He can't even talk. He's never had a nickel or spent a nickel since the day he came into the residence. I cook his food, bring him where he needs to be and get him home again."

There he be agin, talkin' likes I ain't even there.

"Mr. Brown, I'm telling you what you need to understand under the law. Did you write those songs?"

"Well, no."

"Do you have a legal contract that calls for compensation from anyone concerning this matter?"

"No, but I'm telling you I've been taking care of him for almost three years."

"Did anyone make any representations to you concerning this matter?"

"What does that mean, representations?"

"Did anyone promise you, orally or in writing, something in return for any service you provide concerning this matter?"

"Sure. Rick's been paying me."

"Money?"

"Under the table,"

Rick speak up. "I give him a few bucks cash twice a month."

"For what purpose?"

The other lawyer git onta Rick's arm hard, stoppin'm outta talkin' more. "I must advise you not say another word."

Rick throw up his hands. "Fine. You're my lawyer."

"Archer? You accept that a few dollars under the table does not constitute a contract?"

"Let's table that for now. Whatever Rick may have paid Mr. Brown is of limited import to the matter at hand. We need only address the issue of an agreement. That is, if Mr. Jones does not wish to contest ownership."

They all go lookin' ta me like I gotta talk or somethin'. I look ta Archer T. Zane, thinkin' I need a lawyer, too. He read my lookin' real good. Cletus starin', pleadin' for somethin' wit his eyes. Archer T. Zane make a move.

"I suggest we take a break for a few minutes. Let me confer with Mr. Jones."

"What will that do? He doesn't even talk!" Rick talkin' loud.

"Hopefully, it will lead to some resolution. That's what we all want, isn't it?"

"Not if it I don't get something out of it!" Cletus talkin' loud.

Rick kin't hold off. "What do you want?"

"My fair share! I take him where he needs to be. I feed him, make sure he looks good and make sure he has a place to sleep. You pay me for that and it better be a lot more than before."

"Mr. Brown?" Archer T. Zane make the question, "What does Mr. Jones get?"

"I don't know. What does he want?"

"That's why I need to talk to him."

"Archer?" The other lawyer aks, "Do you propose to represent him in this matter?"

"That's his decision."

A course, I want'm ta be my lawyer. I tol' you afore, Dollface, there be a way a seein' who a person be, who they allays be when ya look in their eyes. I bin lookin' inta his eyes an he be a okay man. What he git from bein' a lawyer, I don' know. What I git from him bein' *my* lawyer? A chance ta goes ta California an I take it. I stands up an I nods my head real hard. No question 'bout my answer.

"Does anyone dispute that Mr. Jones has just gestured his ascent to my representation?" Nobody say nothin', 'cept' the other lawyer.

"He seems to understand what we're saying and he seems to agree."

"Are we going to get this straightened out now?" Rick aks.

Archer T. Zane look ta Rick. "You accept that Mr. Jones has taken me as his attorney in this matter?"

"If it will get this resolved."

Archer T. Zane push on Rick. "You accept that Mr. Jones has taken me as his lawyer?"

Rick nod. "Yes, yes. Okay."

"All right. I need a few minutes to confer with my client."

It be settled quick. I write the words *tour* an *San Jose, California* onta a piece a paper. Archer T. Zane aks me if that be whats I want. I write *Cletus come an git paid by Rick.* He aks how much. I writes *more than he git now. You figure.* He aks what or where about San Jose. That man be good. I write *Rick an the Riders play music at San Jose State University.* An there it be! My plan comin' tagether!

Volunteer ladies don' come 'round much no more. Christmas comin' an there ony be me an a ol' lady over t'other side a the house. They come in the mornin' like afore wit flowers, but they don' try talkin' an they don' come 'round in the aftanoons. I figure they don' stay cuz they got other stuff ta do cuz a Christmas comin'. I don' think on Christmas. Never mean nothin' when I growed up an afta, movin' 'round wit the music, it jus' a day that come an go witout thinkin' on it.

Head hurtin' a lot. Sometimes, I git ta shakin' an Edna come quick. I git cold sittin' near the window an lookin' an talkin' inta this recorder. I know it ain't cold in this house. It jus' me fightin' the dyin'. Jus' so much a body kin do. Somethin' gotta give so other parts kin keep workin'. Edna know it an she brung me a blanket ta wrap 'round my shoulders afta gittin' me inta this chair. Yesterday she git 'nother chair not so soft as this one an not so big, neither. She carry it over an put it like there be two peoples sittin' an lookin' outta the window. Then she sit wit me for a while. I don' do no talkin' an she don' talk much, neither. I don' mind. It be good when she sit wit me that little bit. It put me ta thinkin' what come next afta the pill do its magic for the last time.

'Portant ta me that you know I ain't afeared. I ain't nothin' really an that's a 'sprise cuz I allays figured peoples be afeared a dyin' an it be that way for me when my time come. But it ain't an alls I kin do, no... alls I wanna do is git this talkin' out '. It ain't 'bout bein' afeared. It 'bout workin' at what be right afront a me each minute goin' by. 'Cept, an I gotta be honest, I do think 'bout what come afta all this hurtin'. Goin' inta 'nother place somewheres?

Like all them other books, I got the Bible words in my head. Gotta say it don' make a lotta sense ta me 'cept some a the poetry an picture words in Psalms an such. First book, called the Old Testament, an full a peoples gittin' inta trouble an gittin' hurt an gittin' killed. Second book, New Testament, got a lotta that stuff, too. I think on the message other peoples' gittin' but I ain't. Jesus got a message, I think. Them others I don' know. What I seen in livin'? Most peoples jus' workin' on gittin' stuff. They don' much care 'bout other peoples 'cept if they git in the way. Daddy be like that.

I 'spose some be differnt, good, but not a lot. Afta momma you be the first carin' peoples I come on knowin' an Edna be the last one since I ain't leavin' here an no one comin' new afore I gotta die. Atween, I think on Cletus an Rick an Archer T. Zane an Crystal an Dale

Messenger. I gotta figure'em out. Mostly, I got a feelin' I gotta figure me out afore it's too late. Maybe that's why I do this talkin' ta you.

Jesus say somethin 'bout the next place bein' a kingdom up in the sky or someplace that ain't here. A course, there be 'nother place called hell an that 'sposed ta be down. I don' know. It don' come clear ta me like a poem that make a picture. I don' know how peoples kin tell 'bout a place they say we all goin' ta. If them peoples livin' right here like me an Edna an everbody, how kin they know all sure 'bout some place afta dyin? I ain't never heared a peoples comin' back so we kin see'em an they kin tell us what the afta dyin' place be like. Dead be dead an it be the end. Edna one a them, I think. I 'spose if I wanna talk I otta aks her, but that ain't gonna happin.

Jesus say he comin' back. He jus' don' say what time. So, Dollface, that ain't heppin' me know 'bout what come afta layin' in this bed. I let that go an jus' think on what he say 'bout bein' good an bein' bad. He got that right, I figure. Jus' hard ta knows the differnce sometimes.

EIGHT

I try to alleviate the loneliness of dying - Edna Nieves

E dna decided to skip the District Education Office on Midland Parkway. Her conversation with the PS 0875 elementary school principal was too discouraging. Too many years had gone by and she doubted the educational system of New York would cooperate with or even be sympathetic to her purpose. She re-read the e-mail response to the message she'd left on the Rick and the Riders web site. This, too, was discouraging.

Ms. Nieves:
Thank you for your inquiry concerning Rick and the Riders. Yes, there was a backup player with the band named Samuel Jones during its first solo tour nine years ago. That tour was a huge success and proved to be instrumental in the band becoming a national draw. One picture is attached depicting Mr. Jones on a piano. The piano was used during those early performances, but it has since been replaced by keyboards. Mr. Jones appeared with Rick and the Riders only during its initial promotional period. He left the band at the time its original leader, Rick Tilton, was killed in a motorcycle accident in California. The band we know today continues to be very successful. However, only one member remains from the original group. He recalls Mr. Jones as a talented piano player.
Sincerely,
Mary F. MacDonough
Publicist, Rick and the Riders

Somewhere in the audience she was listening. It won't happen during this first set, he concludes. His fantasy, after all, bringing her to him on his terms before the lights of his life went down.

She couldn't get into the party mood. Her sorority sisters held court with a group of frat brothers, enabling her unnoticed escape to the house, large, white and imposing on a hilltop overlooking the buildings of the campus below. In a few days finals would be completed. One more year of college to earn her degree. Then she was determined to teach children like those she had come to know at the residence in Jamaica, Queens. She thought about Lacey. Would the little girl still be there? She prayed from time to time that a good family would adopt her. She prayed for him, too. For his safety and well-being and that they may meet again someday. She did it now as she climbed the stairs into the house.

If there be a time in them twelve years afta knowin' you that come close ta that soul-touchin' feelin' it gotta be seein' them new places I ain't never seen afore cuz a that tour wit Rick an the Riders. Yeah, we done some ridin' on airplanes, but we done a lotta ridin' on a bus. Cletus musta got everthin' he want cuz he don' have no more words wit Rick. Rick thinkin' my songs be his cuz Archer T. Zane give'm my word in writin' an, a course, I git happy cuz we goin' ta California. I ain't gonna say much 'bout that 'cept ta tell you I git good carin' outta Cletus, I git mention on them album covers, I git my name called out like Rick do for them others an I sit under lights same's them. Good 'nuff ta make it so you kin see me when you come ta the concert in San Jose. Rick an Cletus takin' my money? I don' care long's I sees you in California.

That bus gimme a look 'bout what be in places aside a New York. I tol' you 'bout the Jersey Shore an the moon shinin' on the water. It be like that, all new an all differnt. Afta we git onta the highway inta Pennsylvania we see farms wit nothin' but hills goin' everwhere. I ain't never seen nothin' like that. Then we go ways away inta places like Iowa an Kansas, flat an forever an makin' Pennsylvania farms look small. Corn, I knowed, an I go lookin' an thinkin' 'bout the kinda peoples makin' it grow everwhere. A lotta complainin' 'bout the long ridin' an a lotta sleepin' whilst it goin' by, but I ain't sleepin'. No way! Not even if it rain.

We do four shows ever week. I count maybe atween one an two thousand peoples watchin'. Rick do good on his guitar, real good on that harmonica an even good singin' them bad lyrics. I go long on the piano cuz everone knowed I be part a the band afta the meetin' wit Archer T. Zane. Look, I be the best musician an them still my songs no matter what Rick go sayin' on the radio an ta the writin' peoples comin 'round. I knowed it, he knowed it an Cletus knowed it. So, long's Rick figure he got no fight comin' he ain't lookin' ta crowd me outta the playin'. Me goin' hard on them keys an laughin' an makin' like Jerry Lee Lewis be the kinda show them peoples like. Sellin' a lotta records.

Long run, Dollface, goin' 'bout them cities an towns afore we git ta California. I ain't gonna tell you 'bout ever one cuz you knows I kin do it. Jus' the same I gotta tell you 'bout one a them places. We git ta Lawrence, Kansas 'round June an it be hot. We go outside in a stadium, seein' good lookin' women everwheres. Cletus 'bout fall in love.

"OUT!", he go yellin' afta he brung her inta the hotel. We got two bedrooms an 'nother room wit a big television. I git goin' cuz I don' like bein' 'round when he git like that. Fine lookin' woman, I gotta say, an he got a differnt look wit'er from all them others he brung 'round afore. I catch her givin' me a look, too, like she sorry for makin' it so I gotta git outta there an she knowed Cletus ain't bein' nice.

I git onta the street an go walkin'. Lotta cars an peoples goin' everwhere an nowhere jus' like me. 'Cept it ain't like New York. Them Kansas peoples differnt in ways I bin thinkin' on, but ain't clear on how ta 'splain. Maybe cuz they look up not down. They walk easy, too. In New York peoples ain't lookin' ya in the eye. They go rushin' wit no lookin' an no stoppin' 'cept when the walkin' lights ain't blinkin'. Kansas peoples ain't lookin' like they gotta git somewhere quick an there ain't no need ta git clear a cars cuz theys all stop for peoples wantin' ta git t'other side a the street. So, I walk wit'em an I look in windows an stores an I even git a drink a root beer. I come on knowin' outta all that travelin' that America got differnt peoples an differnt livin' an differnt seein' aside what I knowed in New York.

That lady Cletus brung ta the hotel come on bein' real special. Not pushy, neither. She stay wit Cletus an even go ridin' the bus. I come on knowin' she come outta Chicago, catchin' us doin' the gig in Kansas cuz a visitin' wit'er sister or somethin' like that. An when we gotta fly somewheres Cletus git me inta a seat an go sepret wit her, buyin' her ticket an catchin' up afta we git ta a new stage. We all shack up tagether in them hotels, him an her sleepin' in one room an me gittin' n'other that ain't so good. I don' care cuz California comin'. We don' see Rick an them others 'cept when we play. Rick a big star an he got a lotta peoples comin' 'round an hangin'on everwhere.

We git ta San Diego an I be real worked up cuz it ony be a week afore we does your San Jose show - why all a my song writin' git done. Maybe, I figured, if you glad ta see me I quit Rick an the Riders an hang 'round San Jose, California. We bin on the road six months, comin' on September an all them kids back doin' school. I don' never figure you ain't there an I don' never figure I ain't gonna see you.

There be two, maybe three thousand watchin' Rick an the Riders durin' them concerts we done afore movin' up north. Rick gittin' crowded wherever he go. He ain't able ta go outside an he even come up ta git a decent supper outta Cletus. It be the first time I sit at a table wit Rick afta we make that deal wit Archer T. Zane. Up 'til then he sit ways away up front on them buses an airplanes whilst Cletus go pushin' me ta the back. Yep, I knowed Rick ain't gittin' close ta me afta it come on clear ta Mr. Dorman they be my songs. Deal done. I ain't carin' 'bout nothin' 'cept gittin' on that stage in San Jose an findin' you lookin' an hearin'me. It gonna happin'.

Rick an the dumb drummer make a differnt move afta we come onta the bus ta San Jose. They don' even show up. Cletus push me ta my seat an take 'nother one wit his pretty lady. Roadies an all them others hangin' up front. Nobody say nothin' 'bout Rick an I wonders where he be at. It ain't Rick I care 'bout, but I don' want nothin' stoppin' us from doin' that San Jose show. I tell you here if Rick think on scattin' outta doin' it I woulda dropped'm wit the hardest punch I ever throwed. We git ta San Jose an I jump outta that bus. Cletus come lookin' an tryin' ta unnerstan' why I go lookin' all 'round. Then he musta figured it cuz he say,

"Rick's on his Harley. He's on his way."

Then he brung his lady inside up ta the room. I don' go nowheres. I stay right there waitin' on Rick ta show up. He never do.

Edna decided to write a letter to Archer T. Zane. She called his office shortly after encountering the dead-end message from Rick and the Riders' publicist.

"Mr. Zane is traveling," answered his efficient, no-nonsense secretary. "If this is a legal matter please be informed that he is not accepting new clients. I can refer you to one of his associates." Edna paused, deciding that the secretary lacked the patience to properly convey her inquiry about Samuel. Besides, lawyers made her nervous. She said no thank you and hung up.

Her letter was short and simple, mentioning her patient's condition and inquiring if Attorney Zane might assist her in uncovering information about him as well as any next of kin. She posted the letter with little expectation of a response. And, she admitted to herself, with each passing day she was less concerned with the details of her patient's life. Samuel Jones had some prominence as a part of a music group, Rick and The Riders. Who was she to dig any deeper?

The band was well into its first set and the onlookers at Sigma Alpha Phi were caught up in the reverie. She could hear the music, but it wasn't hard to find peace with her thoughts farther away in the sorority house kitchen. It wouldn't be long before a few couples wandered in, looking for a place to be alone.

She sat at a large table with a cup of tea. It wasn't always this way when her sorority threw a party. Most times she joined in the spirit, but recently her thoughts ran deeper. In the past year she had concentrated on her studies, earning straight As and envisioning the career she would pursue; practical experience followed by more study and hopefully, the chance to bring the ideas percolating in her half finished thesis to fruition. Not due until second semester of her senior year, she knew she had time to delve deeper into her research. She had observed classrooms at the local public schools and in the coming year would student teach under the supervision of a veteran out in the valley. She looked forward to learning under real conditions in the real world.

Children touched her. Lacey, of course, was special, occupying a place in her heart, but the others she came to know in New York solidified her determination. Yes, those children had challenges, but after a few weeks, getting to know them and falling in love with them, she recognized that each was unique, full of the same curiosity and hope that all living souls possess. She knew there was a way to open their fertile minds to the love of learning and the beauty of life. Someone had done that for her, the one that remained most profound in her memory who wasn't a child at all. No, he wasn't normal in the way that one would recognize normal in another human being. He spoke, but as far as she knew only to her. He knew by heart every word from every book she read to the children. And, he recited poems and profound philosophical essays with a depth of understanding that belied his circumstance. He touched her more than she knew at the time, but she knew it now as she pondered her future. She remembered kissing him good-bye.

Cletus come git me, standin' outside in the dark the whole time watchin' for Rick.

"Gotta go," he say, but I heared somethin' bad outta his voice. "Come to the room."

"Where's Rick?" I aks with my eyes not my mouth.

"Mr. Dorman wants to talk to us on the telephone."

I follows'm up the stairs an inta lobby ta the elevators. He go lookin' down an shufflin' his shoe on the floor an I figure somethin' ain't right. We git ta the room. His lady open the door then hurry away inta the bedroom. Cletus go git the telephone.

"Sit down," he say.

Afta be jus' a bad hurtin'. Them others listnin' somwheres on the telephone an Mr. Dorman sayin' the names afore tellin' us the bad news.

"Cletus? Do you have Samuel with you?"

"Yes, Mr. Dorman. He's here."

"All right that's everyone. There's no easy way to say this so I'll be direct. Rick was killed in a motorcycle accident about six hours ago."

Ya coulda knocked me onta the floor.

"From what we know he died instantly from massive head trauma. I'm sending a plane tomorrow to pick you up and bring his body back to New York. The concert tour is cancelled and obviously there will be no further dates. I'm very sorry to tell you this terrible news. You all loved Rick and I want you to know that we at Blossom share your grief."

I din' hear nothin' afta. San Jose an doin' a gig an findin' you be all I ever want. I make songs an I make Rick do'em right so I kin see you agin. He go kill hisself an I got nothin'. Simple as that I walk outta that hotel.

NINE

"I've hurt people. I don't have time to fix the wrongs. I'm afraid to die." Reassurance is essential to end of life care – Edna Nieves

I go walkin' an walkin' the whole night an afta the sun come up I git ta San Jose State University. Dumb ta be lookin'. I knowed I never gonna find you cuz a all them peoples everwheres. I look at ever girl wit your color hair. Fat, small, taller'n you an I git onta the next one, 'bout ready ta smash somethin' cuz Rick go killin' hisself. I stay there the whole day, walkin' 'round all them buildins', nothin'. You gotta be somewheres, but you ain't. You know why I knowed? Cuz a soul kin feel 'nother reachin' out. No reachin'.

Night come an I figure Cletus git on that airplane. Good, cuz I be done wit all of'em an wit Cletus for sure. 'Cept that ain't how it happin'. I keep lookin', watchin' it git dark an seein' cars comin' an goin' an for the first time afta hearin' the bad news I git ta feelin' somethin' asides mad an sad. If you was gonna hear me talkin' on this recorder I figure you think I shoulda bin hungry an I shoulda quit on lookin' an I shoulda jus' gone away. But I come on thinkin' I bin lookin' in the wrong place. Somethin' make me git movin' somewheres differnt. An, Dollface, you gotta unnerstan' the powerful knowin' inside a me that say wheres ta go. I bin thinkin' long on that cuz a the Bible talkin' 'bout a times ta ever purpose, Ecclesiastes 3:1.

I go outta them college buildins' an up a hill, seein' big houses an such. I don' have no reason ta go lookin' there, but I got me a feelin' like my soul know somethin' my head don'. I git up top a that hill an 'round a corner lookin' an seein' lights outta them college buildins'. The feelin' be strong an I sees a big white house an a sign. I knowed it like I know everthin' I ever seen in books, Sigma Alpha Phi. You be there! You be there! My soul tellin' me loud. I stand a long whiles, breathin' hard cuz a bein' sure I found you. I knowed you gotta be there cuz our souls sayin' hello. Then somethin' inside make me sit on the sidewalk an wait.

Maybe 'bout two hours I sit waitin' on you. Lotta peoples goin' ta that house an music playin' an keyboard soundin' real good. Coupla girls out front checkin' on somethin' afore lettin peoples in, but they ain't you so I hide offa the side an down a bit. I knowed peoples woulda got spooked cuz a some guy jus' sittin' on the sidewalk like that piece a sidewalk daddy gimme ta do the sellin' in New York. Bodega peoples allays nervous, seein' me jus'standin an waitin'. I ain't dumb an I knowed ya gotta pay 'tention. San Jose ain't no differnt in that way 'cept I din' pay 'nuff 'tention.

She finished her tea just as the first set came to a close. Sounds of applause and shouts for more drifted into the house. She rose from the table to peer out the window. Several couples were approaching the stairs. They held hands and talked softly. She knew it was best to leave the house to them and their private plans.

Outside, she avoided the crowd of onlookers who talked, laughed, and poured more beer from kegs nearby. She circled around toward the front gate where two young pledges were stationed to make sure no uninvited guests made entry.

"Everything all right?" she asked.

"Yes," one of the pretty girls answered.

The other girl spoke. "But something happened down the street."

"Where?"

The girl pointed. "Down the hill about two blocks, on the sidewalk. Two police cars stopped with lights flashing, but no sirens. We thought they were coming here, but they jumped out and grabbed some guy. It all happened fast. They had him in cuffs before we understood what was going on. Then they put him in one of the cars and drove off."

She stepped through the gate and peered down the street. "Who called them?"

"I don't know. I don't think it had anything to do with our party."

"Good," she turned back. "Let me take over. Go grab a beer and catch some music."

The pledges smiled with anticipation. "We'll come back in a little while."

She waved them off. "Take your time."

After they hurried off she went through the gate and walked down the sidewalk. She stood for a moment, looking back up the street and then down at the tops of the campus buildings. A vision of the unusual boy she once knew in New York appeared before her mind's eye. She suddenly feared for him, feeling him near. Uncertainty and confusion made her shudder as she turned back to the sorority house.

Does ya know 'bout jail? I never done no time, not even afta Daddy git me onta the street. I never git rousted by police 'cept one time wit Dale. I'll git ta that. But them San Jose cops got a way a findin' trouble that ain't there jus' like New York's finest ain't findin' it when there be.

Two cop cars come fast up that hill, stoppin' wit a lotta lights an squealin' tires right where I be. Course, I shoulda scatted quick, but there weren't no wheres ta go cuz all them houses got big fences goin' ways up high. I musta bin lookin' ta run cuz them cops come outta them cars real fast an they ain't aksin' no questions, neither. One of'em go grabbin' my arms an turnin' me onta the car near breakin' my face on the glass. 'Nother cop git my wrists an I be locked inta cuffs so fast I ain't got time ta think on the hurtin' in my arms. Twice I don' do what I shoulda afta I seen trouble comin' - that time them brownies come outta the car an that time them San Jose cops come at me wit no meanin' ta aks questions.

Two hours they keep me standin' down ta the station. Two hours I ain't sayin' nothin'. An I gotta tell you here them cops do a lotta a pushin, yellin' an hard smackin' 'cross my head. They don' care

73

nothin' 'bout doin' that an I got no one steppin' ta my side. Gotta take it.

Black ink come next an jus' as hard smackin' wit no thinkin' on hurtin' my fingers, rollin'em 'cross a bunch a papers an takin' a coupla pictures. Then I git shoved down a bunch a stairs inta a dark room wit peoples sittin' an standin' ahind metal doors. Lotta a peoples, dirty, some cryin' an carryin' on an some lookin' like them brownies afore knockin' me silly in New York. Gotta be honest, first chance one of'em git afta I git shoved inside an the cops gone up them stairs, he come at me. I drop'm quick. Lotta shoutin' afta, but I ain't talkin' an nobody come at me no more all night.

I got no wallet an, a course, I ain't carryin' no way a knowin' who I be. 'Cept bein' a part a Rick an the Riders ya gotta have a card sayin' ya kin git inta places ya 'sposed ta be at. I come on thinkin' that musta bin how they find Cletus cuz he come an git me outta that jail next mornin'.

He be alls careful wit them San Jose cops. He say yes sir an no sir ta ever question an I gotta stand offa the side cuz I ain't talkin'. Afta it all git settled up the cuffs come off an Cletus go grabbin' my arm ta git outta that place. I let'm cuz I don' wanna be there no more, neither. I tol' you I be done wit Cletus an afta we git onta the sidewalk I pull my arm an go hustlin' fast, hopin' I kin find that house agin'. Your house top a the hill. Cletus yellin' an comin' afta me, but I ain't payin'm no mind, walkin' fast, him tryin' ta catch up an suckin' hard for air.

"Where are you going? We gotta go to the airport. There's a plane waiting."

A taxi comin' down the street an Cletus go grabbin' me agin, holdin' his other arm up, wavin' it down. I ain't goin' ta no airport so I push'm offa me an keep walkin'. Don' matter, taxi don' stop.

"Hey!" Cletus movin' up ahind. "We have to go!"

I shake my head an keep walkin', but Cletus come runnin' 'round, makin' me stop.

"What is it? You want to stay here? You can't. The concert is cancelled. The tour is cancelled. We have to go home."

I shake, pointin' ta the cement under my feet. He knowed me

long 'nuff ta git my meanin'. I ain't goin' nowheres outta San Jose, California. He open his eyes wide cuz he figured somethin' he din' know afore.

"Everything was about you getting here! What's here in this city that's so important that you won't leave?" He go lookin' inta my face real hard an I looks right back so he knowed. "You *did* make up all those songs for Rick, didn't you? Holy… I was right all along! You're super smart! You made everything happen so you could get here to this place. Why? What are you looking for? Or is it who?" I jus' keep lookin'. "Now I get it. That's why you ran off by yourself and got picked up by the cops. You want to find something or someone." He nod his head. "Yep, you're smart. I didn't pay enough attention."

He go lookin' 'round, wondrin' on what he otta do.

"All right, let's keep walking a little bit. No, c'mon, you must be hungry. Let's eat somewhere. I'll call Mr. Dorman and tell him I need a little more time. He'll hold the plane for us while I figure this out. Jeez, all this for the past three years just to come here to San Jose."

We start walkin', him shakin' his head an even smilin'.

"You made up a bunch of great songs so Rick and the Riders could cut an album and go on a tour. I can't believe it, but," he go puttin' his arm on me. "I do. Outsmarted all of us and made everyone a lot of money in the process."

I bin thinkin' on what happin afta for a long time. Cletus seen a breakfast place an I follow'm inside. He git a table by the window. He git bacon an eggs for him an me an I seen my hands all black an dirty from the finger printin' in that San Jose jail. I git up an go inta the bathroom ta git'em clean. That gotta be when he done it. Breakfast on the table afta I git back.

"Okay, the way I see it is we can stay here for a few days and let you look around for whatever or whoever it is. Or, we can catch that plane and come back later after Mr. Dorman decides what to do about Rick and the Riders. The right thing is to get on that plane so I can protect our interests. And, I promise you right now, cross my heart and hope to die, I'll make sure you get back here to do your looking. I'll come with you. I'll make it happen. And, the good thing is we'll have the money to do it right."

He go chompin' and fidgetin' like I knowed when he ain't tellin' the truth. Like most a the time.

"There's a big payday coming for us back in New York. Rick's dead but there was a lot of money made before we got here. Mr. Dorman's going to have to settle up just as soon as we get back."

He take a piece a bacon, chewin' an lookin' for me ta give'm a answer. I shakes my head an eat. Ain't goin' nowheres outta San Jose, California.

"All right," he say, "if that's the way you want it we'll finish eating and I'll call Mr. Dorman and tell him we'll get back on our own. Can't keep the plane waiting. He'll be mad, but I've got a little money. We can stay for a few days. But, look, we've got to go back soon. If we don't we might get shortchanged."

I give'm a nod cuz, like a dumbass, I believe his lyin'. Last time ever. He finish eatin' an I see a shiny new phone comin' outta his pocket. He push a button an go talkin' like there be Mr. Dorman talkin' on t'other side. He tell it like he say it ta me an I git ta thinkin' on you seein' me an how ta make it so you don' git afeared cuz a me bein' there.

"Are you sure you want to do that?" Cletus talkin' like he ain't sure. "All right, Mr. Dorman. If you want to make a car available for us to use it will be much easier. I don't know, maybe a day or two or three. Yes, he's trying to find something or somebody. No, I don't know where or who, but he seems to be sure. I'll let him lead the way. Address? Oh yes, let me see." Cletus pick up a menu from atween the salt and ketchup.

"Here it is 123-40 East Meadow View Ave., Ken's Breakfast and Lunch. We'll be on the sidewalk out front."

He snap that shiny phone shut an go lookin' 'cross ta me wit a big smilin' face.

"All set. Eat up and we'll go looking for as long as you want."

A 'course, that don' happin. We be standin' on the sidewalk an I git real sleepy. Car come an I jus' 'bout git onta the backseat afore I ain't 'wake no more. I don' know nothin' 'til I git rousted outta that airplane by Cletus afta it git ta New York. He put somethin' in my eggs whilst I go washin'my hands in the bathroom.

Okay, I figure, ridin' a taxi inta the city. I gonna git Cletus offa my back for good. He lied ta me. He go stealin' my chance a seein' you an I bin hatin' on'm alls a while afta.

TEN

Loved ones should try not to show their fear, insecurities or uncontrolled sorrow. A smile means everything - Edna Nieves

E dna unwrapped the box, relieved that the latest delivery had arrived. She was running low on opioids and because she only had two patients and only Samuel needed the painkillers, she worried that the doctors at Jamaica Hospital might challenge her request. He was on the verge of the final stage, needing opioids each day as well as pills to forestall the seizures. Sometimes, she stayed in his room, watching to be sure he responded by falling into the stupor that passed for sleep to anyone who didn't know better. Either way the pain was lessened and she left the room believing a few hours of relief was possible. Soon, one or two weeks, she doubted it would be before the new year, Samuel would enter the throes of agony that would rob his will to live.

She hated cancer. Unrelenting and unfair, those were the words she used to describe her patients' descent into hell in her reports. Those who read them; doctors, nurses and medical administrators already knew. Alone, apparently homeless, mysteriously unknown and speaking into a recording device to a girl who may only exist in his imagination, motivated Edna's determination to prevent him from being forgotten after he passed.

Lately, she found herself seeking God's forgiveness each time she slipped the recorder from Samuel's limp hand. His story captivated her. She guessed that he dreamt as well. Every so often he mumbled or spoke aloud in his stupor or his sleep. The words were about music, a concert and a girl he wanted to find. It must be the same girl he was speaking to on his recorder. The story was touching and perhaps true. Certainly, parts were true. She'd found Mission Foundation and PS 0875. She'd received corroboration that a Samuel Jones was once a member of a prominent band called Rick and the Riders. The picture that accompanied the response from the group's publicist was too indistinct to confirm that it was her patient, but she wanted to believe it was him. Archer T. Zane was a real person, Cletus Brown, too.

She leaned close to Samuel's face, making sure he was asleep. Then she reached beneath the sheet and gently took the tiny recorder. He mumbled something she couldn't understand. As she stepped back and moved to the door he mumbled again. Fitful tonight, but not conscious and, therefore, not consumed by waking pain. Edna sighed and left the room. She looked in on her other patient and when she was satisfied that all was as it should be, moved on to her small office, placed the recorder on her desk, pressed rewind and then play.

I bin thinkin' on Christmas cuz it comin' in a coupla days. I'm gonna make it, but it ain't gonna be much fun. This poundin' real bad. Edna givin' me more pills an that 'bout all she kin do ta make it better for me. She sit wit me everday, sometimes talkin' an sometimes jus' sittin'. The ol' lady down the hall be close ta dyin' too, but she ain't clear in the head no more. I know she wanna, but there ain't nothin' Edna kin do for her, neither.

She be takin' this recorder. Coupla nights back she come inta the room, thinkin' I be asleep. Pill work most a the time, but sometimes it take a while. I act like I'm sleepin' cuz I don' wanna git up. Course, Edna ain't comin' ta make me do that. She jus' lookin' in on me ta make sure. Then she git her hand under the sheet an take the recorder. That's how I know.

I tol' you Christmas ain't never bin much special. Daddy din' do nothin' afta momma don' come home no more an I don' much 'member what she done on that day when I be a little kid. Afta, wit Cletus it ain't no differnt, 'cept the one time in the residence when peoples come an give stuff ta the little kids. Lacey git a bunch a dolls cuz everone thinkin' that be what she like. She take'em, but afta a while that first doll be the ony one she go carryin' 'round that house. 'Cept I otta talk on one Christmas wit Archer T. Zane. I bin thinkin' I gotta say somethin' on it, but first, I gotta finish on Cletus.

We git outta the airport an it ain't long afore I git my head cleared an unnerstan' what Cletus done. Him an his girlfriend shack up in the apartment like it be that way forever. He don' say nothin' ta me an he don' go lookin' at me, neither cuz he be afeared a what I be thinkin'. Next day he gone early an it jus' be me an the girl hangin' 'round the apartment. I ain't gonna say nothin' bad 'bout her cuz she ain't.

"I'm sorry Cletus did that to you," she say. "It's just that he's worried about what's going to happen now that Rick has died. He went over to New Jersey to meet with Mr. Dorman this morning. He said the funeral will be the day after tomorrow. In the meantime, let me take care of you. How about some breakfast?"

She make pancakes, talkin' 'bout where she come from, Chicago. In all a time afta I stop talkin', Sheena, that be her name, be the ony one actin' like she don' even know. She go talkin' ta me jus' the same's she talk ta everbody an she tell me 'bout herself an her feelin' on Cletus.

"I love him and he loves me, but he's all mixed up. That will be hard for us. We both knew from the moment we met after the concert in Lawrence. Do you know I was only visiting my sister who goes to school out there? I'm from Chicago. If I didn't happen to be with my sister I never would have met Cletus."

I be thinkin' better if ya stayed in Chicago.

"I quit my job when he asked me to come on the tour with him. He told me about you, how he takes care of you and makes sure you get where you're supposed to be. Now, he doesn't know what's going to happen. He doesn't trust anybody. He thinks they're going to steal his money."

His money? My money!

"You're special on that piano. Do you know that?" I come on thinkin' she ain't dumb. "I know he's cheating you out of some of that money, maybe all of it. He says there's something wrong with you and that he's the only one who ever cared enough to watch over you. That's what I mean about him being mixed up. He doesn't understand that it's your playing with the band that's taking care of him. I'll work on that. If the band doesn't survive I'll get Cletus to go back to really helping people. He told me about the residence and how he came to know you. That's the kind of thing he needs to do. I'll help him and we'll get married and we'll work together. Helping the less fortunate is noble. I want the man I love to be noble."

I looks at her, wondrin'. She catch me lookin'.

"Somehow I'll get him to go to Chicago with me. That's what I'm trying to say. He's living off you right now and that's not right. You should be sitting in Mr. Dorman's office, not Cletus. He says it's your music the band's been playing, your songs making money for the record label. So, what's he doing in the middle of it all? I hope Mr. Dorman cuts him loose. Then it will be easier for me to convince him to go to Chicago with me. That brings it back to what happens to you." She got'er eyes on me an I go listnin' good.

"First of all, he owes you money. Second, we need to make amends for taking you away from San Jose." She lean 'cross the table a little bit. "I know you didn't want to come back here. He told me you wanted to stay and look for something or someone. If that's true how could there be anything wrong with you? Some of the guys in the band call you an idiot, but an idiot doesn't know his mind or what he wants. Maybe you don't say anything to anyone, but that's your business." She sit back an look 'round the kitchen. "So, I'm going to try to make things right." She git up an go inta the bedroom. In a minute, she come back and put a envelope on the table.

"That's four thousand dollars. It's not enough. I know he owes you a lot more, but it's all he has here in the apartment. It belongs to you and if I get the chance I'll give you more. That is, if you want to stay. Cletus doesn't know it, but you've been good for him. I don't want to get in the way of that, but you're getting cheated out of what you want. That's the dilemma for all of us. If you want to go back to San Jose and look for whatever it is that means so much to you I'll help you. If you want to stay here and see what's going to happen to Rick and the Riders that's fine, too. If the band falls apart and I can convince Cletus to go with me to Chicago, you're welcome to come with us. I'll make sure Cletus doesn't stand in the way. What I'm trying to say is it's your money and your life. I will do whatever I can to make Cletus do right by you. Do you understand?"

I take a bite a her pancakes, lookin' at the envelope. I ain't never gonna trust Cletus agin for sure. Stayin'? No way! Takin' that money be the ony sure thing an I drop my fork ta do it. She smile an pat my hands as I put'em on the envelope.

"Stay and I'll make sure you get the rest that you deserve, but if you're planning to go I can't make any promises. If you want to go back to San..."

I nods my head hard so she don' miss my meanin'.

"Okay, we should leave now before Cletus comes back. I can call a taxi and go with you to the airport." I shake my head. Gotta be a bus. All them miles got a lotta stuff ta see an you still gonna be there afta I git there. She git the dishes offa the table. In a flash they be washed an she make me go inta my bedroom ta git my stuff. Standin' inside a Port Authority by noon. She don' even take none a the four thousand she gimme. She buy the ticket ta San Jose wit money outta her own pocket. She watch me git in line an come up close ta gimme it, New York ta Cleveland first.

"Come back if it doesn't work out. If we aren't here go to Chicago and this address."

She put a paper in my hand. We looks a second an that be it. I never seen'er agin. Cletus neither, an that be okay wit me.

Funny, how my thinkin' on you come on bein' all differnt on that bus ta Cleveland. I look outta the window, but I don' see nothin'. I think 'bout the money. More money than I ever seen afore 'cept for daddy, but that weren't the same cuz he allays take it. This be my money. An I think 'bout findin' you an seein' you an even talkin' ta you like I done in the residence. But somethin' make me wonder 'bout how come I git real close ta you in San Jose an alls a sudden I be right back in New York. I come on thinkin', you know, a time ta ever purpose. If the Bible be right 'bout that, then it weren't the right time. Now I be ridin' a bus, tryin' all over agin. Maybe it still ain't the right time. Worse, maybe there ain't never gonna be a time.

Find me, din you say that ta me? Why ain't I sure? I 'member everthin', but now I ain't sure 'bout nothin', Dollface, you gotta unnerstan' I ony bin thinkin' on that first moment afta you know it be me. I ain't never done no thinkin' 'bout the next part, what be happnin' afta. Specially if I be thinkin' wrong an you din' want me ta come lookin'. I be crushed an you be afeared a me. I dunno, I dunno go runnin' in my head.

I git out the envelope. Inside be alls a that four thousand jus' like Sheena say. Cletus onta a good woman who gonna make'm a better man than the one I knowed. I come on thinkin' you be good jus' like her an I wonder on me bustin' inta your life. Soul talkin', yeah I be sure ta this moment, but it weren't the same as two peoples like that girl an Cletus. She got some work ta do on him an she gonna do it cuz she see it as her purpose. There ain't nothin' I kin figure showin' a purpose for me afta I find you. An that ain't the baddest part. All that time afta figurin' a way, walkin' the sand at the Jersey shore, Dollface, it ony bin' 'bout me. I never think on you. Now, ridin' that bus, I do an there ain't no purpose I kin figure for you, neither.

Alls a sudden I gotta think on ways a makin' sense outta lookin' for you, watchin' your face an knowin' I be gone quick if there ain't no smile. Gone where? I got no answers. An if there be a smile what come afta? 'Spose you got a man you like. I don' wanna git afront a him an you. I don' wanna mess nothin' up. I jus' wanna be your friend like we was in the residence. 'Spose he don' git that. 'Spose he don' like that. An even if you don' have no guy hangin' 'round maybe you workin' hard an ain't got time ta be a friend wit me. I git that an I figure I coulda bin okay jus' bein' 'round close 'nuff ta be sure you doin' okay.

I figure you coulda bin okay lettin' me be 'round like that, but that weren't gonna do right by you, Dollface. I come on thinkin'... no, I knowed it way deep, you gotta git onta what you wanna do wit your own life. Some guy hangin' 'round, waitin' on you ta make time for soul talkin'? Jus' me draggin' on you an I knowed it weren't right. Time for ever purpose. Yeah, my time come an gone. Ain't comin' back. Hurtin' afta that bus come inta Cleveland. Next day on 'nother bus back ta New York City.

Zane paused the program, took a sip of coffee and rocked back in his chair. He remembered the first time he heard those recorded words about San Jose. How the hurt came through loud and clear. In all of his interactions with Samuel he never paid attention to what may have been going on in his heart, the emotions behind his mask of silence. Yet Zane was an observer. It was the forte that enabled him to serve his clients so effectively. He could always read people, he thought. Just not his wife and son. Not Samuel. Not himself.

"I guess you all know who I am." Cletus Brown stood, but avoided eye contact with the others. "I'm the guy who didn't come off so good on Samuel's recordings. My wife made me come today. Sheena said I needed to face you, face myself for who I used to be. Trouble is he had me pegged right. He knew the only guy I cared about was me. All that time I was running that house I had my eye on making a fast buck and getting a Cadillac. I'm so ashamed I can't look at any of you.

I sorta fell into that job, never seeing it as a calling. You know, a chance to do something good for those kids. Really, a chance to feel good about me. It was just a job. I cooked, watched out so nothing got messed up, kinda killed time while I was looking for somebody to use to get what I wanted. That turned out to be Samuel after I heard him play piano and got him hooked up with Rick and the Riders. Believe me, he was special.

"Everything he said about me is true. I put it away in the back of my mind all these years since Sheena and me settled down in Chicago. I didn't want to hear his words about me. I didn't want to be reminded of what I did to him and what I stole from him. And, when she made me listen to that recording it all came back. Not just the money I took, the happiness, too. It hurts real bad. I want to go back and fix it, but I can't go back. It's too late

"The second best thing that ever happened to me was him. The first is Sheena, but if I never knew Samuel I never would have met my wife. And, if I didn't meet her I'd still be the old Cletus, miserable and thinking about nobody but me. I wish I knew he was dying. I wish I could have told him I'm sorry.

"I understand a lot more about real living now. Sheena taught me that. Loving a woman, wanting to make her happy, that's just the start because it leads to other things. For me it opened the door to doing what I can to help other people. Can you believe that? I actually see other people now. And, I want to be of service to those in need. It means everything to me.

"We've got a house in Chicago. We run it together, eleven kids waiting on placement in foster homes or even adoption, but that doesn't happen very often. Money's tight just like it was back then in the residence when Samuel was there. We get half of what we need from the government, but that's not always guaranteed. The rest comes from charity and that's a struggle, too. There's a lot of worthy causes out there.

"We put off having kids of our own because we don't make much money. It doesn't matter. We've got each other and we've got the kids who need our help. There's purpose in our life together. I'm happier than I've ever been. Samuel said 'I be the lucky one.' Remember that when he was talking about reading books in the library? I wish he was here so I could tell him how lucky I feel because of Sheena and because of him." He raised his head and forced himself to look at the others. "Samuel changed my life for the better. I understand that now."

ELEVEN

The longer the dying can do for themselves the less they dwell upon their fear – Edna Nieves

Monday, nine a.m., that's when the surprising telephone call came. Edna obsessed over it for the rest of the day, wondering what she would wear, how she could possibly control her nerves and what she would say in the presence of a prominent lawyer who was sure to intimidate her.

"Ms. Nieves, please." Edna recognized the no-nonsense voice of the legal secretary who'd brushed her off ten days before. "Attorney Zane's office calling."

"Yes, this is Edna Nieves."

"Oh." There was a change in the woman's voice, as if she was unaccustomed to immediately reaching the person she was calling. "Ms. Nieves, Attorney Zane has asked me to contact you. I read your letter to him via telephone last evening and he would like to meet with you. He will be returning from Minneapolis late tomorrow afternoon and wishes to inquire if you might come to his office at seven p.m."

"In Manhattan? I don't think..."

"Avenue of the Americas. I have arranged for a car to pick you up and return you to, let me see, ah... Jamaica, Queens. The car will be at your location at six. Would that be satisfactory?" Edna frowned at the presumptive close.

"I have patients."

"I'm afraid that's the only time he has available."

"I'm sure he's a busy man." Edna summoned her self-respect. "My patients are in the last days of their lives. I need to attend to them."

"I beg your pardon?"

"I'm a hospice nurse."

There was a pause before the voice on the other end softened. "Please forgive me. My mother passed away under hospice care a year ago."

"You mentioned tomorrow evening. I'm on duty, but we could talk by telephone."

"He said in person, quite insistent. Is there any other time you could meet?"

"I'm off on Wednesday evening, but that's the day before Christmas Eve."

"Oh perfect. That's the night of our Christmas party. He hates those things. If you don't mind I could change the arrangements."

Edna thought for a moment. She had no plans. Actually she wasn't intending to take the time off. Her husband was gone. Her extended family was two states away. Apart from buying some small things for the Saint Lawrence Christmas Relief Benefit, she had no other purpose to her time.

"Yes. That will be fine."

"Thank you. The car will be at your door at six. And, Ms. Nieves?"

"Yes?"

"I admire the work you do."

His head hurt. He lay still on his back, arms and hands extending out from his body on the clean sheets of the freshly made bed. He needed help not only to use the bed pan but also to rise again so it could be pulled from beneath him after the chore was done. Then he needed Edna's strength to lie back. Once settled, she bent down, adjusted his legs and raised the covers to his shoulders. She sat with him for thirty minutes then quietly left the room. A low glow pierced the darkness from a night light in the corner.

In recent days the the opioids took longer. He waited for both his pain and his consciousness to subside. Sometimes, he panted in natural reaction to the increasing pressure in his head. More often he was simply exhausted with little appetite for the food Edna brought to his room. In the mornings she still helped him to his chair by the window and sat with him for an hour or so. She told him about Mrs. Walker who lost her battle a day earlier and she occasionally prayed aloud - for the less fortunate during the Christmas season, for her son, for her husband, for herself and for him. He listened.

At noon she guided him back to bed, promising to return and help him to his chair again after he napped. More often he didn't return to the chair, too spent from the pain and too intent upon finishing his last words to a girl he called Dollface.

The second set began with a larger audience pressed together in front of the stage. He slid behind the keyboards and opened with an imaginary song played fast and loud. In his fantasy he often rose from his seat, still playing as his eyes wandered to the face of every girl he could see.

"Dollface, you here?" A mumbled plea before consciousness faded away.

I git back ta the city, pocket full a money wit nothin' ta do an feelin' bad. I ain't givin' no mind ta meetin' up wit Cletus. I ony think on'm bein' lucky he got hisself a woman an he otta go wit'er ta Chicago so she kin make'm a better man.

Them coupla months I go'round livin' on the street. September and October ain't bad in New York 'cept if it rain. Nights git cold an I fixed that quick by buyin' a coat, waterproof an goin' down ta near my feets. Sometimes, I git a good place ta sleep in a park. Take some lookin' cuz there be a lotta a guys like me an they got their places an they ain't lookin' ta share. Deli got food an I got money ta pay so I jus' points ta what I want an I don' gotta figure a way ta git it sayin' words.

Come November, gittin' dark early an I go thinkin' on gittin' outta the cold. Money still linin' my pockets an I think on where ta let the winter go by. I wonder on California agin', but not too hard cuz I knowed I ony wanna find you an that make it 'bout what happin afta. I tol' you I got no answer ta that.

Florida. I does walkin' some, but most a the time I git on a bus. The walkin' happin afta I come on a place I wanna see up close. Kinda like Lawrence, Kansas, cuz a' bein' a city that ain't like New York. Road I seen outta the window aside the highway got a lotta parts goin' flat wit ol' buildins' all rusted up an no peoples 'round. Some livin' places, too, not lookin' so good even if peoples in'em. So, I git outta the bus ta do some walkin' an lookin' cuz I ain't never seen places like that afore.

I come ta a spot wheres the road meet up with 'nother lookin' like a town, but it ony got a coupla buildins'; gas station, store sellin' farmer stuff an a place ta eat somethin'. Lotta ol trucks an tractors ya sees everwheres down there, but like never in New York City. An a bunch a guys hangin' 'round smokin', laughin' an drinkin' somethin'. Seen that afore.

I bin walkin' all mornin' an gittin' hungry so I go up them steps inta the eatin' place. No peoples 'cept a woman readin' a newspaper. She go lookin' me all over an I knowed she wonder 'bout me wearin' my long coat an, a course, I ain't nobody she seen afore, neither. I git a seat and look in the menu. She come over an I point ta the word sayin' hamburger.

"What d'ya want ta drink?"

Water ain't on the menu. I look 'round. Gotta have some kinda place ta git water.

"In the menu," she go pointin' wit a pencil. "We got Coke, coffee, milk, whatever."

"Hello, Alma." One big man in a uniform standin' aside the door alls shined up wit a badge an a round hat an a gun aside his belt. "Got yourself a new customer today?"

"Hey Joe. Just waiting on this guy's order."

Big man come over ta me, lookin'. "Speak up, boy."

Boy? I done readin' my whole life. I knowed 'bout ever part of America an I knowed who say what and who done what in ever state. Sittin' in a eatin' place in a farmer town in South Carolina where the Civil War git goin' an hearin' some big cop callin' me boy!

I kin talk 'bout Charleston, them slave auctions, John C. Calhoun whippin' up the peoples. An I kin tell you 'bout segregation, confederate flag wavin, Ku Klux Klan killin', football, indigo, rice, sugar, cotton an jus' 'bout everthin'. Sayin' it true. An, I kin tell ya 'bout hate. Boy ain't a good word comin' outta a cop's mouth wit a gun aside his hip. Best scat outta that place an I does real quick, him followin' an talkin' loud ta my backside.

"What's your name?"

I git ta near runnin'.

"STOP!"

I do cuz I be some afeared. He come 'round lookin'. I ain't lookin' at nothin' 'cept dirt.

"Son, I'm not trying to make you nervous. Just because I'm a cop doesn't mean you have to be afraid of me. You don't have to run away. Now, Alma's back there cooking your hamburger. Go back inside and she'll have it ready in a minute or so."

I look up an he be smilin'.

"Go on now and eat your food. I'll stick around to make sure you aren't bothered by those fellas over there." He go pointin' an I see maybe four of'em lookin'. "Small town. Not much to do."

That stoppin' ta walk bin wit me a long time. I come on thinkin' it be 'bout me not that big cop. He git me thinkin' on what I allays take for truth outta books. See, Dollface, he call me boy. I heared that word an it be 'bout gittin' hurt, maybe killed by my way a thinkin'. Ain't that what them books say? But that ain't what happin' an that ain't the kinda man he be. Afta I eat my hamburger I scat outta that place an there he be in his cop car smilin'. I look'm in the eye cuz he ain't like them peoples outta them books. He shake my thinkin' cuz I allays bin lettin' books make my mind for me. I ain't sayin' readin' ain't good. Jus' sayin' ya gotta do some thinkin' an lookin' all ya own so ya don' go lettin' readin' make somethin' good or somethin'bad cuz ya ain't seen it up close. Look, I knowed all that bad stuff really happin back in them days an I ain't sayin' it don' still happin now. I'm tryin' ta say I found out it ain't everbody doin' it .

I go walkin' an I ain't lookin' back cuz I knowed he be watchin' an nothin' bad gonna happin'. I stick ta that road an at night I find me a place ta sit 'til mornin'. Back on a bus, but I ain't goin' ta Florida no more. I goes back ta New York cuz I knowed what kin happin' there an I knowed what ta do 'bout it.

I come outta Port Authority an git the subway ta the ferry. Good day, but a lotta wind. I git off an walk inta town, lookin' for what I figured on gittin' whilst thinkin' on that bus outta South Carolina. See, it weren't no good ta be hangin' 'round the city lookin' for a place ta be sleepin' everday cuz it gittin' real cold. So, I git a hot dog an go lookin' 'round Staten Island. It ain't nice everwhere so it don' take long ta find a junkyard place. Fence no trouble afta I seen what I bin thinkin' on. That ol' white van got a lotta rust 'long the bottom an 'round the doors. Nobody hangin' close so I look inside, seein' the seats all tore up. Backside doors come open okay. It got a metal floor for carryin' stuff. Come 'round front an lift the hood. Motor all tore up, too, an lookin' like no hope 'cept there be stuff 'round an I figured on findin' me the parts I need.

Man come lookin' ta roust me, but afore he kin say somethin' I shows a coupla hunnerd an point. Done quick. No papers cuz I ain't talkin' an he ain't aksin'. Gonna make this my sleepin' place outta the wind an rain an snow durin' them days that ain't so good. Lotta them kinda days cuz a winter comin'.

I git ta fixin' the inside, real dirty wit a coupla big holes in the floor. There ain't no windows where I wanna sleep an that be good. The guy ain't 'round an I go lookin' inta jus' 'bout ever piece a junk he got, findin' stuff. Coupla days an afta them holes git covered up I make me a clean floor wit a bunch a ol' rugs makin' a place ta sleep. Ain't gonna keep out the cold, but I ain't gonna be wet an it ain't lettin' in the wind. Wind kin kill a guy tryin' ta sleep 'round New York in winter. Nobody comin' near ta take my pockets, neither.

Staten Island, sleepin' in a piece a junk, readin' books an magazines an newspapers an gittin' food outta pizza places be my livin' right up ta Christmas. I go pickin' my way 'round them other junks, lookin' ta fix the motor, but that pickin ain't no good like I figured. Library books gimme a sense a what need fixin'. Yard gimme nothin' an asides that, I got no tools an it come on bein' too cold. See, I figured on fixin'the heater offa the motor ta git me by the winter. Cold git real bad an it don' matter 'bout the wind bein' stopped. I knowed it be a bad mistake afta a coupla a weeks .I gotta git outta livin' on Staten Island.

I git on the ferry an peoples be lookin' an movin' ways away offa where I be sittin'. Subway be the same an I seen a little kid grabbin' his momma an holdin' his nose. I go lookin' ta my coat and come on knowin' I ain't bin clean for a long whiles. Smellin' real bad 'cept I be the ony one not smellin' me. Next stop, I scat offa the subway an up onta the street. I ain't carin' where cuz a bein' real 'shamed. I jus' knowed I gotta git outta there 'til I kin figure a way a not smellin' bad no more.

I come onta Avenue of the Americas. Dollface, of all the streets a dirty, bad smellin' guy come onta that gotta be the wrongest one. Gittin' dark an I see Christmas stuff hangin' offa light poles an such. Shoulda knowed, but they ain't makin' up no junkyard for Christmas. Guy ringin' a bell lookin' at me an talkin' loud.

"Shelter serving dinner off 42nd behind the theatre."

Yeah, I 'member an it be the most shamin' moment I ever knowed. I go walkin' fast.

I ain't bin much in Midtown. It weren't no place daddy an me done no sellin'. Ony time I ever bin ta that part a New York City afore that Christmas Eve be when I showed them lawyers an Mr. Dorman them songs be mine. Don' matter cuz I ain't thinkin' on that. I jus' tryin' ta figure where ta go so I kin git the smellin' offa me. I cross a corner. Lotta taxis goin' an comin'. Lotta peoples walkin' wit bags an stuff an I git that it be quittin' time. I look 'round for a way outta there so I kin think on what ta do. I scat ways away 'til I be standin' 'gainst a buildin'. I see peoples comin'outta the big door an a guy stoppin'. He go lookin' a long whiles so I be lookin' down ta my feets an thinkin' 'bout what ta do an wheres I kin go.

"Samuel?" I heared that voice afore. "Samuel Jones, is that you?"

If there be a time ta go talkin' ta 'nother peoples 'cept you, Dollface, it woulda bin afta I heared that voice, but I keep lookin' down, seein' dirty hands like the rest a me an knowin' it ain't 'sposed ta be that way. Archer T. Zane come close. I git my dirty hands up, coverin' my face an go walkin'fast, but he callin' loud ta come back.

"Samuel, stop."

Why'd I stop? Gotta be cuz I knowed he be a okay man. A big, black car come up front a the buildin'. A man git out an open the back door. Archer T. Zane go wavin'.

"Samuel, wait here a minute, will you?" He go talkin' ta the man. I ain't hearin' nothin' 'cept there be a minute afore he come back.

"Look," he say. "You have to understand that when you disappeared some of us were worried that something might have happened to you. Are you all right?" He wait on me, but I be scared a lookin' cuz a bein' dirty an smellin' bad. "No, of course not," he say. "From the look of you it's apparent that things aren't well." He look me alls up an down. "It's Christmas Eve and it's very cold outside. Unless you have someplace to go you're going to freeze. Do you have someplace to go?"

I coulda lied but he take my side afta Rick try on cheatin' me. I ain't gonna go lyin' ta Archer T. Zane. I shakes my head.

"Will you come to my home so you can get cleaned up and be warm?"

I nods.

"Good. Car's over there. Let's go."

He take my arm, not actin' like he knowed I be smellin' an dirty. The car man holdin' onta the door an showin' Archer T. Zane a look.

"He's a client fallen on bad times."

I bin sayin' I don' know nothin' much 'bout Christmas an truth be I din' care. This time come on bein' differnt cuz a Archer T. Zane. He don' do much talkin' in the car. I look outta the window an it ain't long afore we come outta the Lincoln Tunnel inta Jersey. Signs goin' by an I git ta worryin' 'bout bustin' in on his peoples. Course, I ain't sayin' nothin' an I figure that ain't gonna hep, neither. I jus' go watchin' outta the backseat, seein' a lotta cars comin' an goin' an gittin' afeared cuz a Christmas an peoples bein' mad.

We git onta a real dark road like ya ain't never seein' in New York City an I see fences an walls an big trees an stuff. Driver go stoppin' at a big box an open his window. He push a coupla buttons an a gate open real slow. I figure maybe ten feet high.

"Bill, when we get to the house I have something for you," Archer T. Zane say an he git a hand inta his coat an come out wit a envelope.

"You don't have to do that, Mr. Zane. You've always been more than generous."

"Of course I do. I want you to have it. It's Christmas."

Car goin' slow up a road wit fences an big trees like I ony seen in Central Park an outta them bus windows whens we was ridin' from place ta place. Maybe afta a coupla minutes the car come 'round a circle wit a statue or fountain or somethin' in the middle an stop. Archer T. Zane got hisself the biggest house I ever seen. Wow, be alls I kin think lookin' outta the window. We git outta the car wit Bill keepin' the motor goin' an comin' 'round ta git the envelope. They talk quiet an I figure it be a present cuz a Christmas. Money. He don' open it, but he go shakin' hands like he mean it. They talk, but I ain't hearin' cuz I gotta look at that big house. I wonder on what come next. One thing showin' up on Christmas, but somethin' differnt if peoples ain't 'spectin' a guy lookin' an smellin' bad. Bill gimme a look afore gittin' back inta that big shiny car. I figure he be thinkin' on me an maybe worryin' for Archer T. Zane, but he be smilin' an sayin', "Go be with your family." So, Bill git inta the car and drive away openin' alls the windows. I be shamed agin.

"Come in, Samuel." Archer T. Zane pressin' a bunch a buttons like Bill done at the gate. Clickin' kinda sound an he open a big door.

I git nervous cuz a his peoples comin' ta say hello 'cept they don' an he gotta turn on lights. The house be real dark. Dollface, I ain't never bin in no house like that, big wit stuff I knowed cost a lotta dollars, but real quiet. If he got peoples somewheres they gotta be a long ways away cuz they ain't showin' an he ain't lookin' like he be 'spectin'm ta come say hello.

"I think the best thing for you to do is take a shower. You'll feel better."

Sure, I be thinkin' whilst lookin' 'round, but I ain't gonna smell no better puttin' my dirty stuff back on afta. He onta that.

"I'll show you to your room upstairs. Come with me."

He take off his nice coat an go up some big stairs wit a soft rug coverin'. Up top he open a door inta a bedroom an git on a light. He don' say nothin' whilst he open 'nother door and git 'nother light shinin'. I ain't never seen a bathroom as good afore and I ain't never seen one as good afta 'cept maybe wit Crystal. I be gittin' ta her.

"I assume you know how to run the shower. Go in and get cleaned up while I find fresh clothes for you. You can leave the things you're wearing on the floor and we'll see about cleaning them later." He go an I don' waste no time.

Afta I gits outta the bathroom there be pants an stuff on the big bed. I kin smell my stuff on the floor stinkin' up the room. Nothin' ta do 'til I git the clean clothes on. Afta I do, I feel like a new man an I go thankin' Archer T. Zane in my thinkin' alls a way down them stairs wit them dirty clothes. I open the front door an stick'em in a pile ahind some growin' stuff, hopin' the air come take away the stink. Archer T. Zane watchin' an smilin'.

"That's fine. We'll deal with them in the morning. I'm glad my son's things seem to fit. Come into the kitchen. You must be hungry."

He go talkin' whilst makin' eggs an bacon smellin' so good I come on knowin' how hungry I bin. Alls a sudden I 'member I got my money layin'in them bushes. I scat quick. Eggs an bacon an toast an butter waitin' afta I git back.

"So, Samuel, by the look of you, all cleaned up, you're still healthy. That's good. You gave a few of us a bit of a scare when you disappeared."

I hear'm but mostly I jus' listnin' for other peoples in that house on Christmas. See, if he ain't got no peoples then he don' need no big house. I din' know'm that night like I come on knowin'm afta, but I figured he be a man who ain't keepin' somethin' if it got no purpose like a big house otta have peoples livin' in it. No peoples. Nothin' 'cept him an me.

"Cletus came to my office just after everyone returned from California. You were gone by then and he was upset. There was a woman with him, a lovely girl. I remember her name, Sheena. Cletus wanted me to find you. He was very insistent. I reminded him that I wasn't his attorney on matters pertaining to you. He didn't like that. He'd already met with Ellis Dorman in New Jersey. He expected a big payday and when Ellis told him there was only money tied to Rick's estate he came to me for help."

There it be jus' like Sheena say it gonna be.

"Do you know what he said to me? He said you stole four thousand dollars from his apartment. Of course, it was your earnings in the first place. We all know you wrote those songs. Rick wouldn't admit it, but Ellis knew and I knew. Cletus just wouldn't accept that he wasn't entitled to any of it. I told him he was fortunate just to receive the generous caretaker amounts you had me put into the contract with Rick. When I said there was nothing I could do for him he left in a huff. That girl, Sheena, stayed behind for a few minutes to talk to me. She asked me to keep a secret. She said she gave you that money and put you on a bus back to San Jose. I asked her why and she said it was the fair thing to do. She said she knew Cletus was using you, but she also said she loved him and believed he was a good man in his heart. She wanted to take him to her home in Chicago and coax him back to helping people. I think that's where they are now."

Archer T. Zane go talkin' bout this an that whilst eatin' an lookin' okay 'cept there jus' be him an me an that big house on the night afore Christmas. Afta we done eatin' he stop talkin' an git the plates an stuff for washin'. I think on that big bed up them stairs. Them days an nights in a junkyard din' gimme no good sleepin'. He come over an sit agin, lookin' an thinkin' on somethin'.

"Samuel, I know you can hear every word I say. I know you understand and I suspect you can talk. Why you prefer to keep silent is perplexing to me. Ellis Dorman called you an idiot savant. Do you know what that means?"

He wait but I figured on lettin'm do the talkin'.

"Idiot means you have some kind of debilitation that... no, let's use a better word, some kind of challenge that prevents you from acting like or maybe thinking like most people. Savant means you have a special, even extraordinary talent. I buy the savant part, but I'm not so sure you're different from the rest of us. Your musical abilities, Ellis concedes, are off the chart. After I sent Cletus away Ellis was the next person to come to me for help finding you. I told him what I believed was true, that you went back to San Jose, California. Do you know what he did?"

I shake my head this time, wantin' ta know.

"He hired a private detective to look for you. Of course, his search was unsuccessful, but the fact that Ellis would go to such lengths makes it clear to me that he holds your talent in high regard. Now, we're sitting here and I'm wondering about that other part of you, why you refuse to engage with people in what I would call a normal way. I suppose I can ask you straight up. Why don't you talk? Is it because you can't or is it because you won't?"

He wait on me, wantin' ta know. Truth be hard ta figure. I talk ta momma. I talk ta daddy, too. Maybe too much talkin' cuz she don' come home no more an he allays mad afta. I talk ta you, Dollface, afta you come inta the residence, but you go ways away an I never sees you agin, neither. An right now I talk inta this recorder. Atween, I ain't talkin' ta nobody an why be a question ta me jus' like Archer T. Zane. All I kin think on doin' is look cuz I got no answer. He go sittin' back.

"Well, no matter. Look, I've got some work to do so I'm going to go down the hall to my office. You have the run of the house. If you'd like to watch some television I'll turn it on for you. Would you like that?"

I shakes my head, pointin' up. Then I git up them stairs ta sleep.

TWELVE

People face death much the way they faced life. We all have a philosophy – Edna Nieves

The limousine waited at the curb directly in front of the hospice house. A young certified nurse's aid accompanied by a volunteer relieved Edna for the evening as was normal one night a week and on Sunday. More often than not Edna accepted the services of these fill-ins, but never left the house. She had little to occupy her spare time other than shopping for food and tidying up her small one-bedroom apartment on the second floor. She worried for her patients and was never truly off duty.

A man named Bill introduced himself with a smile and held the door when she reached the sidewalk. On the drive into Manhattan he said nothing, which actually relieved Edna. She was too nervous for idle chat. It was just before seven p.m. when he brought the black car to a halt in front of a tall elegant building on Midtown's Avenue of the Americas. Edna looked at the huge bronze revolving doors and then at the lights of the many floors above. Bill once again held her door then escorted her across the wide sidewalk to the entrance.

It's not that the hospice nurse was unfamiliar with tall buildings and city lights. She'd lived in the New York metropolitan area most of her life. Still, she rarely went into Manhattan. Its bustle of office workers, sightseers, tourists, shoppers and endless cars, trucks, buses and taxis made her edgey. When her husband was alive they attended shows in the theatre district followed by a nice dinner at one of the many small restaurants speckling the cross streets around Broadway. With him by her side it was pleasure. Without him was unthinkable.

An attractive woman in a red party dress waited in the lobby. She smiled and came forward, "Mrs. Nieves?"

"Yes?"

"I'm Roberta, Attorney Zane's assistant." She held out her hand. "I want to thank you for taking the time to come into the city."

Instantly charmed, Edna lost some of her anxiety. "A man picks me up in a beautiful car and drives me right to the front door. It's all a bit exciting for me."

"He's waiting for you in his office on the twenty-seventh floor. I'll take you. And, when you've finished your business with him I'd like to invite you to our Christmas Party. He always has an excuse to avoid a party. Tonight it's you, but if you'll accept my invitation I'm sure we can shame him into joining us. Do you mind?"

"Oh, I wouldn't dream of imposing."

"No imposition. Have you eaten dinner?"

"No, I thought maybe later."

"Perfect. The food is delicious."

Luxury was Edna's immediate thought when the doors opened on the twenty-seventh floor. The carpeting was deep and plush, the walls painted in calming pastel shades of blue and white, and the vistas out to the city from every vantage point displayed New York at its finest. All was quiet with only a few lights brightening the floor since anyone who might have been working was at the party. There was an occasional desk with computer and screen, but most of the space was occupied by large expensive couches and chairs. Paintings were mounted at several perfectly measured spots along an interior wall. Roberta led Edna past each one before coming to a stop outside a rich mahogany double door, leading to an office on the other side. The secretary noticed Edna's surprise.

"He's the founding partner and still generates more revenue than any of his colleagues. His former wife insisted that the firm spend the money on these doors and the furnishings inside. If he had his way he'd be in a cubicle somewhere down the hall, but it's good to put an attractive veneer on things. Clients expect it."

This was Samuel's lawyer? Edna was astonished.

Roberta knocked lightly then turned the handle, opening the door for Edna to pass. She followed her across the threshold, still holding the handle.

"Archer?" He looked up from behind his ornate desk and smiled. "This is Mrs. Nieves. Would you like me to stay or shall I leave you two alone?"

"Ah, Mrs. Nieves." He rose from behind his desk and quickly came forward. He held out his hand to Edna. "I'm very pleased to make your acquaintance." He turned to Roberta. "Yes, you might stay at your desk for a few minutes. The party will still be going on when we're finished."

"Of course. And, by the way, I've invited Mrs. Nieves to celebrate with us. You'll be our escort, won't you?"

Edna wanted to smile at this ploy, but she held back, taking the attorney's hand and shaking briefly while looking from one to the other. Roberta winked at her.

"You never tire of your shenanigans, Roberta," he sighed. "If you insist."

"I do." She retreated from the office, letting the door quietly close behind her.

"Please, let's sit over here." He gestured toward a plush leather couch fronted by a mahogany coffee table similar in appearance to his desk. Once seated, the silence was mildly uncomfortable. Edna didn't know what to say or even if she should begin while Zane, dressed impeccably in an expensive tailored suit, seemed to gather his thoughts by looking around the room. After some seconds he brought his eyes back to her. "Tell me, Mrs. Nieves, how is Samuel?"

"Edna," she began. "Please call me Edna."

"Yes, thank you and please call me Archer." The ice was broken.

"Samuel has begun to fail. He fights it, but I see the signs, extreme headaches, seizures, unbearable at times. I have increased his medications to compensate."

"When?" The question needed no clarification.

"Maybe two or three weeks, mid-January. The original

prognosis was Christmas. It's not an exact science."

"No. Life and death never are. I understand from your letter that you want to know something about him. How did you come to find me?"

Edna explained the recording. "I'm ashamed. I know I shouldn't listen."

"Then he *does* speak. I've always wondered."

"Only into the recorder and only when he thinks no one is near to hear him."

"May I ask what he says about me?"

"I don't remember his exact words. My impression is that he trusts you."

"What else is he saying?"

"He's speaking to a girl he met when he was young and living in a residence in Queens. It was a place for homeless children with special needs funded by Mission Foundation in College Point."

"There was a man named Cletus who looked after him there," replied Zane.

"That's right." Edna looked up in surprise. "He talks about a Cletus Brown. I had no luck finding him."

Zane leaned back on the couch and crossed his legs. "I don't know who he really is. I mean his legal name is Samuel Jones. The surname, Jones, was given by Cletus and established in the appropriate legal and governmental records at the time of his release from that residence."

"Yes, I know. The Director of Mission Foundation told me. In a few days I intend to order a gravestone for him. I'll use Samuel Jones. He seems to like that name and, like you said, it is his legal name."

"Is that what they do for the patients, provide gravestones?"

Edna shook her head. " No, this is something personal that I want to do."

"Out of your own pocket?"

"Yes."

Zane considered this for a moment. "Forgive my candor, but head stones and burial plots are expensive. Why would you do this for him?"

"As far as I can tell he has no one. I want him to be remembered at least for little while. When people come to the cemetery they might see his gravestone and know he's missed."

The attorney nodded his head. "That's very admirable."

"Thank you, but it's not why I wrote to you. I'm still hoping he has family or friends who care for him. That you might be able to help me locate them."

"I doubt we could find any family. As for friends, my only interaction with Samuel was for legal purposes. Cletus Brown was closest to him, but that relationship appeared to be based upon selfish advantage. When the money dried up Mr. Brown lost interest."

"Yes, Samuel doesn't seem to care for him."

"Cletus had a girlfriend. She wanted to take him to Chicago. They might be there if they are still together. I could inquire if you wish."

Edna shook her head. "At first, I wanted to speak with Mr. Brown, but I think he wouldn't care and Samuel should have people who care for him."

"The girlfriend's name is Sheena. She told me she gave Samuel money and put him on a bus to San Jose, California. She thought he might have been trying to find someone or something out there when Cletus got in the way. That's the last contact I had with either of them. I did come across Samuel another time later at Christmas. That would have been around eight years ago."

"The girl he speaks to, he tried to find her in San Jose. Do you think there might be a way to identify her?"

Zane's face lit up. "So, that's the mystery behind San Jose. Everybody wondered. Do you have any information about her?"

"She read stories to the young children in that residence. He calls her Dollface, that's all."

Zane shook his head. "I doubt it." He rose and went to his desk to retrieve a pad and pen. When he was seated again he posed some questions. "What does he say about this girl?"

"They were the same age I think, seventeen. She had blond hair and blue eyes. He mentions a little girl named Lacey who had a favorite doll. That's the way he describes this girl, she looked like that doll. From what I can tell she came to read in the afternoons with two other girls. Maybe from a school nearby."

The lawyer wrote quickly. "Why do you think she came from a school?"

Suddenly Edna understood that he wanted exact details. It shouldn't have surprised her. His profession depended on facts, all the facts.

"I'm sorry," she responded. You need details."

"Yes, that would be best."

"Maybe you should come to the hospice house when Samuel is sleeping. I could let you listen to his recording."

"No, no. I don't want to do that. And, I recommend that you stop listening. I have no reason to think your concern for him is anything but genuine, but if others become involved they might take a different view."

"Oh my God! I'm breaking the law?"

"Please don't be alarmed. It's just that when certain kinds of people get involved with anything for the wrong reasons they often try to use the law to do what it shouldn't. Better to give them nothing they can latch onto. Let's say Samuel has some assets and for strictly noble reasons he leaves them to you as his final caretaker. Someone like Cletus Brown who only seemed to be interested in taking money from Samuel, if he found out, he might try to wrestle it away. That opens the door to legal actions and that can lead to all sorts of mis-representations."

"I would hate for that to happen."

"It probably never will. Just the same skip the listening."

"Believe you me," she fidgeted. "I'll never listen again."

"So, about this girl…"

"The residence burned down several years after Samuel left. A brick building stands on the spot today. As for the girl, he describes a uniform of some sort that she wore. I'm guessing there must be a school somewhere in the area."

"Okay, that helps. What else can you tell me?"

"I suppose I should start from the beginning."

She went on for five minutes, reconstructing everything she could remember from the recordings. The attorney continued to take notes. When she finished he stood and opened his office door.

"Roberta, see if you can find Kip. Ask him to come down."

"Certainly."

He closed the door and came back to the couch. "Let me review a few things to be sure they're correct. He said his father was a prize fighter who was suspended from the ring?"

"Kicked out. That's the way Samuel put it."

"They sold drugs together on the street?"

"I'm afraid so. Until Samuel was beaten and robbed. That's when his father hit him again and abandoned him on the subway."

"He mentions his mother not coming home one day?"

"Yes. He seemed very sad."

"Continuing," Zane looked at his notes. "There was an elementary school, PS 0875."

"Yes. I went there and met with the principal. I was hoping there might be someone who remembered him or some records. Nothing."

"No surprise there. It was years ago."

"Yes. The principal told me to go to the district office, but I never did."

Zane rose from the couch and placed his notepad and pen on the desktop. He turned, leaned against the front of the desk for a moment then looked up at Edna.

"I have to ask you why."

"I haven't told you about his involvement with music. He talks about a singing group, Rick and the Riders and a man named Ellis Dorman. I received confirmation..."

"Yes, I know everything about that part of his life. That's how I became involved."

"What then? What do you mean why?"

"What is your reason for asking me to help you? Why are you trying to locate his family and friends? Why would you go to considerable personal expense to bury him and give him a headstone?"

Edna recoiled in a combination of shock and irritation, replying in a formal tone that felt like a rebuke to the attorney. "Mr. Zane, he's a sick young man dying alone. No one comes to visit him. It isn't right. There must be someone who cares for him. Maybe this girl, Dollface." She hesitated. "And, I want him to be remembered. The least I can do is see to it that his last days are as comfortable as possible and that he has a proper burial."

"What happens to your other patients?" Zane tried to act unmoved.

"Most have family. There was one other like Samuel, a woman, just after I started working at the home. She was completely alone like him. After she passed away her body was cremated and her ashes disposed of."

"That is the normal procedure?"

"Yes."

"You are a religious person?"

"Yes. Why do you ask?"

There was a knock on the door. It opened and a tall, good-looking young man, perhaps thirty entered.

"You wanted to see me, Archer?"

Zane stepped forward. "Kip, yes. This is Mrs. Edna Nieves." The young man approached her with a sincere smile. Edna rose and shook his hand, recognizing a measure of good manners and good will in his demeanor. "I'd like you to gather some information for us."

Zane's mind returned to the present, recalling Edna's words during the luncheon. Again, he paused the program:

"From the moment he came under my care I felt that it was meant to be." She pushed her chair back and stood, glancing at her host then turning her attention to the others. *"I'm grateful to Archer and Kip for all they have done to help me know more about Samuel. One unexpected benefit is all of us coming together today as friends.*

"After I heard him speaking to an unknown girl and discovered his recording device, I was so surprised and curious that I waited every day for him to sleep so I could secretly replay his words. Was I guilty doing this? Yes. Only upon hearing the full recording after his

death has my guilt diminished. Now, I know he knew I was listening. He didn't mind.

"When a person comes under hospice care loved ones show many emotions; sorrow, relief, love, impatience, frustration, denial. Some, as the very end arrives, need to be reminded to say good-bye. Very few come under my care completely alone and speechless. Over the weeks, as I cared for him, he became my child. It's not supposed to be that way. The role of a caretaker is not to interfere, but simply to make a patient's final days as comfortable as possible. I confess that I could not keep to that purpose with Samuel. Call it intuition. In my heart I believed he came to me for a reason. That's why I was determined to learn everything I could about him. I wanted to know so I could remember him. So, I could make it possible for other people to remember him, too.

"Over a short span of time I lost my only son and my husband. A kind of numb despair and loneliness became a part of my everyday existence. Then, gradually, after Samuel arrived I began to feel again. Everyday, caring for this unusual soul, hearing his story and watching him fight against the inevitability of his illness so he could finish all that he wanted to say renewed my faith in life." She lifted her eyes to Rebecca. "He cared so deeply for you, a girl he affectionately called Dollface. He missed you, wanted to see you one last time, believed it could not be, but never yielded to despair.

"I was instilled with an unquestioned religious devotion at an early age. It has remained with me, a source of comfort and a shelter from uncertainty. I was taught that blind acceptance of much that cannot be proved requires faith. There are mysteries in life. That is all. My religious belief has helped me to accept the mystery of Samuel Jones. God sent him to me. My life is renewed because of him."

Music from the sorority party grew softer, unusual as the evening revelry progressed. Most times the students went into high gear, urging ever more sound from the band. She stayed by the gate, preferring her solitude and mildly disappointed that her private time was abruptly interrupted by a young man appearing on the sidewalk in front of her.

"You must be the gatekeeper," he said lightly.

"Do you have a pass?" she asked, looking up.

There are moments that are never forgotten, instants that force a rush of all-consuming concentration that temporarily denies awareness of all else The background music was silenced, but only in her ears. Her eyes widened in recognition that fought for remembrance. Her body tensed as she tried, but could not turn her face away. He, too, was forced to stand still and gaze only at her, hearing nothing, noticing nothing but her. The momentary silence was not awkward. It was necessary so they each ould find equillibrium again.

"Pass?"

"It's a private party. I can't let you in without a pass."

"I heard the music and decided to investigate. No, I don't have a pass."

"You're welcome to stay here and listen. I wish I could let you in, but I can't."

"No. I understand. You have to be careful."

They continued to stare at one another. She searched his face, heart fluttering and hoping the darkness hid her blush. Only once before had she been so startled by the appearance of another person. She knew she couldn't stare forever. She had to break the trance. She sat down on the curb. The lights from the party shifted to a silhouetted view of the boy.

"Are you a student?" She asked.

"Was. I finished my course work today."

"Graduation is still two weeks off."

"I'm afraid I won't be able to make it. I leave for New York tomorrow."

"Why?"

"I start law school at New York University in the fall. Fortunately, I landed a job in Brooklyn, working construction for the summer. The pay is good, but I have to report in six days. I'll drive cross country and find a place to live."

"I'm from New York."

"Yeah?"

"Born and raised."

"I've never been. California guy all the way. I'm excited, but a little nervous. I hear New York is very different. What brought you to San Jose?"

She wanted to talk to him. His eyes, voice and casual friendliness captured her, but she was still reeling, not nervous or uncomfortable, but somehow certain that this boy was different, special. She needed time to think. "I guess it will be okay."

"What?"

"You can go in." She stood up. "There's beer and the music is good."

"I suppose that must mean you don't want to talk to me."

"Come back if you get bored."

"My name is Kip." He held out his hand.

"Rebecca," she answered, taking it.

"Maybe one beer. My last hours in California."

"Enjoy." She waved him in.

Sometimes there jus' ain't no reason why somethin' happin' or don' happin'. Yeah, well maybe that's wrong. There's allays a reason. We jus' don' knows it. I wake up in that big bed an I don' know where I be. I look 'round, tryin' ta figure it out an then it come ta me, Archer T. Zane. Clock on a table sayin' two in the mornin'. Then I 'member it bein' Christmas.

I go lookin' out the window an down. Lights on an there he be, sittin' in the cold in a big coat wit the collar up 'round his face. I wonder, no peoples 'round, no stuff showin' Christmas, him workin' whilst I sleep. Nothin' lookin' right. I git on them clothes he gimme an go down the stairs. Dollface, it be real cold outside, him sittin' an me wondrin', lookin' an gittin' cold soon's I open the door.

"I'll get you a coat." He make me go back inside an he git a black coat outta somewheres. Then he stop an git somethin' outta the kitchen. "Might as well enjoy the night air on Christmas since neither of us can sleep. There's a fire pit."

It don' take long. He git some wood offa a pile on the side

an go makin' a light. Smoke risin' then a lotta fire faster than ya think. He pull on 'nother chair and we brung'm up close. The way rich peoples do Christmas - I ain't complainin'. Smoke comin' outta Archer T. Zane, too. He got hisself a big cigar like my daddy used ta smoke. A minute go by afore he git onta talkin'. He don' go lookin' ta me. Jus' the fire. Somethin' weren't right.

"I made a call earlier after you went upstairs. Ellis Dorman would like to see you the day after tomorrow. He might have some work for you on the piano. I told him I'd mention it. If you're interested let me know." Makin' music agin be nice an havin' a warm sleepin' place pressin' on me. Archer T. Zane knowed my mind. "Blossom Records has some bungalows with kitchens, efficiency apartments if you understand what that means. You can stay in one of them." I nods my head.

He go puffin' that cigar an the fire givin' a nice warm ta the air. I keep lookin' at Archer T. Zane, wondrin' an feelin' lucky cuz a maybe makin' music agin. He go rockin' his chair a bit an I does it, too, slidin' back real easy an real soft. Gotta cost a lotta dollars, them chairs, same's everthin' in that house.

"Odd to you, I suppose," he go sayin' an I keep my eye on'm. "This empty house on Christmas Eve. Well, Christmas Day since it's after midnight. He take 'nother puff. "I've got plenty of cigars in the house. Would you like one?"

I shake no. He rock back an keep puffin'. I wanna aks, "Archer, what be wrong?" His eyes gittin' red, fire maybe or somethin'. Long while afore he say more.

"I never smoke in the house. My wife won't tolerate it. I like a good cigar now and then. Special occasions like when I've successfully closed a case. That and a nice single malt. That's whiskey. Now that's something we both should have. What do you say?"

I nod cuz showin' no two times ain't right, him bein' nice ta me an all alone on Christmas. He git up quick. Whilst he be gone I git more wood onta the fire. Shootin' up high afta he git back. Never drunk no whiskey afore, neither. It ain't like beer. Better ta my way a tastin'.

"Where was I?" He go rockin' agin. "Oh yes, the oddity, me alone here on Christmas. We're getting a divorce, my wife and I. It should come through by the end of January. Right now she's up in Vermont celebrating Christmas with our son. We have a house at a ski area. It's a big place at the foot of the mountain in a valley on a golf course. I've been there a few times, Christmas and Thanksgiving, but that's all. She's a bit of a socialite up there. Does fundraising for worthy causes. Did I mention that she's beautiful? We've been married for twenty years. She's nine years younger than me. Our son, Tim is his name, is nineteen. He's in his first year at Bowdoin College in Maine."

He take a drink a whiskey. I quit lookin' at'm an turn my eyes ta the fire.

"She's the one who wants the divorce. I'll admit it came as a shock, although in retrospect, after I read her reasons, I understood. It must have been on her mind for a long time. My son is the one who finally tipped the scale. Anyway, I'm not contesting it. She'll get half of everything and the house in Vermont.

"So, now you know why we're sitting here on Christmas in a quiet house, no decorations, no lights, no tree and, as I think about it, no presents. Over the years she was the one who made sure those things were done for the holidays. I never paid much attention, simply paid the bills. Just after Thanksgiving the professional decorators would show up. They'd have everything finished in a couple of days; thousands of lights, very tasteful I might add, three trees, quite large and beautiful. She'd have them placed in the foyer, great room and one out here on the patio. All of this was in preparation, not for Christmas Eve or Christmas Day, because we didn't spend that time here. It was meant for our friends to see and anyone else who happened to visit. And, it was done for our annual Christmas Party every year on December fifteenth. One of the reasons she cited in the divorce papers. I often missed our annual Christmas party. I'm a workaholic. Do you know what that means?"

I nod, but it be the first time I ever heared that word.

"I was thirty-eight years old when I married her. The reason is simple enough. I worked all the time and never put any effort into meeting women. From law school onward, right to this very moment I derive pleasure only from working. I've got fifty-three clients who give the firm sixty-five million in annual billings and that's down from two years ago when I peaked at seventy-five. There's an army of associates working strictly for me and my portfolio. You can imagine I'm plenty busy and I've made a pile of money.

"My very first client was Blossom Records where Ellis Dorman is the boss today. The man who hired me was his predecessor, brilliant and a workaholic just like me. The difference is he saw the light a few years after his only child was born. He put Ellis in charge of things and spent the rest of his life devoted to his wife and son. I've never slowed down. All the holidays and every other special occasion, even if we were together, I always had work to do. You saw it earlier, Christmas Eve and I'm wandering down the hall to my office. I did that to my wife and son. Selfish, that's the term she used in the divorce papers. It's also the term my son used in his valedictory speech when he graduated from prep school last May. I wasn't there to hear it.

"I'm sure you're familiar with 9/11, the day the twin towers came down. Everyone knows where they were and what they were doing that terrible morning. I was on an airplane at LaGuardia, on the tarmac about to take off for Minnesota. Of course, the plane never flew. I grabbed a cab back to the office. When I arrived everyone was either gone or on their way out. I could see the smoke from the towers in the distance, but I didn't even think about my wife and son or going home to be with them here in New Jersey. I went directly up the elevator to my office and called my client. I was working on an acquisition, a company they wanted to buy.

"I worked through the day alone in my office, never thinking about the pandemonium down on the streets. My wife called several times, frantic, worried about me and fearful for our son who was four at the time. She kept pleading with me to come home. He's safe I told her. You're safe, too. I never understood how frightened she was. All I cared about was the pressing work I wanted to get done. I keep several suits, shirts, ties and underwear at the office. I stayed there for two days on the phone back and forth between my client and the attorneys for the other side. The deal got done. When I finally did go home there was a note on the kitchen counter, one word all capital letters, *BASTARD!* My wife had taken Tim to the house in Vermont. I should have driven up to be with them, but I never did. Next day? I was back in my office.

"I don't know if she ever loved me. That's not a knock on her. I never gave her the chance. We met at a business function at the Plaza in New York. It was one of those rare moments when I was relaxed and not thinking about things I needed to do at the law firm. We were married six months later. I let her dictate our lifestyle. There was plenty of money and she has exceptionally good taste. From my warped perspective she was the perfect partner, few demands on my time if you understand what I'm trying to say. Just after Tim was born she made me buy the house in Vermont. I liked the idea of her being away so I wouldn't feel guilty about working all the time. Now I've begun to understand that she wanted the house as a way to get time with me. I believe she thought that if we spent vacations and holidays up there I'd relax a bit like I did when we first met. A relationship needs to be nurtured with time together, intimate conversation and closeness. Our reasons for buying and keeping the Vermont house were diametrically opposed.

"Tim went to school here in New Jersey until he turned fourteen. Then she enrolled him at a prep school in New Hampshire. Intellectually, he's very much like me. Emotionally, he's his mother. They're very close. I hate to admit it, but I hardly know the boy. Last May he graduated at the top of his class, valedictorian. I missed the ceremony just like I have allowed work to interfere with every other meaningful occasion of our family life. I shudder when I think about it now. Can you imagine a father not being there for his son's valedictory speech? There's a transcript of what he said attached to the divorce papers. I can't bring myself to read it. I do have some understanding of what he told his classmates because my wife wrote about it in a bitter letter to me some weeks later.

"The title of his speech was 'Life Without My Father'. The opening sentences read, 'My father is not here tonight. My father wasn't here yesterday. My father won't be here tomorrow. That's what my wife wrote in her letter to me. There were a few more paragraphs and then the simple sentence, I'm filing for a divorce."

Archer T. Zane take all the scotch an the glass be empty. He suck on that cigar and drop his head low. I be real sad for'm. When a man come on knowin' the truth an it ain't what he bin thinkin' all along it hurt real bad.

"I'm back." The words startled her, coming from behind as she sat on the curb playing with some pebbles in her hands. "Kip is my nickname." He held two plastic cups filled to the brim with beer. "You're right about the music. Guy on the keyboards is terrific." He sat down and handed one of the cups to her.

"Why did you come back?"

"Why are you sitting here by yourself when there's a party going on?"

"Just doing some thinking."

"Always in deep thought or just now?"

"So, what's your real name?"

"Waldo."

"Waldo?" she chuckled.

"That's the reaction I always get. Goes with my last name, Emerson."

"C'mon. You're playing with me."

"It's true. Insisted upon by my paternal grandfather."

"Now I'm interested." She smiled. "What did your grandfather have to do with it?"

"He and the famous philosopher were distant cousins, although my grandfather was much younger, just a baby when Emerson died. When I was born my grandfather was ninety-four years old, but he still had all his marbles. My mother told me he insisted that I be named after his famous cousin. Do you know much about my ancestor?"

"A little. Someone recited some of his poems and essays to me. Why not Ralph Waldo like it's supposed to be?"

"Mom planned to call me Wally."

"So, where did Kip come from?"

"After I was born, she changed her mind. She decided Waldo could be an invitation to ridicule so, she came up with Kip as a nickname and it stuck. Now, whenever I have to sign something, you know a formal signature, I write W. R. 'Kip' Emerson. Works reasonably well. "

"I like it."

"Do you have a nickname?"

"Just Rebecca."

"Sounds literary."

"I'm at the School of Education. I plan to teach."

They talked for an hour with the music from the party barely catching their ears. She decided he was charming in an easygoing way. He confirmed her beauty.

"I better go back to the party." She stood and brushed sand from her dress.

"I should be going, too. I've got a long day behind the wheel tomorrow."

"You must be excited about law school."

"I am. It's all I've ever wanted, to be a lawyer. Where will you teach?"

"Wherever I can find a job. Back home in New York if I'm lucky."

"Well," he finished his beer and moved toward the sidewalk. "Til we meet again."

"Not likely, I'm afraid."

"Oh, it will happen. Don't know where or when, but we will definitely meet again."

"How can you be so sure?"

He started walking, hands in his pockets, face cast away to hide the color rising in his cheeks. "Because you're the one."

THIRTEEN

Two years I goes livin' in one a them places Mr. Dorman gimme. Like a apartment in the city, but better wit a bedroom an a kitchen an a place ta read an look at a television. I likes it alot an if I ain't on a piano in the studio I go inta town ta the library, readin' alls the time.

I be called a studio musician accordin' ta the contract Archer T. Zane gimme. Money be good cuz Mr. Dorman ain't no cheat. I'm clean an I eat good. An, I ain't worryin' on bein' safe in that nice livin'place. Best part, Dollface? I git ta do what I like ta do, make music. Happy time 'cept knowin' I ain't never gonna see you agin.

Other peoples comin' an goin' 'pendin' on the kinda music we makes. 'Cept none of'em livin' at Blossom like me. They all got places and peoples. We do rock, pop, jazz, R&B, a bit a hip hop an rap, country an even some classical stuff when a lady called Reina come wit her violin. Them times be special.

There be a big guy, Whitehurst, an he allays come ways away outta Australia wit'er. I seen'm maybe three times whilst livin' an workin' there. Whitehurst be a big music star an if he comin' there be a lotta runnin' 'round in them offices up the hill. Somethin' good atween'm an Mr. Dorman cuz he be smilin, jokin' talkin' ta everone an bein' in a good mood jus' afore Whitehurst show up, all the whiles he be 'round and even for a coupla days afta he go away. Then Mr. Dorman git back ta bein' the boss he allays be.

Whitehurst married ta Reina Das an I figure they don' go nowhere sepret. If he come ta Blossom ta do music she come wit'm. If it be her music he be there wit'er. An Mr. Dorman ain't doin' nothin' 'cept tendin' ta them. Tight kinda likin' they got.

One time other peoples come from Australia, too. A guy

named Buckman an his wife, Les. Wow, Dollface! When they all come tagether; Whitehurst, Buckman an Mr. Dorman, it be a happy time. Peoples come that musta done somethin' in the times afore. A nice lady named Cindy an guys named Sonny an Eugene, they all come 'round - everbody laughin' an havin' a good time. I don' do no talkin', but I gotta say them peoples gimme a happy feelin'.

Right afta I git there, Mr. Dorman talk on gittin' me back on the piano wit Rick an the Riders. I gotta tell it here, I done a lotta thinkin'on doin' it cuz I had me new songs in my head. But afta I got'm goin' good on that harmonica, the ony guy that coulda played my songs good 'nuff wit me be Rick an he killed hisself so I jus' shakes whens Mr. Dorman aks. He don' push.

I ain't clear on ever song I done over them two years. Truth be, singers I git ta playin' wit ain't Blossom's big names. Jus' peoples doin' auditions afore talkin' 'bout a contract. Most of'em ain't gittin' no contract. I seen a lotta wishin' an hopin', but not a lotta gittin'. Bunch a recordins' wit me on the keys, but it ain't on big sellin' songs so ya gotta do some lookin' ta find my name somewheres. I never done no lookin'. Don' mean nothin' ta me no more. I knowed Archer T. Zane make it right. Mr. Dorman, too.

Asides bein' in a good place an playin' piano likes I likes, an readin' books outta the library, the days be jus' 'bout the same alls a time. I ain't sayin' it git borin' cuz I knowed I be real lucky an I knowed what it be like on the street.

I got songs in my head an I got me a key ta them studios. Sometimes, at night if I git tired a readin' an there ain't nothin' on the television I go walkin' ta the studios an play my songs. I figured out the recordin' 'quipment easy quick an afta I had'em jus' the way I like I record'em. I 'member maybe fifty good 'nuff ta keep hearin' an I left'em on the tapes so I kin hear'em agin if I want. Gotta still be there cuz I heared Mr. Dorman talkin' 'bout that Buckman guy tellin'm ta never git rid a no music on them tapes. I din' go pushin' them songs ta nobody. They be mine an that were 'nuff for me. I like makin' songs.

Come on the cold time a the second year an I git itchin'ta see somethin' differnt. I ain't sayin' I stop likin' Blossom cuz I din'. Jus' me thinkin' on somewhere I ain't seen afore. I wonder 'bout other peoples an if they git feelin' like that, too. Bein' in one place alls the time ain't for me. I know it now. Jus' din' unnerstan' afore.

'Round that time Reina Das 'sposed ta be comin' ta Blossom. I git a knock on the door an it be a pretty girl outta Mr. Dorman's office up the hill. She got a big envelope in her hand an she gimme it, smilin' but not sayin' nothin' cuz she musta knowed I ain't talkin'. I take it, wondrin' cuz I ain't never got no big envelope afore. I go closin' the door, but not afore I catch a look like she wondrin' on what kinda peoples I be. Lotta that kinda lookin' from peoples in the studio when I gotta play, too. The envelope got music sheets an a paper from Mr. Dorman:

Samuel:
Reina Das-Whitehurst requests your presence on the piano. She will be in Millburn next week. Please familiarize yourself with the enclosed material.
Ellis Dorman

I sees them chords an notes an figure on it bein' easy. Next week, I git the word ta go inta Studio A, the big one an there be other peoples settin' up. I git ahind the baby grand onta the seat, waitin'. More peoples comin' an settin' up instruments. Practice. The piece be new cuz I ain't heared it afore an I ain't seen it in none a the books in the big room in the back. Maybe twenty session peoples fillin' that room. They git up on the platforms in groups; horns, strings, drums an me offa the side an back a bit on the floor. Reina ain't showed.

A man come inta the studio an go ta the front, carryin' a stand an a bunch a sheet music. He don' look at no one whilst settin' up an movin' them sheets 'round. He git somethin' outta his nice lookin' jacket an I figured he be the boss. He got hisself a baton an go tappin' it on the stand, makin' it so's we pay 'tention. He look 'round, sayin' nothin' 'til he come on seein' me ahind the piano.

"You are?" he aks, like I ain't 'sposed ta be there. I ain't talkin' an he look real hard like my daddy afta momma don' come home no more, makin' me afeared like a little kid.

"Where is our piano player?"

He go lookin' at them session peoples, waitin' on somebody ta say somethin', but none a them knowed me an none a them talkin' neither, jus' like me.

"Has Ms. Das arrived?"

Lotta mad comin' outta that voice. It make them peoples itch 'round in them chairs. His eyes tellin' somethin', too. I tol' you afore 'bout seein' inta people's souls. This one ain't happy.

"This is unacceptable!" He shout, makin' everone jump, 'specially me.

I git it quick. Conductor man ain't likin' his place. I mean the kinda life he got. I knowed all 'bout that outta livin' wit my daddy. A course, he ain't gonna do no punchin' like my daddy, but it be the same. See, Dollface, I come on knowin' all peoples got a picture a who they wanna be. Daddy seen a boxer winnin' in the ring an bein' a champ. I seen you an bein' friends. Rick seen bein' a big star. Cletus seen bein' rich an Archer T. Zane seen bein' better man ta his wife and son. You? I dunno an I wished I do cuz we all got a picture.

I ain't seein' a bad man. Jus' a man who ain't doin' the kinda livin' he 'spect for hisself. He ain't in a place he wanna be. An, cuz it hurt he go turnin' all that mad inta makin' other peoples feel bad. It come on bein' my time cuz I ain't lookin' like the guy he be 'spectin' ahind that piano. Alls a sudden he go out. Them other peoples lookin' my way like I done somethin'. A coupla peoples go walkin' 'round, others lookin' at music sheets an two of'em on strings talkin' quiet. I watch, thinkin' I ain't wanted in Studio A.

Does ya know the name Rachmaninoff kin end in a coupla 'fs' or a 'v' an be the same guy? It ain't 'portant ta know that, but I come on knowin' it cuz I go readin' 'bout'm an a piano man, Van Cliburn. See, Dollface, we all think somethin' ain't right afta that conductor man go slammin' the door. Me? I gotta say here I think I ain't 'sposed ta be sittin' ahind that baby grand. Them others jus' doin' a job cuz they need money an it ain't lookin' like they gonna git none cuz a me an cuz a that conductor man thinkin' I ain't 'sposed ta be there. See, them peoples ain't like workin' peoples. Ain't a lotta steady gigs for'em. Who be out there waitin' on hearin' a bassoon? An I kin say the same 'bout oboes, piccolos an a lotta instruments. So, them peoples gotta do session work cuz it be the ony way they kin make money doin' what they do best. I gotta show'em I be good 'nuff ta be waitin', too.

I bin tellin' you 'bout Jerry Lee Lewis, but I never tol' you 'bout some a them other records up in that attic an there be one outta 1972 by a piano man name a Van Cliburn. It ain't the same kinda piano playin' as Jerry Lee Lewis, but jus' as good. In 1934 Rachmaninoff, make a piece a music called Rhapsody on a Theme of Paganini. I knowed cuz I go readin' up on it afta I heared it up in that attic. He be real good at writin' music an I come on thinkin' he make that piece for hisself. Look, a guy that good kin do music for hisself all he want. So, what I heared in that attic aside a Jerry Lee Lewis an them others, be Van Cliburn playin' Rhapsody by Rachmaninoff an conducted by a 'nother guy, Kirill Kondrashin, an made inta a record in 1972.

There be twenty-four parts outta three sections an it take maybe a half hour ta git it done. None a them three sections be the same an I gotta say here the piano work be real hard. But, Dollface, it be the best way a gittin' them peoples thinkin' I kin play. An I din need no music sheets, neither. I kin 'member stuff. You knows that.

Edna listened just outside the door. His voice faltered at times and she could hear him wheeze as he thrashed from side to side, rustling the sheets. She knew the throbbing pain came earlier each day, especially upon waking, and she feared that soon she must make a decision that would haunt her prayers.

There had been no word from Archer or the young man, Kip. She had a sense for people and concluded both were sincere, but eight days had passed. The New Year would come and go and Samuel was near his end. Time was running out. Suddenly, his voice trailed off. She cautiously opened the door and peered into the room, catching a glimpse of her only patient asleep at last and relieved of his deathly march for a little while. The recorder remained clasped in his outstretched hand.

"He's an auto mechanic. Owns a shop over in Queens,

Belrose." Kip sat with Zane in the founding partner's large office. "I expected him to be the easiest to locate since Mrs. Nieves was able to give us his full name."

"Dale Messenger." Zane consulted his notes. "According to the recording he was the one who left Samuel at the emergency room. What else can you tell me about him?"

"Afghanistan, two tours, single, no siblings, both parents passed away. I checked the service records, lots of visits to the VA Hospital. I couldn't access the medical records so I don't know what his condition is or was. All I know is he worked construction here in the city after he left the military, hauling bricks so whatever ailed him wasn't physically disabling."

"But he's an auto mechanic now?"

"Yes, with plenty of business. Apparently, an honest guy."

"What about Samuel's father, the boxer?"

"I have a list of all the suspensions from the last thirty-five years. There's quite a few. I'll have to research them one by one. It may take a while."

"Samuel may die before we know."

"I think so."

"And the girl?"

"My alma mater."

"What?"

"San Jose State."

"I thought you went to NYU?"

"Law school. I did my undergrad back home, University of California at San Jose, same as the girl he's talking to on the tape."

"Coincidence."

"Yes. I'm going through alumni records, but frankly, Archer, I've got nothing to go on."

"The high school uniform, Edna said he mentions it and that maybe she went to a school in the area. What's around Jamaica?"

"There are several private schools; Catholic and Jewish. Again, a needle in a haystack."

"Why do you suppose this Dale Messenger fellow simply left him at the hospital. Why didn't he stay and why hasn't he surfaced at the hospice house?"

"It's a mystery to me, too."

"Go see him. Try to do it as soon as possible. I'll hold off on calling Edna until you tell me what he has to say. And, chase down his father. As for the girl, I'll see what I can do myself. It's too much of a long shot and I don't want you to get scattered."

"Archer, what exactly are we doing here?"

Zane looked at the notes in his hand, shaking his head. He took a breath, looking up.

"I asked Edna that when she came to see me. She seemed irritated by the question. 'He's dying all alone', she said. For whatever reason, she's concerned that he'll be forgotten. There's something personal going on, I think. Of course, I knew Samuel intermittently over the years, but strictly for legal matters. I'm quite surprised that he mentions me on his recordings."

"That's the reason? Because he remembers you?"

"I suppose. And, I'd like to help Edna. I think she's sincere."

Kip rose from his chair. "I'll see if I can catch up with Messenger today."

She returned to the party, keeping to herself as she slipped by onlookers gazing at the stage. A lively jam was underway. The two pledges spotted her and nodded toward the gates. She nodded back, wordlessly telling them to return to their assignment.

Who was that boy? What was that fleeting sense of recognition that grabbed her the moment their eyes met? She was thrilled when he returned and sat down to talk. Kip, she rolled the nickname off her tongue.

Edna comin' in 'bout an hour. I bin sleepin' an, funny, my head ain't so bad. Rhapsody on a Theme of Paganini got a openin' tempo. I rises ups a bit, lookin', tryin' ta see if I got alls a instruments. Got most of'em an I think on sittin' or standin' like Jerry Lee Lewis afore I hit them keys. I sit cuz this ain't no rockin' like Rick and the Riders.

Rachmaninoff musta bin real good on a piano an he musta bin wantin' ta make music that go bustin' onta ever one a them keys. I like that an in my head I thank'm for it. It be no time afore I git them peoples quiet cuz this ain't no foolin' 'round ta see if that baby grand got a good sound. This ain't practice an it ain't no warm-up, neither.

I work them middle keys, movin' my fingers an crossin' my hands over, makin' sound them that knowed kin hear wit all the learnin' they got. It ain't the kinda piano sound Rachmaninoff go makin' for money. He couldn'a bin thinkin' on that whilst pressin' them keys, tryin' ta find notes an chords fittin' good. This be a present his brain make for his fingers. It be for hisself an cuz a that it come out real good. Ain't nobody wit a good ear not knowin' it.

I don' go lookin' at them keys afta the first coupla minutes. If ya got the feel ya jus' let ya hands do what they gotta do. Jus' the same I wanna say it throwed me off afta I seen them peoples lookin'. I coulda missed some a them keys cuz I near stop. Does I belong? I ain't' tellin' outta them faces, but I keep playin'. Git inta the end a the openin' section an it come on time ta drop down jus' a bit. Here, that conductor man woulda pointed ta the strings ta come in an a girl take up her violin, lookin'. I shoulda looked back so she knowed I want her ta play, but I ain't sure an I don' so she put it down agin.

So, it jus' be me playin' for real, thinkin' on Van Cliburn. Alls inta the second section I play 'til the door open an that conductor man wit the mean face come inside. I keep playin' but them others go lookin', 'spectin' somethin' gonna happin. I keep my eyes down, but I knowed he be lookin' an wondrin' on me. I press on them keys, tellin' all them peoples I be the piano man - ain't gonna be nobody 'cept me! An I kin't hep myself no more. I gotta look, liftin' my eyes. If there be a meetin' it be cuz that conductor man lookin' back. I ain't seein' mad no more an I ain't seein' sad, neither. He be inta that Rhapsody, me playin' an him hearin'.

It be wrong a me ta say Rhapsody on a Theme of Paganini ony got one pretty part. It ain't true, but I ony knowed it cuz I knowed the high Rachmaninoff musta got outta ever press a ever key. I never heared him play it, ony Van Cliburn an that ain't no bad thing, but it musta bin somethin' special when Rachmaninoff do it. See, there be a lotta up an a lotta down tempos, but the best part come outta the middle, Opus 43, Variation 18. I tol' you I git up in that attic for a week afta you go. I tol' you 'bout Jerry Lee Lewis an his happy playin' on them records. I never tol' you 'bout Rhapsody an Variation 18 that suck some a the hurtin' outta me so I kin git back livin' agin. I played it once for Lacey, sittin' on my lap. This be ony the second time it come 'round.

I slide inta that part nice an easy, thinkin' on you. It don' matter no more if them peoples don' want me sittin' there. It don' matter cuz Rhapsody an Variation 18 an Opus 43 be my world right then. I wish it now, too. I wish you was here so I could play it for you afore I gotta go. You ain't here. It ain't a long part, maybe three minutes like a song on a album. It jus' ain't like what Rachmaninoff put inta them other variations - beautiful an I let it take me ta you.

Afta, I stop. Maybe I bin on them keys twenty minutes an there be ten minutes more, but the conductor man lookin' an it come on time ta know if I be stayin' or goin'. I sit wit my hands on my lap. Them others go lookin' at the conductor man, but he ony lookin' at me. Afta a coupla seconds he come offa the wall an take his baton ta his music stand. He go tappin' it hard, lookin' at everone.

"Ms. Das will join us shortly. We will use the time before she arrives to warm our instruments. I suggest we continue with The Rhapsody under full accompaniment. Mr. Jones, from the opening."

FOURTEEN

Private thoughts replace interest in the here and now. Perhaps listening to deeper messages from the body or, as I believe, the soul - Edna Nieves

E dna was up before the sun. It was Christmas morning and she happily prepared the makings of a large breakfast for her only patient. Pushed far to the back of her mind was her underlying reason as she layed out strips of bacon, poured muffin batter into a pan and retrieved eggs from the refrigerator. Instead, as she hummed a favorite christmas melody, she banished all reality, including the responsibility of her caretaker role, letting her mind relive those joyful Christmas mornings at the breakfast table with her son and husband. Soon, all would be ready. She'd peeked in on Samuel, giddy with the thought of her surprise on this special morning and spying where to place their trays after he awoke and she triumphantly entered his room with her feast. Sure she knew better, but today was Christmas! Her beloved Eduardo was always so excited on Christmas!

I gotta say somethin' 'bout Christmas. First, a course, I'm still here talkin' ta you like I bin hopin' cuz I ain't done sayin' all I wanna be tellin'. Now, comin' on New Years an I kinda knows I'm gonna be 'round for that, too. Ony Edna an me in this house an I don' think she otta be stayin' here wit me alls the time. She gotta have peoples, 'specially on Christmas, but she don' go nowheres.

I ain't sayin' it be some kinda big day wit peoples laughin' an talkin' whilst openin' presents. That ain't never bin the kinda Christmas I knowed 'cept one time when momma gimme a big breakfast an stay home wit me an Daddy most a the day afore goin'

124

out at night like she allays done. Edna go makin' a big bunch a food like that time, eggs an bacon an blueberry muffins wit a lotta butter.

A course, eatin' ain't real 'portant ta me no more. She brung it inta the room early on Christmas day. Pills be workin' jus' for a little bit these nights an I bin wakin' up a lot more than afta I first git here. I kin tell she thinkin' on givin'me more. Achin' head gittin' real bad an she know. She hep me git outta the bed an inta the chair over ta the window. She go puttin' a tray on a table she brung outta n'other room. Then she git me a blanket an come sit aside me wit her own bunch a food.

"It's Christmas, Samuel!" She go sayin' real happy. Me? I jus' think she otta be havin' a good time wit other peoples.

She threaded through the partiers for a few minutes, rising on her tiptoes to see the stage so she she could make out the face of the man on the keys. She was too far away and the throng was just tight enough to block her view. The song wasn't familiar, but it had a happy sound. Even she, with no musical training, knew he was very talented. The music pulled her. The others all around were dancing. When the song ended she weaved through more groups, mostly paired up boy and girl, and made her way to the front steps of the house. She sat down to listen. The music, or was it the man making it, took hold of her concentration.

Edna don' push, but I eat some eggs an a piece a bacon. I does it cuz I knowed she be feelin' somethin' special 'bout me even if I gotta be goin' soon. Dollface, I dunno, maybe Edna jus' gotta do good for peoples. I look sometimes an I kin see a kinda hurtin' ahind her smilin'. She missin' somethin', I think. Maybe someone an I sure don' wanna do nothin' ta make that hurtin' worse. Kin't hep myself.

Thing 'bout food right now - it don' stay down. Afta 'bout ten minutes them eggs an bacon come outta me an I make a big mess. Edna git it cleaned off real fast, but I kin see'er bein' real mad at herself cuz she go makin' all that stuff an watchin' me eat even afta she knowed it ain't somethin' I want no more. She stop bein' happy. An me? I git real sad cuz a takin' it from her on Christmas. A course, throwin' up knock all I got outta me an I be sleepin' in that chair faster than even the pill kin make me. Aftanoon afore I wake up an there she be still sittin' next ta me whisprin' somethin. Prayin', maybe. An that be the differnce 'bout this Christmas, the last one I ever gonna know, Edna.

Dollface, I don' wanna die. A whiles back I ony think on talkin' ta you an I know I tol' you I weren't feelin' afeared like I allays figured. Now, I bin thinkin' on what be comin' an I'm gittin' afeared cuz I dunno. I bin tellin' you 'bout all them books, Ralph Waldo Emerson an them others. Them peoples don' know more than I does 'bout t'other side a not wakin' up. An I don' know nothin'. Edna go makin' Christmas food an hepin' me outta bed ta eat. I see her smilin' eyes, but she be afeared, too. Cuz a bein' a nurse she knowed all kinda stuff 'bout livin' an dyin', but she don' know nothin' 'bout afta the dyin' jus' like me.

'Round that time playin' the piano for Reina Das I tol' you it be time ta move on. Two years 'bout all I want outta stayin' in that nice place at Blossom Records. Most times I jus' move on witout tellin' nobody. A course, nobody ta tell cuz it jus' be me. "Cept now I knowed Mr. Dorman be countin' on me ta make music. An, a course, he a fair man. Maybe a month I go thinkin' on ways a tellin'm I gotta go, but I din' have ta say nothin'cuz he already knowed.

An ol' guy come 'round Blossom sometimes, a big talker, wearin' nice clothes. He allays got a fine lookin' woman on his arm. Somethin' atween'm an Mr. Dorman cuz they done a lotta talkin' evertime I seen'em tagether. The ol' guy doin' most a that talkin'. Them women be singers an he git on Mr. Dorman ta let'em record in Studio B. Mostly they be all looks an no voice. Mike Winfield be the ol' guy's name.

None a them women git no contract in all the time I be at Blossom. Mr. Dorman knowed everthin' 'bout music an what be good. He ain't no fool. Lotta times he git me on the piano backin' them women. I do my best playin' them times, but it be hard ta make somethin' good outta voices that ain't.

Mike Winfield? He ain't no dummy, neither. There come on times, sittin' an waitin' on them singers ta git goin' an I heared

Winfield tellin'em what they gotta do. It be easy ta see what he be gittin' outta them ladies, him bein' a ol' guy an them bein' young an fine lookin'. It weren't 'bout carin'. I don' know nothin' 'bout that, but I listen real good them times he go talkin' music. There ain't nothin' he don' know 'bout ever song. He tell'em who done it first, when, where an how many records git bought. He tell'em how come peoples like them songs and he tell'em how it gotta come out when they sing'em. An he be right evertime. Good learnin' for me cuz there be a lotta stuff I don' know 'cept I knowed I gotta listen if there be a guy that do.

I dunno, maybe Mike Winfield brung seven women inta Blossom them two years. He don' stick wit any of'em long. Or, maybe they ain't stickin' wit'im. I back most of'em on the piano til' it git clear he bin aksin' Mr. Dorman for me ta be doin' all the backup. No Blossom contract comin' so I figured Winfield go takin' them tapes somewheres afta. If I gotta say what I think, it musta bin him lookin' ta make money quick afore the other stuff he be gittin' outta them ladies run its course.

At the end time, afta I bin thinkin' on leavin' for a whiles I git called inta Studio B for 'nother session wit one a Mike Winfield's ladies. This one be older'n them others, maybe 'bout the same as momma when she don' come home no more, but she ain't no girl. She be small an her hair be black an shiny an good lookin' like her. Thing 'bout'er is she got a scary kinda carin' 'bout singin' even if she ain't so good. You ever seen peoples carin' 'bout somethin' so hard they ain't thinkin' on nothin' else? I seen that in Studio B whilst he go talkin' in'er ear. I ain't sayin' I got somethin' agin' Mike Winfield. Truth be, I din' know the man an I never come on knowin'm afta, neither. He jus' the one that gimme a way outta Blossom cuz he brung that woman inta the studio 'round the time I bin thinkin' on doin' somethin' differnt.

That woman go singin' wit me on the keys. I don' 'member the song cuz it weren't 'portant ta me like all the other stuff I do 'member. She got a okay voice, sometimes workin' it too hard ta hit the high parts. It be clear she ain't got no trainin' an she ain't 'specially got no talent like Rick. Soul? Yeah, that she got somewhere deep. I feel it even if I ain't hearin' it. She wanna be a singer real bad an I knowed it weren't for money. It jus' who she be. Lotta peoples out there dreamin' an hopin' an tryin' real hard.

We do a coupla songs an she go lookin' at me runnin' my fingers 'long that baby grand. Winfield standin' an lookin', too. I catch'em a coupla times, but it don' matter cuz I ony thinkin' on what it gonna take ta git that woman soundin' like who she be down deep 'stead a some other peoples she ain't. That day an for most a the time afta we go workin' tagether she ain't the singer she coulda bin 'cept the one time. I be gittin' ta that.

She come ta Blossom maybe six sessions an I allays git called inta Studio B ta back'er on them keys. Winfield wit'er, but somethin' ain't good atween'em. He tryin' ta hang on'er an she ain't havin' it. Afta, he don' show no more an it jus' be me an her. Funny, all that time she don' say nothin' like she knowed I ain't talkin' an she knowed I kin run them keys onta any song she got. A course, I kin an I do.

Last day she got Mr. Dorman taggin' ahind. No singin' this time. She go standin' up front, eyein' me whilst Mr. Dorman come over.

"Samuel," he say, smilin' nice like most times, "let's go up the hill to my office."

Archer T. Zane be there an he come outta his chair, smilin' and shakin' my hand. I smile back cuz evertime he come 'round somethin' good happin' for me. Mr. Dorman go sit ahind his desk. Crystal be her name an she got a job.

"Samuel, I have asked Archer to join us today because he has represented you in the past and we have a proposal for you to consider."

Archer T. Zane aks, "Is that acceptable to you, Samuel?" I nod, lookin' ta Mr. Dorman talkin' agin.

"You've been backing Crystal on the piano for what, six or seven sessions now?" I nod agin. "She," Mr. Dorman go lookin' ta her. "has signed a contract to perform as a singer on a cruise ship. She has asked my permission to speak to you concerning this and I have agreed. I want you to know that there will always be a place for you here at Blossom. You've done a wonderful job on everything we've asked you to do. Lately, however, I've sensed some restlessness in you. Perhaps I'm wrong, but I understand that living and making music here might not be enough for someone who is accustomed to moving about and seeing other places. So, if you care to hear more and choose to pursue this opportunity I will not stand in your way. In fact, I'll do whatever I can to help you."

I look at'er, wondrin' 'bout her makin' a record at Blossom. If she got a contract she sure ain't gonna take no gig on no boat ship. But, Dollface, I knowed the answer. Nope, she ain't good 'nuff for Mr. Dorman ta be makin' no contract wit an, yep, I be goin'. I shoulda bin wondrin' 'bout other stuff. How I be livin'? What I gonna be playin'? What she gonna be singin'? I don' think on none a that. It jus' be time. I stops lookin' at'er an I don' look ta Mr. Dorman, neither. I look ta Archer T. Zane cuz he allays knowed my thinkin'. He make it all come tagether on paper an such. Oh, an there be one big 'sprise afta we git done workin' on jus' what I gonna be doin' wit Crystal on that boat ship.

"Samuel? There's also the matter of your earnings here at Blossom Records. Do you understand what I am saying?" I don' an Archer T. Zane kin see it on my face. "You've been earning a salary for the last two years. Since you've been living in one of the apartments most of that money has gone unspent and remains on account, but now that you will be leaving Blossom's employ you need to take your earnings with you. Accounting for rent on the apartment and tax withholding, it comes to a net amount of one hundred and nine thousand dollars."

I git it right there cuz I knowed no studio piano man gonna git a big pile a money like that 'specially afta rent an such come out. So, Dollface, I come on thinkin' it be a deal atween Archer T. Zane an Mr. Dorman ta gimme money cuz a me not gittin' nothin' outta my songs afta Rick go takin'em for hisself. Maybe I got'em wrong, but I figured it then an I figure it now.

Chase Manhattan Bank, Archer T. Zane an me go puttin' my money there an I git a little book sayin' it. I carry that book everwhere 'til it come on a good reason ta go spendin' it. That come afta.

She wasn't really alone because there were dozens all around, listening with a beer in one hand and more often than not the hand of someone else in the other. Kip lingered in her mind like she'd always known him, but this time it felt like they'd come together too soon. Mysteriously, like the timing wasn't right. *'Until we meet again. Oh, it will happen. You're the one.'* That thought suddenly made her impatient. She looked up at the stage. Who is this musician riveting everyone's attention?

There was a knock at the door. Edna heard it from her office next to the foyer. It was two o'clock in the afternoon. Samuel was sleeping as she wrote her notes, describing his deteriorating condition accompanied by another order, this time for the morphine drip she knew had become necessary. The phone rang.

"Edna."

"Archer?"

"Yes, I'm calling to let you know we've located..."

"Excuse me. Can I call you right back? There's someone at the door."

"Yes, of course. Call me when you have a moment. I have a progress report on our findings."

"It should only be a few minutes."

She hung up, rose and stepped into the foyer, looking through the chiffon curtains for a glimpse of who stood on the porch. Another knock. She opened the door. A large, burly man in his early thirties quickly removed his soiled baseball cap and stepped back almost to the steps, self-conscious. Edna looked him over. He had a two-day growth of red stubble on his cheeks and chin. His hair, also red, was long and mangy with tufts curling up around his ears. His jacket, unzipped and grease stained, was olive green, matching his pants also stained. He looked at her uncertainly, lacking in self-confidence as if he wasn't sure what to say. Edna was about to speak when he blurted out the words.

"They told me to ask for Edna. I'm Dale Messenger."

FIFTEEN

When that special person arrives, the husband, the wife, a son, a daughter, brother, sister, friend, the patient knows and responds to what that person is feeling – Edna Nieves

Dale musta come outta the shop cuz he got them greasy clothes we all weared for fixin' cars. Funny, I bin wondrin' on'm comin'. He git me quick ta the hospital that time, but he don' hang 'round. He afeared 'bout me for sure, but he afeared a wantin' pills, too. So he ain't hangin' 'round no hospital. He git me onta a chair an scat quick. Good cuz we both knowed he coulda got hisself onta scammin' pills that ain't never done'm no good.

He sit wit me 'til afta Edna brung supper. She git us onta chairs, lookin' outta them windows wit trays so Dale kin eat. Me? Edna brung a tray for me, but afta Christmas she ain't puttin' nothin' much on a plate cuz I ain't eatin' most a the time. He go talkin' like he allays gotta do, but he be jumpy. Head achin' real bad an I ain't sittin' a whole lot no more. Edna knowed. Dale hep'er git me inta bed, but he don' stay ta watch'er git me up for sleepin'. Don' know if he gonna come back. Cryin' a bit cuz a me lookin' real bad. Lookin' like a dyin' person I 'spose. I dunno.

Crystal be differnt from other peoples I knowed. Pretty 'nuff, jus' not young pretty like you. Gotta say I unnerstan' how come Mike Winfield lookin' for action outta her. She got a movie star body an she use it sometimes singin' on that boat ship.

I come on knowin' it be a special boat ship cuz rich peoples livin' on it alls a time. They got apartments, some real big, an Dollface, I gotta say I ain't never seen livin' an sleepin' nice as them places 'cept Archer T. Zane's big house. So, 'cept for more rich peoples comin' onta that boat ship afta it stop somewheres, there jus' be the same rich peoples alls a time.

We go everwhere. Sometimes, that boat ship wanna stop, but it gotta stay on the water a whiles afore it kin git inta a dock. It got 'nother small boat called a tender hangin' up top an it git dropped down the side so them rich peoples kin git ta the shore. I git on it, too, but ony afta them rich peoples ain't usin' it no more. Boat ship got a helicopter, too. It don' git used much an I gotta say I ain't never git on it cuz it ony be for them rich peoples. Sometimes, we go by somewheres witout stoppin' an it go inta the sky ta git peoples who wanna git onta the boat ship. Nothin' a lotta money ain't buyin'.

Crystal an me work tagether a real long time, 'bout three years. Longest I ever done somethin' witout movin' onta somethin' differnt. She ain't talkin' ta me 'cept ta figure songs an afta a whiles we slip inta 'bout sixty, doin' fifteen or twenty per set. Afta maybe three months she git onta figurin' differnt songs ta be doin'.

The signs were clear to Edna, near constant severe headache and more frequent seizures that came on anytime. His voice was changed - lower, huskier, words spoken into the recorder with halting, breathless effort. He seldom let her coax him from the bed. The last time, with the arrival of Dale Messenger, sapped every bit of strength her patient could muster. He didn't touch his food. Dale helped her get him back under the covers. Then he left with tears in his eyes. Sedatives helped only as an aid to sleep. Signs of the final stage had arrived as she expected. Eventually, it would be the coma that took him. She prayed for this, a death absent of anxiety and conscious pain and one that would not require her to fully open the morphine drip for the final time.

Zane filled her in when she called him back. Dale Messenger had already arrived, she told him. The lawyer seemed pleased. The young man, Kip, found the automobile mechanic and gave him the details of Samuel's condition and where to find him. Now, Kip was digging through the New York State Boxing Commission records, hoping to get a lead on Samuel's father that might reveal potential relatives. She cared less about all this with each passing day. Zane seemed to want to know Samuel's background more than Edna.

"While Kip checks out the boxing angle I've taken on the search for the girl. I'm looking into private schools around Jamaica Estates. It's a longshot after all these years."

Should she tell him? He told her to stop listening to the recorder. Surely, Archer T. Zane knew of the man Mike Winfield, the connection to music, which is the basis of Zane's involvement with Samuel. Still, three years, is that what Samuel said? That's a long time to be associated closely with someone. Maybe the singer mentioned by Samuel, Crystal, should be found and alerted to his fate. She may be someone who would care. Edna kept silent.

He hovered in semi-consciousness, constructing more of his fantasy. The California night air was cool and dry, soft is the word that came to mind when he finished playing a selection and sat back to rest his fingers. He pondered where she would be, preparing the scene and how she would appear. The rest of the band looked to him for a cue. The lead guitarist turned back to the partiers. "Back in ten."

Crystal git the star treatment, livin' in a nice apartment on a deck ways up from me an eatin' real good wit them rich peoples. We do two sets a night, on a nice stage at nine o'clock jus' afta dinner an 'nother 'round eleven in a lounge wit a bar an dancin'. Five nights a week for her, Sunday and Monday off. Me? I gotta play six nights no matter what. So, I git on the piano wit my own set on Sunday, makin' a different sound for them rich peoples drinkin' an wantin' ta dance. It ain't hard an I like playin' my own songs.

Them three years gimme the whole world! Ralph Waldo Emerson unnerstan' stuff witout goin' far ta see it. Yeah, I knowed he done some travlin', but most a the stuff he knowed come outta books an, a course, him bein' a smart man. Peoples call it wisdom. Me? I wanna see it. I jus' don' never 'spect seein' the whole world like I done.

'Cept for workin' nights me an Crystal go sepret. Truth be, I don' know what she done wit her time, but I figured it be workin' on her singin' cuz, like I bin tellin', it be all she care 'bout. Lotta guys comin' 'round afore an afta the singin'. I watch'em an sometimes she even git ta laughin' wit'em. Theys rich peoples wit a lotta time an a lotta dollars. Nothin' new ta them, 'specially a fine lookin' woman. Rich guys git bored an go lookin' ta Crystal ta spell it a bit. I ain't sayin' she done that. I don' know what she done all them days when we ain't workin' 'cept once. I be gittin' ta that.

Me? I git on that tender boat ever time I kin. In port there allays be a run at seven in the mornin' so them kitchen peoples kin git fresh stuff for the lunch an dinner servin'. Them rich peoples ain't goin' nowhere at seven in the mornin'. I be on that tender near ever time. Wheres I go? Everwhere!

Dollface, I seen all them places I read 'bout – Greece, Italy, England, France, Norway, Sweden an everwhere atween'em. I go walkin', eatin' differnt kinda food, hearin' peoples talkin, seein' faces, smellin' flowers, lookin' in windows and sometimes museums, ridin' buses an trains an not one time does I git afeared an not one time does I feel alone like I does right here in New York. There be a lotta stuff I come on seein' an knowin' an it be way better than jus' readin' all them books. Japan, China, Viet Nam, India, Australia, Hong Kong, New Zealand, Peru, Argentina, Brazil, you don' need me tellin'em all. The whole world an the best kinda learnin' I ever knowed.

An you know what? It come on bein' the ony time afta you gone away ta California that I ain't allays thinkin' on seein' you agin'.You gotta unnerstan' it weren't like that at the beginnin'. I go lookin' at all them faces cuz I hope maybe, maybe. But bein' on that big boat ship an travlin', sometimes goin' a lotta months afore comin' ta America agin' git me thinkin' 'bout more. Thinkin' on you slip jus' a bit. Maybe the word be happy. Do you hate me for tellin' that? Even knowin' you ain't never gonna hear this I hope you don'.

A lotta times we jus' go sailin' on the water an that tender boat ain't goin' nowhere. I do more readin'. There be a library that git used by them rich peoples. Most a them books in my head outta other places, but there be more I ain't read afore an I like that. Dollface, makin' music wit Crystal five nights an n'other one jus' me, catchin' the tender boat ever chance I kin, an readin' anythin' new outta the library be my livin' way them three years. I eat sepret in a kitchen place, but the food be the same's them rich peoples an Crystal eat an tastin'real good I gotta say.

I tol' you Crystal got soul but it don' never come outta her. I wonder on ways a fixin' it for a long time whilst we be workin'. Rick be the ony guy I ever git onta doin' good, but he already got the passion an he knowed how ta git it outta hisself afront a peoples. I ony gotta blow hard on that harmonica ta git Rick goin' right. Crystal ain't the same an she ain't takin' no notice a me, neither. I ain't even there afta she lift that microphone up close. Nobody in that room ta Crystal not even them rich peoples' listnin'. Good 'nuff for them maybe. Not good 'nuff for me.

I otta be tellin' 'bout the world I seen cuz a that boat ship an them years a movin' 'round them oceans. If my head ain't tellin' me my time comin' I be talkin' on that. Dollface, I'm real tired an I got other stuff I gotta be tellin' you afore I kin't do it no more. I come on a way a gittin' ta Crystal an, truth be, I weren't thinkin' on doin' it, neither. Jus' happin an I gotta say I git ta wondrin' why there be times when ya kin git ta peoples way a thinkin' witout even knowin'. So, I gotta talk 'bout it afore I ain't got time ta tell you the other stuff I bin thinkin' on. I kin see outta the way Edna lookin' an the way Dale lookin' my time comin' quick. I ain't never gonna see you an alls a waitin' an alls a hopin' ain't gonna change that. Jus' gotta finish my talkin'.

Come on the end jus' like me wantin' ta git outta Blossom. Do you feel it sometimes? Them times when somethin' else callin'? Maybe it jus' be me and I wonder on that a lot, but I seen other peoples changin' an I come on thinkin' we all lookin' for somethin', growin an knowin' more.

Crystal an me 'bout done ever song we ever knowed, hunnerds of'em 'til we come on doin'em all over agin. I 'spose it be okay cuz Rick an the Riders din' have a whole lotta songs, neither. Ya git used ta it. 'Cept near the end Crystal git edgy afta we come 'round ta playin' an singin' stuff we bin doin' a long time. If I gonna talk I woulda aks, "What do you want?" Even afta three years a makin' music I din' know that woman, but I allays watchin' an waitin' on'er ta be who she otta be, herself. I knowed she git it on wit a coupla them rich guys over them years. I knowed one of'em make her cry afta he don' come 'round no more. I knowed music be her everthin'. An I knowed it ain't cuz she real good doin' it. Jus' her way a hidin'. Peoples gotta be who they be. They kin't be somebody they ain't forever.

I make up a bunch a songs over them years jus' like I done at Blossom. Nothin' special, jus' somethin' I like ta do. Near the end I figured there be ten a them songs Crystal coulda done if I git ta writin' words. A course, she don' know nothin' 'bout me makin' songs, but somethin' new that ain't bin done by other peoples woulda bin good. Boat ship come inta New York for fixin'. Them rich peoples git off cuz a lotta workin' goin' on all over the decks an it weren't no nice place ta be hangin' 'round.

Crystal gone cuz we ain't doin' no playin' an I take some time, too, goin' back inta the city an lookin' 'round. I check on my money in the Chase Manhattan Bank, wondrin' on stuff ta buy, but there ain't nothin'. Nights I come back for eatin' an sleepin'. I git ta thinkin' this run be near over an don' git me wrong, I like travlin' round on that boat ship. I like makin' music. But, Dollface, New York allays bin the place I knowed an it go tellin' me ta git onta somethin' differnt, that's all. Maybe Crystal thinkin' on it, too. She be wantin' more outta doin' music.

Afta a month she come back. Work near done an sailin' time comin' on. She got a whole lotta a different songs an I git onta knowin'em quick so it weren't real hard ta git a new act tagether. I don' do no talkin', but she used ta that an she knowed she kin gimme the sheets an I jus' git on the piano, no fuss. Like I tol' you afore, this woman got all the curves an she knowed how ta look real good on that stage. So, it ony be the singin' she gotta git right. No, that ain't what I gotta say. Gittin' it so them rich peoples don' know no better be jus' 'bout it. I woulda liked ta do somethin' ta make her find that soul I knowed she got. No talkin', but I git it done.

When he left with tears in his eyes Edna wasn't sure Dale Messenger would return, but he telephoned in the morning, more composed.

"Ma'am, I'm sorry about the way I came and went yesterday." Edna noted sadness in his voice. "He's my friend and it's hard to see him like that."

Edna didn't know the nature of the relationship between this man and her patient. This ignorance didn't alarm her because she believed that Kip from Attorney Zane's law firm would never have sent him to the hospice house if there was any question about his character.

"I understand. Please call me Edna. Will you come by again?"

"Yes, Ma'am, er Edna.That's why I'm calling. Can you tell me how much time he has?"

"It's hard to predict. It was supposed to be Christmas. Now we are past the New Year and he's still with us."

"He looks so bad."

"Yes, he's in the final stages. A week maybe. Not weeks."

"Can I stay with him? I won't be any trouble. I can sleep in a chair in his room. I'll go out for food and clean up back here at my place." Edna sat up in surprise. Never, since she became a hospice nurse, had anyone asked to stay with a dying patient. She was unprepared to respond. "Look, if it's against the rules I get it, but if you can bend them for me I'd sure be grateful."

Edna thought. There were rules, only next of kin. Still, the post New Year referrals had yet to materialize. Apart from Samuel the hospice house was empty, plenty of room to accommodate Messenger. "You understand the final days and hours may be difficult?"

"Yes, yes I do. I promise not to get in your way."

"All right, Mr. Messenger. Bring some clothes."

During the band's ten-minute break she decided to leave the steps and wander closer to the stage. Most of the others were gathered around the kegs, leaving open space through which she could navigate. She wasn't embarrassed to be one of the few girls still unaccompanied on this quintessential California night, cloudless and comfortable with an occasional light breeze. That wasn't on her mind except for the brief interlude with the boy preparing to leave for her New York hometown. No, she decided to enjoy the evening. The music did that for her, changing her mood and her thoughts from serious to carefree if only for this last set about to begin.

I come on thinkin' this be the last sailin' for me. Crystal off doin' what she do durin' them days an I git sorta lost for the first time since comin' onta this gig. See, Dollface, it all come back ta you. Alls a while I jus' like the sailin', makin' music wit Crystal an seein' the world like I never figured I woulda. But we bin ta most a them places an this sailin' jus' goin' ta most of'em all over agin'. There still be a lot I din' see afore, I knowed that, but it weren't gonna be new no more. Afta we git outta New York we go sailin' east ta Bermuda agin' an I don' git offa that boat ship. For the first time in a long while I come on wishin' I could see you agin' real bad.

A course, that ain't gonna happin'. It bin a long time afta I tried on findin' you an, funny, that boat ship never git ta California in alls a times it go everwhere else. So, I keep ta myself kinda like afore, stayin' in my little room an readin' books outta the library. No Ralph Waldo Emerson an that be hard cuz I woulda liked readin' on his thinkin' agin'. I 'member everythin' he say in them books so it be kinda funny ta wanna read'em agin. In 'Conduct of Life' he connect everythin' tagether 'bout how what we does an what we think make us who we be. I think on you all my life afta them two kisses. I don' know why I done it an I don' know why you kiss me back. If it be 'portant why ain't I never seen you agin'? An if I think on you alls a time afta, what do that make me? Right here layin', dyin', talkin', feelin' my head an wondrin' what be comin' on t'other side a not wakin' up no more, I don' know nothin' 'bout who I be. An if I come inta your life an you come inta mine ain't that 'sposed ta mean somethin'?

We git outta Bermuda on a Saturday aftanoon. Crystal an me doin' two shows an the lounge full a rich peoples cuz they all come onta that boat ship for sailin' 'til Christmas. Sunday be my night ta jus' run my fingers onta the piano for thems showin' up. More of'em watchin' an listnin'than most times cuz it ony be the second day. I git onta playin' my ol' stuff outta the Rick days cuz some a them ladies wanna dance wit their man. I go 'bout two hours, no stoppin' cuz takin' a break jus' mean walkin' 'round for a bunch a minutes waitin' on gittin' back onta them keys.

Crystal talkin' wit some guy at the bar an payin' me no mind. I git thinkin' 'bout them songs I make up an I start playin'em. Thinkin' on it now I know I played'em for Crystal. Doin' my own stuff be 'bout good's it kin be for me on a piano. Kinda like Rachmaninoff musta bin feelin', but I ain't sayin' I be good's him. No way! First time I ever git that feelin' be down the Jersey Shore wit Rick an I sorta bin chasin' it alls a time afta. Jus' me, Dollface. My soul sayin'; 'this be me!'. An that be it 'bout Crystal. She ain't sayin' who she be outta her singin'. She got who she really be somewhere locked up an she ain't lettin' it out.

Ten songs, I 'member. First time I go playin'em for peoples an cuz a the dancin' I makes a coupla changes an up the tempo, but I keep the best ones jus' the same. No words, a course. I ain't singin' an I thinks now if Crystal din' git some lyrics ta sing'em wit maybe I woulda got some a Ralph Waldo Emerson's poems:

> If I could put my woods in song
> And tell what's there enjoyed,
> All men would to my gardens throng,
> And leave the cities void.

'Member that one? 'My Garden'? I tol' you all five stanzas at the residence. First time you come on knowin' Ralph Waldo Emerson. First time it be 'portant to me that somebody know I ain't no idiot.

I git ta dreamin' whilst my fingers work them keys, hearin' the loud clappin' afta each a my songs cuz the room be full up. I 'member cuz, tellin' it true, it be the first time I figured them rich peoples even knowed I be there. Afta the last song I look an Crystal ain't talkin ta that guy no more. She be standin' offa the side, lookin' at me real hard like she tryin' ta figure somethin' out.

SIXTEEN

Death is imminent when food and drink are rejected – Edna Nieves

"Rabbit Red." Kip sat on the couch in Zane's ornate office. "That was his ring name. Suspended twice for sucker punching his opponents after the bell. Put a few guys in the hospital. Always went for the back of the neck, rabbit punch."

"Where is he now?"

"Dead. Drug deal gone wrong a few years ago just after he was released from prison."

"You're sure he's the father?"

"Are you ready for this?"

Zane looked up. "Ready for what?"

"His real name was Charles S. Jones."

"No."

"Yes, Archer. No confirmation yet, but he has to be the father."

"I'd like to know for sure."

"I checked marriage and birth records. If Samuel was born in a hospital in New York there isn't any paper to prove it. No marriage certificate, either."

"Edna was hoping to locate relatives or friends."

"Dead end."

"What do you mean?"

"Both the Boxing Commission and prison records show place and date of birth as unknown. No way to quickly trace him. I mean it can be pursued, but it will take a lot of time with no guarantee. DNA might confirm he's the father, but it won't speed up locating any living relatives."

"With his father already dead? No way to get a DNA sample. Maybe there are other records somewhere."

"I wouldn't know where to look, but there has to be DNA through the prison system."

"I'll tell Edna and see what she wants to do."

"I found something else."

Zane looked up, interested. "What?"

"I sent an email to a friend of mine in sports radio, asking about Rabbit Red. Next thing I know there's a reply with a short audio attached from thirty years ago when he was still in the ring. An old radio interview."

"Before Samuel was born?"

"Maybe a year or so before if Samuel is twenty-nine like we believe. But that's not the point. You know how Samuel speaks on his recording?"

"Sure."

"I mean the odd vernacular. Look, here's a guy who can recite poetry, essays, all kinds of words and phrases from the best writings in the world. He understands proper English and it comes through whenever he utters something from a book."

"So?"

"So, why doesn't he always speak that way?"

"You think you know the answer?"

"Maybe."

"His father?"

"Yes. When I listened to the interview he sounded like Samuel; slang, mispronunciations, confused tenses. Hard to tell them apart. "

"So, another mystery about Samuel."

"Mother disappears. Father beats him up and abandons him on the subway. Lousy childhood if you ask me. I'm no psychologist, but for all his abilities, his reading and music, he seems to be emotionally stuck back there in that part of his life. Anyway, the son speaks just like the father, which for me is another data point confirming what he says on his recording."

"Doesn't help us much, but interesting." Zane changed the subject. "I might have a line on the girl."

"Yeah?" Kip sat up.

"Catholic High School right there in Jamaica Estates. All girls. I have an appointment with the principal tomorrow morning."

"What makes you think this is a lead?"

"Sister Genevieve, that's her name, surprisingly open and pleasant. Fortunately, she's been with the school for over twenty years. She says there's a tradition of community service and they keep records."

"You think they go back that far, twelve years?"

"She's looking into that and will let me know when we meet."

"You told her why?"

"Had to, of course."

"Still a crap shoot. No name to go by."

"We'll see. Anyway, it's all I could turn up."

"Can I do anything?"

"After I meet with her, if something looks promising maybe you could chase it down."

Zane returned to the present, pausing the recording again. He opened a drawer and pulled out a thin folder containing a single sheet of paper. The letter was dated six months before and written in the personal hand of Mavis Radnor.

Dear Archer:

Since your query was personal my reply is the same. My opinion of the recordings you have provided falls under the category of contrivance. I refer, of course, only to the younger man's word usage and pronunciation. It shares no parallel to linguistic norms associated with any sections of greater New York, including neighborhoods that have seen rapid turnover during the past fifty years. Thus, in my view this man has generally created his own language. I use the term generally because the radio recording of the other man contains a number of similarities.

However, unlike the first recording, the radio recording does correspond to lower income neighborhoods in several parts of Queens and, more importantly, to language elements unique to the boxing profession in the metropolitan area. It appears that the younger man labors to copy the forms of word usage and pronunciation we hear in the radio interview.

However, as similar as they may seem to the layman's ear, I assure you one is contrived and the other is genuine.

Further, I am more comfortable with the authenticity I hear when the younger man recites phrases from various books. There is relaxation and ease with the words, suggesting it is native to the speaker whether through environment or some other influence such as education. It is indicative of knowledge and intelligence.

Archer, as a linguist I am occasionally consulted by other professionals; physicians, psychiatrists and psychologists seeking to gain insight about a patient or client. If I may be candid I perceive a psychological root to the choice of language used by the voice we hear on the recording. Perhaps there is trauma, stress, a psychological challenge of some kind. I suggest you consult a psychologist if you would like to know more.

With warm regard,
Mavis

Zane recalled Kip's immediate response after sharing the letter. "I prefer the mystery."

He drifted in and out of consciousness, needing the drip from time to time, but more often merely exhausted and too weak to stave off sleep. With his eyes closed and body still, his fantasy was as real as the surroundings that greeted him when he awakened. This time, with only a few songs left to play after the break, he slipped behind the stage and came around the side to survey the audience. He knew how she would come to him. She was there.

We go sailin' the ocean outta Bermuda maybe three days, Crystal singin' the same but actin'differnt, lookin' at me a lot like she never done afore. I ain't sayin' she pull out the soul I knowed she got. She jus' tryin' hard ta unnerstan' somethin'.

I git onta the piano early most a them nights cuz there ain't nothin' ta do an it be borin'. Gotta git offa that boat ship an go home. One night I git ta the lounge early an see Crystal sittin' in my place at them keys. She a tough woman an she don' go stoppin' afta I give'er a look. Truth be, maybe she don' even notice me lookin'. She hit a note an write somethin' on a piece a paper. Then she do 'nother an 'nother 'til I come 'round an see it be one a my songs cuz readin' the music tellin' me right there. She don' look up an I git that she wanna be alone. I goes away.

Near on three years. I seen a lotta this world. I knowed I be lucky ta learn 'bout peoples an places no book gonna never show me sittin' in no chair. I don' know how ta 'splain why three years be 'nuff. I don' know 'cept it come on bein' time, simple's that.

Afore that last sailin' I git some dollars outta the Chase Manhattan Bank. Archer T. Zane make good on alls a workin' I bin doin'. Money outta Blossom an alls a money workin' the piano on that boat ship. Daddy woulda bin 'sprised I got that money an I ain't done nothin' bad ta nobody.

I wonder on Dale doin' okay witout me. He hurtin' real bad that first time I come on knowin'm. Afta I figured what I gotta do ta hep'm git better he done real good, but now I'm afeared he gonna go slippin' cuz I ain't there ta make sure he don'. Best friend I ever knowed. Ony friend 'cept maybe you, Dollface. I don' know. Does ya think on me?

Two days afta I seen Crystal workin' on my songs she go puttin' one under my door. I be readin' an I go lookin' afta hearin' somethin'. There it be comin' onta the floor. I open the door, but she movin' quick, me seein her backside afore she go 'round the corner.

I read it, my notes and chords wit words fittin' good. Nice handwritin' like I come on knowin' women got. She done good, ony missin' a coupla parts cuz she musta heared hard that night. Them lyrics sayin' loud she wanna sing'em. Not gonna happin' if she don' git onta showin' what she got. I fix them parts she don' git right an go lookin'. Funny, I ain't never seen inside a where she live a coupla decks up from my little space. I knowed she live good on that boat ship cuz I heared them kitchen peoples talkin'. Me too, but it ain't like her cuz I ony be her piano man. I don' care. I think on puttin' the music under her door like she done ta me, but I don'. 'Stead, I brung it back ta my place. My music.

She ain't lookin' at me afta she git onta the stage that night. That ain't no big 'sprise. I never go lookin' much ta her, neither 'cept now we got this song sittin' atween us an I come on thinkin' maybe we gonna hear the real Crystal if she git onta singin' it. So, I start lookin' an I keep lookin' 'til she gotta look back. I wave them music sheets high so she gotta see'em, but she shake'er head an take up the mike in that shiny dress tight 'round all her good parts. Same ol' Crystal singin' okay, but not givin' no piece a who she be ta nobody. Next day, I make ready ta git offa that boat ship.

Edna took the recorder from under the covers and placed it on the night stand. Then she removed the tiny needle from his vein. She rolled the drip stand to the side and returned to retrieve the bed pan with only a few drops of dark urine inside. She set the bed pan on the floor near the door and proceeded to pull the sheets from under the mattress, gently turning her patient onto his side then rolling the sheets into a ball and tossing them into the hall. She placed fresh sheets near his feet, unfolded each and remade the bed with the same efficiency. As she retrieved the bedpan and soiled sheets from the floor and carried them to the laundry room, she went over her conversation with Father Miguel, pastor of her church.

"Is he Catholic?" the priest asked.

"I don't know very much about his upbringing. I doubt he's had religious training."

"Last Rights. Schedule permitting, I might be willing to perform them at his deathbed, but a Funeral Mass here at Saint Lawrence is out of the question."

"Why?" Edna knew little about the archaic rubrics of her faith.

"He isn't a Catholic. He isn't a member of this parish."

"He's a human being. He's about to die."

"Has he asked for a blessing from our faith?"

Edna shook her head. "He doesn't speak."

"Unwilling or unable?"

"What difference does that make?"

Father Miguel rose from behind his desk. "Last Rites, perhaps. I can look at my schedule if you wish."

"How can you be so cold?"

Father Miguel came around the desk. "Mrs Dowd?" He went to the door, looking down the hallway for his housekeeper. "Are you there, Mrs Dowd?"

"Yes, Father?"

"Would you see Mrs. Nieves to the door?"

Edna stood to leave, shaking her head in disgust. "Really? You're a priest?"

"The church has its requirements. In good conscience I cannot go against my faith."

"If I went to Saint Michael's or another parish the answer might be different?"

"Not if their priests follow the dictates of Rome. Mrs. Dowd will see you out."

I wakes up, seein' this recorder on the table. I knows Edna done it. I got nothin' left an it be too hard ta git outta this bed afore she go puttin' new sheets on. I figure she go turnin' it on for herself cuz she hearin' me talkin' sometimes. Ain't no secret an I don' care no more. Hurtin' an real tired.

Sometimes ya gotta push. I push on Rick an I knowed I gotta push on Crystal. Truth be, I wanna be hearin' my music comin' outta peoples aside me on a piano. Wit that song sittin' atween us she ain't lookin' my way never. I knowed she be afeared. No missin' that. I wonder why she go writin' it on paper an puttin' it under my door. Look, Dollface, Crystal ain't like you. She ain't thinkin' 'bout peoples an tryin' ta do somethin' nice. That ain't her way. So, if she go puttin' my song ta words on paper it gotta be cuz she want somethin' for herself. Maybe she knowed she gotta sing it. Maybe she afeared a who come out. So, I gotta push an I do.

Lotta times we jus' go movin' song ta song not takin' much time atween'em. Peoples like it that way. I ain't sayin' we don' mix it up fast an slow, but Crystal allays be the one takin'em there. I jus' follow like a piano man 'sposed ta.

Ain't doin' it no more. Soon's we done wit one song I jump onta the one she gimme, bustin' the piano keys an lookin' ta see if she gonna go wit it. A course, she allays bin the boss an she ain't happy 'bout bein pushed. She gimme a hateful look an don' do nothin' 'til I go slidin' back onta somethin' we done afore.

Late mornin' I come 'round the lounge, seein' Crystal on my piano. She go bangin' a note an writin' stuff, makin' the best she kin outta my songs. I knows it be hard cuz she ain't 'membrin'em too good. A course, I ony played'em one time an she be too proud ta aks me ta play'em agin. Good, cuz I knowed right then I gotta git on them keys early afore we do our set afta dinner. Maybe a half hour I git onta playin'em agin for a coupla nights. She ain't there aside me, but she ain't far 'nuff away so she ain't hearin'em, neither. I figured she kin git the parts she ain't 'membrin'. She wanna git more of'em onta paper wit her own words? Okay wit me.

Boat ship go dockin' at Southhampton, England. I git on the tender in the mornin' cuz I ain't gonna stay for the next sailin'. Gotta see 'bout gittin' home ta New York. Lotta airplanes outta England an I got me a schedule in my pocket ridin' that tender boat back.

She put six a them songs under my door. Most done okay an them lyrics she go makin' up ain't bad. Better'n them words Rick done for sure. I look'em over real good cuz I gonna git offa that boat ship an it come on time. See, Dollface, I tells ya she be a hard kinda woman, but she ain't no bad peoples. I seen alls a world cuz a her an bein' on that boat ship. I wanna give'er somethin' back. If she got somethin' inside it gotta come out afore it git too late. Big red letters on the last song. *'This one'*.

Sister Genevieve could offer little information. "Yes", she told Zane," we sponsor reading programs in the area. We encourage our girls to be of service to the less fortunate."

"On the phone you said you keep records."

"I checked, but I'm afraid we don't go back twelve years. Society is so litigious these days. We are forced to record everything. Twelve years ago, before all this controversy arose with priests and children we weren't so concerned." The reference to the many shocking revelations of recent years was obvious. Zane grimaced inside, but let it pass.

"So, it's a dead end."

The nun turned in her chair to face a large, multi-tiered bookcase behind her desk. She stood, reached up to one of the shelves and took down three volumes. "These yearbooks cover the time you believe she may have attended our academy." She returned to her chair and placed them on the desk in front of Zane. "Maybe your client will recognize her picture."

"I doubt it." Zane shook his head, ignoring the volumes. "He doesn't speak and he's near the end."

"I wish I could be more helpful."

He rose and smiled. "It was a longshot. Thank you for your time, Sister." He extended his hand as she also stood. She took it then hurriedly gathered up the yearbooks before he could turn to leave.

"I have a feeling..."

"What?"

She thrust the yearbooks into his hands. "God works in mysterious ways."

So it come clear Crystal bin thinkin' on singin' one a them songs all along. It be a pretty one. I gotta say that cuz I make it thinkin' on you. I brung them sheets ta the lounge jus' afore the rich peoples git done eatin' dinner. Soon's that boat ship git inta a new port a lotta peoples git off for a coupla days an don' come back at night. The lounge din' have so many drinkin' an dancin'. Crystal show early, too.

We git outta the first set an I wonder if she gonna take up my song. Nope. Second set almost done an peoples startin' ta leave cuz it gittin' late. An, after watchin'em all them times afore, it be kinda easy ta figure what they's thinkin' on doin' next. Ol' rich guys an nice lookin' women. Drinkin' done its magic an I gotta say the music hep, too. Maybe twenty or thirty peoples still there afta we come on the end. Crystal lookin' good an there be a ol' guy hangin' at the end a the bar, eyein'er like he got hisself a plan. I seen it afore 'cept Crystal don' go lookin' back. Lotta times afore she do cuz there be money on that boat ship an she ain't no fool. Jus' not this time.

Last song git done an Crystal go steppin' back, takin' a bow like ever night afta it come on the end. The ol' guy bin drinkin' hard an he come offa the bar onta the stage grabbin' Crystal like he wanna dance an yellin', "one more song, one more!" Crystal seen it afore. She give'm a little touch on the face an push'm easy offa the stage. Bartender come 'round an hep the ol' guy back onta a barstool. All quick. Nobody gittin' riled. Crystal lookin' ta me an I knowed that one more song gonna be mine.

I don' need no music sheets, but she do cuz we ain't never practiced an she gotta sing them words she put down. I got me the sheets so I git up an brung'em ta her. She take'em an smile at me. First time ever. Then she run'er hand over the top a mine in a way I seen'er do ta that guy that go makin'er cry a coupla years back. This ain't the Crystal I knowed.

I start slow, jus' tappin them openin' notes sorta like a intro on a record. I does it cuz Crystal gotta git the key an git clear on them words an where she wanna start singin'em. We bin workin' tagether long 'nuff ta know. Then she git goin'.

Dollface, there be a differnce atween singin' an real singin'. Feel, like I heared outta your voice readin' ta them little kids. You got a voice comin' inta my ears like I knowed you afore an our souls be happy. I gotta git that kinda singin' outta Crystal. Singin' she got, but don' never do afore. Rick do my songs wit all he got. Crystal kin do it, too. I gotta make sure.

Singin' come out no good an I quit playin.' Crystal standin' on that stage, lookin' an wondrin' why I go embarrassin' her like she never bin afore. She shake her head like she don' unnerstan'. I touch my chest, pointin'. I ain't talkin' 'cept inside I'm tellin'er *Ain't gonna be your song 'til you take it.* I wanna hear Crystal do it cuz I wanna feel like that first time I heared your voice. I gotta say that be the ony time I ever seen Crystal afeared. Her eyes git wet an twinklin' cuz a them lights. Peoples watchin' an, Dollface, I'm tellin' you I heared somethin' even if'er mouth ain't open.

"Help me."

It be jus' like the time I heared you say, *"Find me."*

So, that be it. I knowed she got soul afta I git onta playin' wit'er. Maybe Mr. Dorman knowed, too. But he ain't wastin' no money if she ain't gonna show it. Why ain't she lettin' it out so everone kin hear? She gotta be Crystal an I come on thinkin' I kin't let her sing like other peoples no more. An, Dollface, it weren't 'bout me wantin' ta hear my song no more, neither. *"Help me,"* come 'cross that lounge. I gotta do it."

I bin thinkin' on that a whiles. In them two words she make me unnerstan' peoples comin' tagether. It be nothin' 'cept ta hep if the goin' git hard. Archer T. Zane done it. Edna doin' it. Crystal thinkin' she alls alone, standin' on that stage afeared cuz she ain't never knowed who she be. She ain't gonna be alone no more.

I git onta them keys an it ain't for them rich peoples no more, ain't for me, ain't even for you, Dollface. I do it for Crystal soft an easy, lettin' sound come inta the air jus' the way it gotta for as long as it take for her ta git ready ta be herself. No lookin', neither. The hepin' gonna come outta the music so it kin touch her inside an come back out for peoples ta know. Oh, Dollface, ya shoulda heared her that night.

In all a my thinkin' she got soul I ain't never 'spected singin' so good. Soft song 'bout wantin' ta see someone agin. She go makin' them words, not me. An she go singin' 'em like they got meanin' ta all peoples an they got meanin' ta her an they got meanin' ta me. Eyes be closed. She ain't movin' an swayin'. She ain't slippin' that mike outta one hand ta 'nother. Jus' Crystal an my piano backin' an ta tell it true, she don' need no piano. I kin hear 'er whiles talkin' now an I sure wish you could hear it cuz it be my song 'bout you an Crystal musta knowed. I got my eyes closed an my hands movin' on them keys, seein' you.

Peoples alls standin'. Like I tol' you afore, not so many but clappin' like they never done afore in them three years we bin playin' that boat ship. It go a long whiles. I don' wanna open my eyes cuz I'm livin' in my song. Crystal, the real Crystal brung me close ta you's I ever bin afta Cletus cheat me outta findin' you. Clappin' go down an loud shoutin' for more, but there ain't gonna be 'nother song that night. I open my eyes an Crystal standin' right there aside me, lookin', smilin' an cryin'. She git my hand an pull me up, makin' me look at the peoples. Bartender talkin' loud.

"Let's hear it, folks!"

An they all start clappin' agin. Crystal make me bow. Then she go pullin' me outta that place ta her nice apartment coupla decks up. I kin tell you what happin' afta, but it ain't right ta talk on it. Crystal make me feel good like I never feel afore or afta. In them hours afore the sun come up I git the meanin' a them poems an them songs 'bout a man an a woman bein' happy tagether. On a airplane ta New York afta mornin' come.

I bin thinkin' on that singin' alls a while afta, right ta this moment talkin' on it. I gotta let you go, Dollface. I wanna stay in that song seein' you, but the song gotta end. I gotta let you go cuz I gotta go.

Zane paused the recording again, picturing Crystal Singleton as she appeared on the cover of her debut album for Blossom Records. Ellis Dorman signed her to a standard contract except for several tweaks she requested. Zane made the changes; fifty percent of her earnings to go to the charitable endeavors bearing Samuel's name.

Archer T. Zane didn't know the early Crystal described by Samuel and confirmed by Ellis Dorman. He didn't know the stubborn, hard-edged, but attractive singer who rarely laughed or smiled, chasing an elusive dream that would never be. He only knew the Crystal of today, cheerful, enthusiastic, bright-eyed and happy. Her public persona simply went by the name Singleton. It dominated the album cover and, since her debut recording went double platinum, the Singleton he knew was much in demand not only onstage, but also on the talk show circuit. No charade. Viewers saw and heard a genuine personality devoted to her music and thrilled that it pleased.

Ten songs attributed to Samuel Jones. Two more and the lyrics to all twelve written by Singleton. Produced by veteran Cindy Crane-McCabe, among the most respected music producers in the industry who came out of retirement at the request of her friend Ellis Dorman. A second album was in the pipeline.

"I paid very little attention to him during the years we performed together. Apart from his skill on the piano, he made

himself easy to ignore, never saying a word to anyone. I was surprised when I heard the recording, that he could actually speak and, of course, what he said about me. Oh, everything was true...is true. I freely admit that.

"Since my first memories as a child I wanted to be a singer. I can list all the greats I emulated; Ella Fitzgerald, Etta James, Diana Ross dozens more who achieved stardom and are household names. I wanted to be them. I practiced hard, studied their techniques and mannerisms, sang their songs, dressed like them. I read everything about their lives, where they grew up, how they grew up, comparing me to them at every turn until I had mastered who they were, or who I thought they were and made myself into as near a copy as possible.

"I auditioned constantly, picking up a lounge gig here and there along with plenty of men. I used some of those men, thinking that's what it took to get ahead. The years went by and slowly my dreams dissolved into what they had always been, just dreams. When it became clear that I wouldn't be offered a recording contract by Blossom Records, my last chance Mike Winfield told me, I took the cruise ship offer. I decided to hide. Samuel came along to play the piano.

"We rotated material from time to time and we had seasonal songlists, but to say we collaborated is wrong. I gave him the lists. He took them and played them. It didn't dawn on me just how talented he was until I realized we never practiced. Not once. And yet, we never skipped a beat.

"He talks about the songs he wrote. When I heard them for the first time I knew they were written about someone special to him. I guess the best word to describe that first hearing is stunned, each song so beautiful that I wanted desperately to sing them as if they were mine. Gradually, as I labored over the lyrics I began to realize I was writing words for all the others I was trying to be. All those years of imitation... those songs deserved the Crystal he believed I could be. Not the Crystal I was.

"As he describes, I started to sing the one I liked best. I couldn't get through the first stanza before he stopped playing. I was furious at him. How dare he? But when we looked at each other his eyes burned into me and suddenly the veneer of all those greats I could never be fell away. I was naked and frightened in front of that small audience. I wanted to run away. And, yes, I did look at him for help. He started to play again. The notes and chords went on for what seemed like forever.

"I know it sounds impossible... I mean to be so in tune with another person that he can wordlessly make you understand what you must do. For the first time in my life I just sang - the most wonderful feeling I have ever known. Samuel gave that to me."

SEVENTEEN

Loved ones and friends need caring, too. Explain, describe, encourage, console – Edna Nieves

"Archer, how's the finest lawyer in New York? You'll be retiring soon, true?"

"I'm well, Your Eminence. Yes, in sixty days."

"It won't be the same."

"I'll still be prowling the city."

Zane shifted the telephone to his other ear and picked up the note his secretary had placed in front of him. He searched for the pastor's name as Cardinal Wolfkawitz told a quick joke in his trademark, jovial style. Able to read and listen at the same time, Zane laughed at the punchline.

"I'm sure you have a reason for calling, Archer." The powerful Catholic leader could be as intimidating as he was charming. Zane felt slightly uncertain whenever they spoke.

"I need a favor." He gave a quick description of Edna's meeting with the pastor of her local parish. "A Father Miguel, that's the name she gave my secretary."

"Yes, I know the name. He's new. Bishop Francis is recruiting from South America. Rolls are thin here in the states. Not many vocations. I haven't met him yet."

"She cares for the terminally ill. A hospice house in Queens."

"Hence, her request for a Funeral Mass?"

"Yes."

"And, what is your involvement?"

"He's been my client from time to time over the past decade."

There was a pause. Over his lengthy career as a negotiator Zane had learned to wait as those from whom he sought a concession formulated a response.

"Our Catholic faith is in transition. Within our ranks, from Rome to the rest of the world, there are forces on the side of tradition struggling against change. Those of us seeking a more modern view face a legion of hard conservatives just like politics."

"I hope I'm not asking too much of you."

"How much money have you raised for the church over the years?"

"I don't know. It's not important."

"Ten million and change. It most certainly is important. You're not even a member of the faith."

"You do good work."

"People like you make it possible. I wasn't aware that Father Miguel was part of the old guard. Please don't hold it against him. Like most of us he's acting in good conscience according to his interpretation of church doctrine."

"I understand. I'm merely pursuing this matter on behalf of Mrs. Nieves."

"Why is this important to her."

"When I have asked she gets irritated, like it's obvious and everyone should know."

"Is she hiding some ulterior motive, some other purpose?"

"Oh no. If you met her you'd recognize immediately that she is a good person. No hidden agendas. However, I do think it has special meaning to her. Something symbolic beyond simply caring for him."

"And the young man? He agrees with what she would like us to do?"

"I don't think she's told him yet. He's mute, doesn't speak. No religious affiliation as far as she knows. He had a difficult upbringing. Mother disappeared when he was very young. Father abused him."

"You say he is your client. Do you know him well?"

"He's a gifted musician. To my knowledge he has never hurt anyone. I sense compassion and understanding." Another lengthy pause. Zane waited. There was a sigh on the other end of the line.

"We, in positions of leadership, cannot curtly overrule our priests. We must take a slow, gentle path to change, justifying why it is necessary and bringing it about through our actions not our orders. I'm sure you understand."

"Your Eminence," Zane replied carefully, "I can't ask you to do what is not within your power to do. I am aware that what may seem simple to me is far more serious to a man in your position."

"Yes, of course you do. If there was time and I was inclined to follow the rules I'd tell you he must become Catholic. That is the accepted path."

"He only has a few days. Perhaps not even that. A deathbed conversion? Is that necessary?"

"If I was a traditionalist, yes, but, I am not. Our little secret. Nevertheless, for my own spiritual comfort you must obtain the young man's consent. If you can do that I will personally say Mass for him in Saint Patrick's Cathedral."

"In writing? I'm not sure..."

"We've known each other a long time. Your word is good enough for me. Get some signal of agreement from him that you believe is sincere."

His fantasy came alive with the drip's pulse. California, he dreamed, San Jose just as he wanted with no mixing of reality from Rick and the Riders and his failed attempt of years before. No, this was his fantasy and he willed his thoughts only to the positive. The song was carefully drawn in his mind. Of such melodic beauty that he was certain she would know it was him. He would play it for her, watching, drawing her near. To be close to her again, see her face, perhaps touch her hand. His body told him the moment approached. Souls talking one last time.

Head hurtin' alls a time an I ain't got it in me ta git outta this bed. I git offa that boat ship an go ta the airport. Ticket home ain't hard cuz I got money. I git inta JFK, showin' my passport an gittin' a taxi inta the city. Style it be for me, spendin' money setup right cuz a me knowin' Archer T. Zane.

I find a hotel for sleepin', but I gotta say here it weren't easy cuz most of'em lookin' for a credit card I ain't got. Midtown, 'round the square wit alls them big signs showin' peoples singin' an laughin'. You know, plays an movies an stuff. I ain't talkin'. I jus' hold up a wad a cash an show my passport, payin' a lotta dollars. Livin' an eatin' good cuz Crystal git me feelin' good an I wanna keep it goin'. I sleep a long time afore goin' down ta the street.

Coupla days I go walkin' the city, lookin' at everythin' an eatin' outta them carts on the corners. I seen stuff in the windows an that be the time I git this recorder. I don' know why I done it but, a course, it be so I kin tell stuff ta you like I bin doin'. Jus' din' know then.

Three years, I bin knowin' Dale Messenger. Big guy, strong like my Daddy, mostly wearin' a tee shirt an talkin' a lot, but not allays stuff other peoples kin unnerstan'. Maybe the same years old as me, he come outta the army an he got some stuff outta them days that mess'm up, runnin' wrong for a whiles 'til I git'm ta do what he allays bin wantin'. He be real good at fixin' cars.

I allays like watchin' them guys puttin' up big buildins'. You know, guys doin' brick work an stuff, climbin' 'round up high. Afta them coupla days walkin' 'round I come on a buildin' goin' up on West 27th street, hotel runnin' real high. I git a standin' place 'cross the street an watch. Dale haulin' bricks an talkin' ta them other guys an talkin' ta hisself the whole time. Truth be, nobody payin' no 'tension ta me 'cross that street. Peoples comin' an goin' on the sidewalk, but I ain't standin' in nobody's way.

Second day I git ta my watchin' place maybe 'round eatin' time. Lotta peoples walkin' 'round. I sees Dale pickin' at a bunch bricks offa the ground 'round the fence an alls a sudden I git a hard shove. They got cops doin' stuff in New York that I come on thinkin' ain't right. Peoples call it stop and frisk an I knowed cuz I seen it on TV an it happin' ta me right where I be standin'. No good reason, Dollface, me gittin' rousted by two a New York's finest. All them years gittin offa that boat ship an walkin' an lookin' 'round the whole world, I don' git shoved by no cops never!

"ARMS UP! SPREAD'EM!"

Rough smackin' 'round my privates an in my pockets, takin' my passport an wad a cash maybe countin' five hunnerd.

"WHERE'D YOU GET THIS?" One of'em shoutin', holdin' up my money. Peoples stoppin' an lookin'. I ain't talkin' but I sure be mad.

"Can't be his," say the other one. "I'll call the wagon. We can sort things out at the station"

"OFFICER!" Dale Messenger lookin' both ways an comin' fast 'cross that street, stoppin' cars wit his arms wavin'. "OFFICER?" He come up ta them cops, lookin' alls nervous an talkin' like he got a place in what be happnin'.

"This guy's okay. Army buddy. We did two tours together in Afghanistan. Look, he's not right from the last tour. He's just waiting around for me to get off so I can take him uptown for his weekly check at the VA. Brain got screwed up." He smile an wink his eye at the cop holdin' the money.

"Who are you?" The one holdin' my passport say.

"We were in the same unit together. He doesn't have any family. My name is Dale Messenger. Like I said, he's a little screwed up in the head. I've been taking care of him since he got out."

"What about this?" The other one holdin' up the cash an lookin' at me.

There come on bein' a time, 'specially afta I come on knowin' peoples like Archer T. Zane an playin' for rich peoples sailin' 'round the world, when what ain't right ain't gonna be takin' good. Never shoulda let my daddy hit me the last time an I come on thinkin' I ain't gonna let no cops roust me for doin' nothin'. I brung my arms down, lookin' that cop in the eyes. There ain't no Dale Messenger standin' for me. There ain't nobody standin' for me 'cept me. I make my fists ready ta do what I gotta do. Them two cops ain't takin' my money an they ain't takin' me.

"Talk, fella," the cop come up close. "Where'd you get this money? Where'd you steal it from?"

I stay in my standin' place even afta he go reachin' for a stick on his belt, even afta he git so close I coulda dropped'm. Mad's I ever bin. I ain't 'fraid no more, Dollface. First time I git mad 'nuff ta take what be comin' long's them doin' the comin' knowed they got a fight in the way.

"Easy, officer. Please, sir, he's just a little messed up from the war."

"I want to hear it from him!"

The other cop holdin' my passport step up. "His name is Samuel Jones. According to the stamp he cleared customs from London four days ago. Came through JFK."

"That's right, officer," Dale talkin'. "He got his medical discharge and pay and came home from the war through London. I picked him up and brought him to my place. That's where he's staying until the VA figures out what they can do for him. The money is his from the army. Look, I can't leave him alone at my place while I work all day. You know, kinda sick in the head like he is, not good for him to be by himself too long. I bring him with me and make him wait here. My fault. Give him a break and I'll make sure he's no problem."

"Seems legit to me," the other cop say.

"All this money in cash from the army? It didn't work that way when I got out."

"It's cash over there, sir."

Dale workin' this like a pro. I go turnin' jus' a little bit, lookin' at'm an wondrin' why.

"No banks like other places. We all got some cash when we shipped home. By the way, it's the only money he's got. I'm trying to help him make it last."

"Sam," Dale say, lookin' ta me, "I told you not to carry all that money around."

"Nothing here," the other cop say an turn ta me. "Good thing you had your passport with you. Here," he hold it for me ta take an go lookin' ta the cop holdin' my money. "Give him the cash. Let's go."

"I dunno…"

"C'mon. He's a soldier. So were you."

"Yeah, but…"

"C'mon."

I tell you now I woulda dropped'm. Dale musta knowed cuz he step atween me an that cop. "He won't be any trouble, sir. I'll make sure of it."

"All right, here." He hold out the money ta Dale. "I'm giving it to you so he won't lose it. You better keep an eye on him. He can't loiter around anywhere he wants. Next time he's gonna wind up in jail."

"Thank you, sir. I'll take better care of him from now on." Dale touch my arm. "C'mon, let's get some lunch."

Dale Messenger don' know nothin' 'bout me, but he make it so I don' go doin' somethin' stupid. An I woulda, too. Funny 'bout that. I git onta returnin' the favor afta.

Before calling Edna, Zane leafed through the three yearbooks from Sister Genevieve. He glanced half-heartedly at the faces of scores of high school girls, mind wandering to his conversation with Cardinal Wolfkawitz. Saint Patrick's Cathedral, he marveled. Quite an honor. Of course, Samuel will be dead. It won't make any difference to the young man. Zane wrestled with the thought of saying nothing to anyone and merely advising His Eminence that Samuel had agreed as a last wish. Why does the Catholic church insist upon all these rules that contradict the very teachings of Jesus Christ?

Zane understood little of religion and confessed to even less interest in the spiritual side of life. Edna was the one who mattered. It was her desire to see that Samuel had a Catholic Mass. Another question, why? Zane respected her. He could read people and their hidden motivations. He knew she was a good woman, giving more than she received. The work she did each day was proof. He guessed her motives were pure. He just could not reason out her dogged determination to see that Samuel be remembered after his death. He picked up the phone.

"Edna, I think Kip has found enough information to confirm the details of who Samuel is. I mean he is Samuel Jones."

"I thought so. His recordings have to be the truth. Have you found any family or friends?"

"We're satisfied that his father was the boxer also named Jones. Still, if you want to be absolutely certain we'd need to do a DNA test."

"Was the boxer?"

"His father died shortly after being released from prison a few years ago. As for relatives or friends we can look, but time is running out. It might take a while." He waited for her reply.

"No, you've done enough. I've been thinking about this and I realize I've asked too much of you."

"Edna, don't worry about that. Remember, Samuel was…is my client. I'm sorry he's dying."

"Thanks to you his friend, Dale, is here with him. I can tell it means a lot to him. That's what I'd hoped for and it's enough."

"I'm still trying to identify the girl. It doesn't look promising, but I'll let you know if something turns up."

"Thank you, Archer."

"And, regarding a Funeral Mass I've spoken with Cardinal Wolfkawitz."

There was a pause as she drew a long breath in utter shock. "You spoke to the Cardinal? About Samuel?"

"We've known each other for a long time."

"Please, I'm so sorry. I didn't mean to cause you so much trouble."

"Edna, it's perfectly all right. His Eminence is a friend."

"Will Father Miguel get into trouble because of me? I don't want that."

"No, no. These things happen. There won't be any repercussions for anyone."

"What did he say?"

"He offered to personally celebrate a Mass for Samuel at Saint Patrick's Cathedral."

A soft sob.

"Edna, please don't be upset. It's an honor. You should be happy."

"I don't know what to say."

"There's one condition."

"Anything, yes what must I do? My Lord, Saint Patrick's!"

"He wants my assurance that Samuel agrees. It's for the Cardinal's peace of mind."

Edna come, but she don' go given me a pill or stickin' the needle inta my arm quick like afore. 'Stead she go sittin' on the bed an run'er hand 'cross my cheek, smilin'. She got somethin' ta say.

Head hurtin' real bad. Wishin' for that drip ta take me away forever. Git that, Dollface? No wakin' up no more! Near ta shoutin' why! Near ta yellin' it loud ta alls a peoples I know, ta Archer T. Zane, ta Dale, ta momma, ta Edna, ta YOU! Why? Why? Why I gotta die? If Ralph Waldo Emerson be standin' right here aside me I go shoutin' at'm ta gimme the answer. Maybe he know. Maybe he got the reason. Who be God takin' his time makin' me hurt so bad? Is he waitin' on me? Gotta be laughin' cuz there ain't no good reason for killin' me this way. If I see'm I'm gonna tell'm, too.

"Samuel? I want to ask you something. I know you can't answer me with words. It's all right. Just nod your head. That can mean yes. Shake if the answer is no. Will you do that for me?"

I nod, hopin' on it bein' quick. God ain't quick 'cept on sayin' no.

"When you leave us. When you fall asleep and don't wake up and your pain goes away forever, do you understand what I mean?"

After I be gone, sure. Don' take long ta unnerstan' what Edna be aksin'. Some guy prayin' on me in a church. I give'er what she want quick so she gimme what I need quick.

Dale take me by the arm, crossin' the street. He don' say nothin' 'til afta we git inside a that big fence.

"Bastards!" He grab a brown bag, tossin' it ta me an sayin' 'catch'. Then he make me sit on the sidewalk. He take the bag, look inside an brung out a sandwich. "Here." Then he git one for hisself an go sittin' down aside me. "I hate it when cops make trouble for innocent people. You didn't do anything. I saw you watching me work yesterday. You stayed back and out of the way so people could get by on the sidewalk. Same just now. I don't know why they gave you a hard time. How's the sandwich, okay?"

"Yeah, good," I coulda said if I gonna say somethin', but he ain't really aksin'. He jus' talkin'.

"You need to be more careful around here. Whole city now that I think about it. Maybe not in some of the bad neighborhoods. Cops aren't too pushy where the street gangs are operating. Pain in the ass everywhere else for people who don't look like they belong where they're hanging out. Know what I mean?"

Peanut butter and jelly. Funny, I kin 'member how it taste jus' like it be in my mouth right now. Dale take a bite an go talkin' an talkin' alls a while. I look at'm some so he think I be listnin', but he don' care. Talkin' be his way. Ta me, ta hisself, ta nobody in particular.

"Got this job right after my dad died because I'm a vet. I don't think it even took two days and here I am hauling bricks. Unemployment office has a whole list of construction sites all over the city looking for vets. Had to join a union, of course, Bricklayers Local 1601. What's it been eight or nine months? Yeah, just about. Dues aren't bad. Come right out of my paycheck so I don't miss what I don't see. I stay away from the hall over on thirty-second street. Guys are nice an all, but they don't want us members around. Tough looking bunch. I'll tell you that. Mostly Italian. They've got all the locals sewed up tight. Long as I get paid I don't care. Don't mess with me and I sure won't mess with you. That's my motto.

"Dad had a nice little car repair business in Belrose. Ever go over to Belrose? Used to be nicer than it is today. Nothing big, but he could fix anything so people in the know came from all over. He got sick when I was in Afghanistan. Geez what a hole! Anyway, mom's dead, nobody to take care of him. I put in for a hardship discharge so I could get back here to watch over him. Worked out. I only had six weeks to go and since my unit got tore up and I was the only one left, they let me go.

'No insurance, you know. Look, Dad had a little business, that's all. He fixed a car, got some money, paid the taxes on his garage and ate soup. He didn't know anything about health insurance and he never got sick anyway. Mom dropped dead of a heart attack. About the only thing he knew was paying for a funeral, not lying on a bed in hospital. When I got back, he's been in a hospital for a coupla weeks. Pancreatic cancer. The worst kind you can get. And the bills! Soon as he saw me he said, 'Get me outta here!' I took him home and got a friend of mine from the VA hospital to get him checked out. He already knew he was dying, but I wanted a real doctor to say it. Six months, maybe more, maybe less. That's what I found out.

"You know you can't figure out what's wrong with a car just by fooling around anymore. You have to have a computer that plugs into places and all kinds of special tools to fix the problems. All that costs a lotta money. Well, stuff that's going to fix Cadillacs, Mercedes and Jaguars. You know, all the big money cars. Dad had everything he needed in his shop. He was proud of it. Rolled that computer around and watched it light up with all sorts of messages saying what's out of whack. Tools were all neat and organized. Thing is, we're looking at a hundred grand just to pay the hospital bills. Then I need a nurse to come in near the end to make sure he isn't suffering too much. Geez, I woulda pulled the plug for him if he wanted, but he's tough. Religious thing. No suicide or you go to hell or purgatory or limbo or some place. Old school guy. So I sold the computer and all his tools, paid off half of the the hospital bill and got the nurse. Got me a plan, though. Year or two I'll have enough money to payoff the rest of the hospital bill and get new tools and a new computer. Then I'll put the business back together and I won't be hauling bricks ever again."

Dale keep on talkin' like he knowed me 'til he gotta git back workin'. He ain't no slouch.

"Look, you stay here inside the fence so the cops don't bother you anymore. Just make sure you keep out of everybody's way. I'll watch in case anybody asks questions. Got that?"

I nods.

"Shift ends at four."

Dale allays talkin' an movin' fast like he gotta keep hisself out front a somethin' so it don' catch up wit'm. I din' know what ta make a that, but I seen somethin' outta his way a lookin' an talkin', how he come 'cross that street actin' like he knowed me wit them cops. So, I stay inside that fence 'til quittin' time.

EIGHTEEN

Silence is an expression of good-bye. It should be respected - Edna Nieves

E dna showed Dale Messenger to a room next to Samuel's. "He's sleeping, but if you'd like to sit with him it will be all right."

"Yes, m'am, I would. Thank you."

Dale wit me. Comin' on the end cuz he got a look showin' it. Edna hep'm unnerstan' cuz he seen peoples dyin', but me lyin' in this bed ain't the same kinda dyin' 'cept maybe his daddy. Good him bein' here cuz he need ta talk. Like I tol' you, that be Dale's way. I come on thinkin' Edna like'm an they like talkin' whilst she think I be sleepin'. They goes talkin' and drinkin' tea in the kitchen. Good cuz it gimme time ta finish on tellin' this stuff ta you. Time runnin' out. Body sayin' it.

Quittin' time an we git on the subway ta Belrose ta his place not so far from this house. He got a buildin' wit three big doors openin' inta dirty places where fixin' cars used ta happin'. His daddy's workin' place. Lotta junk all 'round an stuff for fixin' tires. Some stuff hangin' outta the ceilin', too. Afta, I knowed that workin' place real good. Lotta books sittin' on the wall like they be in a library. I go readin' ever one. An Dale got a truck, real long. He musta knowed I never seen one afore cuz he go walkin' over an tappin' the side.

"My dad's wrecker, a tow truck. See the flat bed? It tips down so a car can be pulled on top. Easy and fast. Dad was proud of this truck. I probably shoulda sold it with his other stuff, but I couldn't bring myself to do it. Come inside."

Coupla hamburgers for supper. Cooked up on a dirty stove in

the upstairs. Afta, he git me inta his daddy's truck an brung me ta the hotel. I check out, payin a lotta dollars an carryin' shirts an stuff I buyed afta gittin' offa the boat ship.

Zane sat with scotch in hand, considering the hold Edna's request and his own curiosity had taken over him. Normally, he wasn't a sentimental man except during those low moments when he thought about the failure of his marriage and the lost years with his only child. Was that it? A chance to redeem his failings?

Retirement, he understood, was inevitable. But what next? What would he do with himself? He thought about traveling for pleasure. That's what many of his peers do, but they all have intimate partners, companions to travel with in renewed togetherness. Archer had no one. Work had always been his mistress. Never in his life had he faced the future without a plan. It was not the carefree feeling he anticipated.

Ellis Dorman returned his call an hour earlier. Yes, there were a number of recordings that earned residuals for all involved, including Samuel. He would also do a search for any music in Blossom's huge repository that might have originated by the savant's hand.

"How's he doing?" Dorman asked.

"Soon. I'm going over this afternoon to talk to him about a will. I should have done it long ago, before his decline. Odd, I'm usually on top of things for my clients. Never thought about it."

Long poem called "Howl" by a guy name a Ginsberg. Maybe you knows it. Jus' that word, 'splain the hurtin' comin' outta Dale Messenger. I ain't never heared the kinda screamin' a man kin make 'til that night layin' in a room aside his in that car fixin' buildin'. It wake me up, givin' me a shakin' like ya read 'bout in books. That first time I sure be scared, listnin' an wondrin' 'bout gittin' myself inta somethin' bad. Next night the howlin' git so loud I gotta go look. He ain't layin' in a bed. He be sittin' on the floor in a corner, legs up tight, arms holdin'em, rockin', cryin', yellin' an not seein' nothin' 'cept inside his head. I ain't there. Room ain't there, neither. Dale ways away somewhere. Hell maybe.

The sudden tingling of recognition swept over her with a chill that made her shiver even on this warm California night. It was in the music, intuition. She angled closer to the stage. Who?

Edna sat with Dale Messenger over tea in the kitchen.
"How do you know him?" she asked.
"He was watching me work in the city, hauling bricks on a construction site. I'd been back from the war for almost a year. Hardship discharge from the army to take care of my dad. He was dying of cancer, too. I saw Sam getting rousted by a couple of cops and went over to get them off his back. I told a few lies. Said we served together and he was messed up. They took my word that I'd take care of him. Didn't really plan to to do it. I just thought he was being unfairly treated. I brought him back to my place. We wound up working together. It's been years, now. Truth is, he took care of me. Straightened me out without ever saying a single word."
"Straightened you out?"
"Bad things happened in Afghanistan. When you're there right in the middle of it, it's hard to describe, but it takes a toll. Stuff I saw, stuff I did... I came home messed up."
Edna fought to keep her composure. Army and Afghanistan were the two most dreaded words of her life, conjuring endless heartbreak.
"And, Samuel helped you with your problems?"
"Yes."
"How?"
"Stayed with me when I would lose it. Mostly at night. I was being treated for PTSD at the VA hospital. Look, I get it. The military doctors and nurses are overwhelmed. It's not like what you do here. Not peaceful and quiet. When I'd get an appointment, and believe me that wasn't always easy, I'd show up and have to wait for hours and hours, watching all these other guys, some like me, looking ok, but most of the others in horrible shape, I'd feel guilty. You know, what was I doing there when all these other guys needed the doctors

more than me? Didn't matter, though. I was just looking for pills to get me through the nights. And, if that meant getting me out of there quickly the docs were glad to oblige. Anything they could prescribe. I tried them all. Nothing worked for long, but some of the stuff got me hooked."

"Addiction? The VA doctors caused you to become addicted to drugs?"

"No ma'am. I used them to get what I thought would calm my nerves. Like I said, the hospital was a busy place. They were just trying to cope with the demand. If I walked in and played the game, told them I needed something to feel better, they gave it to me so they could get on to the next guy who needed them more than me. I got myself hooked."

"Are you taking anything now? Addicted, I mean?"

"No, not anymore. Took a while, but I'm doing good. No pills. Not even aspirin. Sam helped me get off the stuff."

"PTSD?"

"Oh, much better. I sleep okay. Sometimes, I remember things, but it isn't like it used to be. I can live with it now."

Edna pondered the man seated across from her. She lifted her cup, sipped then put it down on her saucer. "You left him at the hospital but you didn't stay with him. Why?"

"Addiction never truly ends. Once I was off the pills I never went to the VA hospital again. I knew if I ever did get near a doctor or a nurse, set foot in another hospital, I'd be back in that bad place looking for relief."

"You said he helped you. How?"

"After about a week, him coming into my room to sit with me while I was having my bad dreams, I started to trust him a bit. Look, I want you to know I'm not a bad guy, but I did some things back then. Tricking the doctors for pills was one, but my dream was to restart my dad's business. What with his leftover hospital bills and the cost of new tools and a diagnostic computer I just didn't have the money to do it. So, a couple of nights a week I took the wrecker, my Dad's flatbed tow truck, out of the garage and drove around the boroughs stealing things I knew I could resell. I'm guilty about it now, but back then I was determined to get the money I needed. My dad had everything, but I sold it to pay off as much of his debt as I could. Hospitals and doctors aren't too patient when there's bills hanging out there.

"I took Sam with me and showed him the drill. Spare tires were the easiest to steal. Pull up, jump out quick, ratchet the trunk, pull the spare out, throw it onto the bed of the truck and drive off. Sometimes, most times, I could do it in thirty seconds. Twenty to fifty bucks for each tire depending on size and brand. Dealer over in Brooklyn took everything I could bring him."

"Samuel helped you do this?" Edna tried to hide her shock.

"A few times after I showed him how, but I could tell he didn't like it. He'd come with me, but he gradually stopped getting out of the truck. He'd just watch, making sure nobody was around. Sorta like a lookout."

"How long did this go on?"

"That's the thing and the reason I owe him so much. After a month I could tell he was getting edgy. Do you know how smart he is?"

"Brilliant, yes."

Messenger nodded. "My dad had a a shelf loaded with original manufacturer repair books. You can tear down and rebuild an entire car or truck just by reading those books and having all the right tools and equipment. During the days when I was working Samuel read everyone of those manuals. Mrs. Nieves, some of them are more than a thousand pages with diagrams and words that even a seasoned mechanic can't understand. German cars, Italian, British, Korean, Japanese, he went through twenty-seven volumes in a couple of months."

Edna smiled. "I'm not surprised."

"I sure was. And, you know what? He knew the page numbers and everything on them by heart. I still shake my head when I think about it. Amazing."

"You said he became edgy."

"Right. One night I got ready to go out with the truck. I had this black tee shirt and pants I used to wear. He was downstairs in the shop standing by the truck when I came to open the garage. Just shook his head no. I figured he meant that he wasn't going with me and that was all right. I wasn't into using him. If he didn't want to go I wasn't pushing. I came around to the driver's side and he stepped in front of me. I didn't see the little book in his hand until he waved it in my face. Then he grabbed my hand and made me take it. It was one of those savings books you get when you have money in a bank.

"I opened it because that seemed to be what he wanted me to do. Inside was a sheet of paper. He took it from me, unfolded it and held it up to my face. It was an order form for a diagnostic computer, brand new and far more advanced than the one my dad owned. It was all in my name and address at the shop. Delivery due in two weeks.

"He used his own money to buy you that machine?"

"Yes, and a lot more. Look, I'd been telling him about my plans. He knew I was stealing to get the business going again. He was watching me with the pills, too. All the while counting how many I was taking and probably reading up on which ones were addictive. The shop was one thing. Getting me straightened out must have been the other thing he had in mind. I don't bother asking why. He never spoke a word. Best friend a man could ever have.

"I remember telling him he was making a mistake. Truth is, I had this dream of reopening the shop, but it was only a dream. I was really stealing to keep myself in pills. They're expensive and I was needing more and more all the time. Good thing, I thought right about then, because not long after Samuel showed up the VA doctors stopped giving the prescriptions to me. Maybe they caught on to my scam. I don't know. I was beginning to need the pills too much to concentrate on anything else; fixing cars or even hauling bricks."

The doorbell rang. Edna reluctantly stood to answer it, leaving Messenger at the table in the kitchen.

"Archer?" She spied a thick manila folder under his arm. It was snowing lightly and the lawyer brushed the shoulders of his overcoat.

"I have some material to review with Samuel. Actually, if he's resting I can leave it with you. He can go over it when he's more alert."

Edna pulled Zane into the foyer. She realized that this was the first time he had come to visit Samuel since learning of his illness. "I wondered if you would come to see him."

"It's a legal matter. I certainly don't want to disturb him or you."

"You've known him as well as anyone." She held out her arms, beckoning him to take off his coat.

"My driver is waiting at the curb."

"I'm sure he's waited for you many times."

Zane shifted his weight from foot to foot, looking nervous. "I've wanted to come. I don't know, it was easier to stay away."

"Go sit with him. I'll bring you tea."

"He's not in his office," Zane's secretary said as Kip approached the ornate door.

He took the door handle, but stopped for permission before entering. "He has some high school yearbooks. Mind if I go in and have a look?"

"Go ahead. They're on his desk." She went back to her typing.

Dale Messenger watched as Edna poured hot water over a teabag into another cup just like the one in front of him. She dipped the bag until the water turned deep red, placed the cup on a tray and carried it to the door. "I'll be right back."

Sound from the keyboard filled the air as the crowd drew closer to the stage. A few couples danced in front, others in place wherever there was enough space. In concert style, some boys near the back hoisted girls onto their shoulders. There was clapping and whistling boosted by hours of drinking, but nobody was acting aggressive. She edged as close to the stage as she could, turned to look at the others behind her and smiled in relief that nothing was getting out of hand. Then she turned back.

The needle numbed his senses, but not his imagination. He

could feel it coming near, hovering over and in him - demise, death. He was less afraid. The weeks of gradual weakening stole his resolve. He wanted to be free. His fingers danced along the keys of the keyboard. His fantasy would be fulfilled in these final visions of life. Each song was his, created for her. Does the spirit know when another is close? Does a dying man know when he must wake? A friend entered his space.

Zane stared down at his client. Samuel appeared to be sleeping. The lawyer lifted his eyes to study the room. He'd avoided situations like this before, never present when someone approached death. Not even his parents. He always arrived after the fact. Only professional duty made him stand where he stood now. Yet, he respected this young man, someone special and unusual who had come and gone from time to time in Zane's life. He spotted the chair by the window, went over and dragged it close to the bed.

"Here is your tea." Edna entered the room and placed the tray on a small table near the bed where Zane could reach it.

He looked up. "Thank you."

She smiled, nodded and left.

He sat down and opened the folder filled with papers. He re-read his proposals while he waited for his client to waken.

Messenger continued to talk. Edna had returned and sat opposite him at the table.

"I'm staring at my last couple of pills and he's watching me. I swear he was reading my mind, knew I was going to do something desperate. Of course, he was right. All that time we cleaned up the shop together while we waited for the computer to arrive, he's got his eye on me. Never said a word, never does, but he knew I wasn't thinking about what he did for me. He knew that wasn't my real priority. You know he stayed up with me every night. I'd be shaking and moaning, but I knew he was there ready to keep me from doing something to myself. And, sometimes I wanted to. Sometimes, I just wanted to end it all, put myself out of my misery. That's what Afghanistan did to me. It's a bad place."

Edna fidgeted in her chair, wanting to know Dale Messenger's story, but not eager for details that might bring back the tears that had finally subsided. She was all alone. The joyful love of husband and son missing from her life despite the memories of them that, if focused solely upon the happy times, could give her the solace their permanent absence had taken away. This calling, ushering people through decline to their inevitable departures from life, doing all she could to give them peace and comfort, filled only a partial void. Empty loss controlled the rest. She thought of Samuel, oddly her only patient at this time when most of her beds should be filled. He touched something deep in her and she felt that his passing would be unlike the others. It would happen soon.

"With only a few pills left I knew I had to get more. I tried to make another appointment at the VA hospital, but the best they could do was three weeks out. I couldn't wait that long so I dusted off my old uniform and put it on. I figured I could sit in the Emergency Room until someone saw me. Most guys aren't in uniform when they go for treatment. I'd stand out. I didn't know what I'd do except I wasn't going to leave without more pills. You know Samuel was watching me. He let me think I was going to slip out unnoticed. I thought he was in his room reading. No, he must have been watching from somewhere."

Where you bin? I woulda aksed if I was inta talkin' ta Archer T. Zane. A Course, I figured he din' know I be sick. Good seein'm. He got my back jus' like Edna. He come up close, not knowin' what ta say ta a dyin' man.

"Samuel? How are you, son?"

I nods, him lookin' real nervous. He read me good cuz he allays done that. Nod outta me alls he need ta git back ta bein' ok. He got a bunch a papers in his hand. Seen that afore. I listen cuz evertime he got papers I git what be mine.

"I'm sorry I didn't come before now. And, I'm sorry you have to go through this. I wish there was something I could do." I tries ta smile cuz he need it. Don' know if it look that way. He go holdin' up them papers. "Most people have wills. You don't really need a lawyer to make a will, but under your circumstances, everything you've done and the assets you've accumulated in your life... well, I gave it all some thought and, if you care to hear them, I have a some proposals for you to consider."

Kip sat on the leather couch in his boss' office, turning the pages. He had no expectations, but his boss mentioned the yearbooks and Sister Genivieve's insistence that he take them. Kip was curious. In his mind the identity of Samuel Jones was confirmed. He was certain the dying man was the son of Rabbit Red, the drug-dealing, disgraced boxer. There wasn't much more to uncover except the mystery girl Samuel spoke to on his recording. That she was set in San Jose intrigued the young lawyer. In truth, he couldn't be sure she was real. Samuel was dying. He was mute except for words spoken secretly into a recording device. Little of what he said could be verified except that everything that could be chased down checked out. That was the enigma that made this whole matter hard to understand. Also, his normally objective boss seemed to be emotionally invested. Something Kip had never seen in Archer before.

He recalled the girl he met at the sorority party all those years past, that night before he traveled east from San Jose to this life in New York. The memory of her, the picture of her in his mind, how he felt the very instant he saw her, the sound of her voice, all remained vivid. He'd had a few relationships in the nine years since, but nothing touched him like that fleeting time with her. He had not forgotten.

He studied each picture, scores of them from page to page, setting the first two volumes aside and absently picking up the third and last. Kip, he thought to himself, you don't even know who you're looking for. He came near the end where each graduating senior is depicted. Twelve photos per page. The Catholic high school was not large, some eight hundred girls total and a graduating class of just under two hundred. He thumbed these final pages; ten, twenty, thirty, forty, fifty, sixty... girls in the prime of their beauty, happy, eager to start adulthood. There she was.

"So, I'm in uniform, heading for the door on my way to the VA Hospital. Sam steps in front of me, looks me in the eye and shakes his head no. I'm a lot bigger than him, but I could see something in his eyes. He wasn't backing down.

'I need pills,' I said. He stayed right there, shaking his head. I put my hands on him and tried to shove him away. I had my army training, but nothing I ever learned worked. I even raised my fists and shouted at him, 'Look, I don't want to hurt you! Get out of my way!' The guy's got moves like a prize fighter. I'd get him off balance, but he'd pop right back every time. I couldn't get by him.

"Here's the odd part, I really didn't want those pills anymore. I just wanted to feel better. I got so frustrated, but I couldn't take a swing at him. He was only trying to be my friend. So, it all came out. I started to cry. He came up close, took my arm and made me sit down right there on the floor. Then he sat down beside me and we just waited it out for a long while, me crying and him making sure I didn't do something stupid."

"Did you get more pills later?"

"No. It took a month. Worst time of my life. The first two weeks I nearly went crazy, but he stayed with me through all the nights. Shakes and sweats ended after that and it got easier. He cooked for me. We got the shop in real good shape. The machine arrived and it was another couple of weeks before we had it all figured out.

"Not all of that money went to the computer. We needed tools and it'd been a while since my dad got sick and, well, there was still the last part of his hospital bill hanging over my head. Sam insisted that we use his money to pay it off. Like always, he didn't actually say anything, but we were so used to each other by then that knowing each other's mind came easy. Also, my dad's old customers, once he got sick, had to find another place to get their cars fixed. Sam made me get on the phone and call as many of them as we could find from my dad's old records. I don't know, maybe I was able to reach half of them, but it was my father they counted on. Most of them didn't know me and they'd already found another place. Not much came of it and I was beginning to worry that I wouldn't be able to make a go of it. Besides, I wanted to pay Sam back.

"You know what he did? I mean even after everything else he still had some money in that savings account. He gave me all of it and made me take out ads in newspapers, buy commercials on the radio and do two nights of big ten-second pitches during the six o'clock news on WPIX. Unbelievable. We started getting business right away and now I've got four more stalls and six mechanics working for me five and a half days a week. And you know what else? Sam and me, we worked side by side right up until he got sick and couldn't do it anymore. I tried to keep the books at first, but he took over so I could concentrate on the cars and trucks coming in. Now, I have an accountant who handles all the finances. I tried to pay Sam back, but he wouldn't take it. Just a paycheck like everybody else. After he passes away," Messenger paused, "yeah, after he goes I'll think of some way to do something good with the money I owe him. Something in his name."

Zane helped Samuel sign the necessary pages. After agreeing to the proposals, all assets to be devoted to charitable causes of Zane's choosing, he could see that his dying client was exhausted. He packed the papers into his folder. What to say? This was likely the last time the lawyer would see him alive. He felt pangs of remorse. He stood to leave. It was supposed to be a handshake, but Samuel held it longer and more firmly than his condition suggested he could. Zane looked his into eyes. He saw something more, a bond the lawyer didn't realize meant so much to him until that moment. The gesture was natural. He leaned down and kissed his friend on the forehead.

NINETEEN

Occasionally a patient will speak aloud with someone who has died before – Edna Nieves

K ip burst from the office, carrying the yearbook with his finger on the page.

"Where are you taking that?" Zane's secretary asked.

"I might have found something."

He kept moving fast. Of course, the girl in the yearbook had nothing to do with Samuel and that wasn't Kip's motivation. All these years since their brief conversation. It was her! Back in his own office he took a chance, jumped behind his computer and searched on her name, hoping. He clicked on several links, dead ends except for one recent reference to an elementary school in Queens. He clicked on the title:

'Experimental Education Program Gets Underway'

The drums kicked in followed by the guitars. He ran his fingers expertly over the keys. The crowd edged together more tightly and closer to the stage. She was squeezed to the periphery still able to hear, but prevented from a clear view. The best performer remained obscured behind the keyboards. She was getting impatient, frustrated by the pressing crowd that thwarted her every attempt to see.

Unlike the earlier songs, all covers of well known hits by famous groups and artists, she had never heard this one before. It had to be an original. She was no expert, but she knew what she liked and she could see what others liked. Everyone swayed to the unearthly sound. All other thoughts left her mind. The music took control.

"He wants to go outside, sit on the porch." Dale Messenger had gone to Samuel's room to sit with him after finishing his conversation with Edna. She was in her small office, reviewing notes on three new patients who would be arriving over the next several days. The hospital called with the information shortly after Zane departed. The lawyer's eyes were red.

"It's cold outside," Edna was reluctant.

"We could bundle him up." Messenger urged. "I'll carry him and put him in a chair, stay with him, okay?"

"I don't know. He's so weak." Edna looked out the window. Snow flurries danced on a slight breeze. "Are you sure that's what he wants?"

"Well, he didn't say it. You know that. I know him well enough. Come ask him yourself."

"No, no. I know you'll watch over him, but only for a short time."

"I think he's ready. Wants to die."

"Soon."

PS 0875 in Jamaica, Queens was fourteen miles from from the Manhattan downtown offices of the Zane Law firm. Subway, taxi, private car – Kip knew he could get there in forty minutes. He'd already called the school and confirmed that she was teaching there, but not under the supervision of the elementary school's leadership. The special needs program was separately funded and monitored under a grant from the U.S. Department of Education.

Samuel displayed a hint of a smile as Edna and his friend wrapped him in thick comforters. No longer strong enough to attend to himself, he was content to let his caretakers do everything. When Edna was satisfied she nodded to Messenger and smiled at Samuel. The big man carefully slipped his arms beneath his friend and lifted him into his arms. Edna held the door. She shivered when the cold air rushed in, but Samuel's eyes widened with pleasure. She could see it. It was the right decision. Messenger carried him onto the porch where he settled him into a cushioned chair.

Kip rehearsed what he would say as he impatiently weaved through traffic to the Queens Mid-town Tunnel. He pressed the accelerator to get through a yellow light before it turned red. Please, please remember me, he prayed. An opening to the right and his car broke free from the snarl. He sped to the ramp, sighing with relief when he saw only a slight backup at the tunnel's entrance.

Dale Messenger talked about the repair shop mostly to fill the silence. He knew Samuel wasn't listening. He wondered what a dying man thought about. He wondered why he'd been so lucky to have Samuel as friend. He already missed him.

Samuel sucked in fresh air, momentarily relieved of his condition and the creeping fear of death. Soon, he dozed in the semi-aware state that had become his norm when not under the spell of the drip or pills. He could hear Messenger talking, but the meaning of his words did not register. Instead, the imaginary concert played on in his imagination. How would she know it's him? Would she need to see his face or will the music be enough? Suddenly, his mind was somewhere else. It was no imaginary vision. It was real and it made him happy.

Intuition? Experience? What caused Edna to know the end was imminent? She simply knew. After staring through the window at the two men on the porch she returned to her office, removed some papers from her desk drawer and called the cemetery administrator, reconfirming for the final time that all was in order. Then she dialed Zane's number, reaching his secretary and asking her to alert him.

PS 0875 was located on a busy, congested block. Kip looked for a place to park, circling the school three times before spotting a car leaving a space at the curb. He slipped quickly into the vacancy. He could tell that school was still in session. He checked his watch. Fifteen minutes and the pandemonium of escaping children would begin. He refused to wait, exiting his car and taking the steps up to the school's entrance two at a time. Once inside he hastily walked the hall and spotted the principal's office at the far end. He made for it, but not without glancing into each classroom right and left as he walked. It was noisy except for one room to his left. The door was closed, but he could see inside through the upper half of glass. She was no different to his eyes than the moment he'd seen her in San Jose. He stopped, knees buckling as his nerve suddenly left him.

"Edna called." Zane went into his office, removed his overcoat and dropped it onto the couch.

"I was just there. What does she want?"

"She said to let you know it's time. Samuel will die soon."

Zane sighed and shook his head. His voice was low when he spoke again. "See if you can get me through to His Eminence and ask Kip to come down."

"Kip went out. He took one of those yearbooks. Said he might have found something."

Zane came back out of his office and stood over his secretary. "The girl?"

"He wasn't specific."

She was at the front of the room, addressing her class when she stopped, turned and spotted him looking. Kip could see her eyes widen. He couldn't move and for the first time in memory, had no idea what he would say as he watched her turn back to her class and issue an instruction. Then she came to the door and entered the hallway. She never took her eyes from his. A smile crossed between them as she approached.

"Rebecca," he half whispered.

"Kip." She nodded, mouth open in surprise.

Messenger droned on in the breezy cold outside on the porch. Occasionally, he turned to look at his friend, seemingly asleep in the chair next to him. He knew Samuel was close to death, but he fought off his remorse as he forced himself to keep the one-sided conversation about the repair shop and anything else far from the impending departure of the best friend he'd ever known. It had been thirty minutes and he'd risen several times to re-arrange the comforters around Samuel's body, up and around his neck and shoulders and down around his legs and feet.

"Ah, Sam," he whispered. "I know you're going to a better place. Save a spot for me when my time comes."

Samuel stirred, eyes droopy. "Momma's here," he said in a clear voice. "Daddy's wit her, waitin' on me an smilin'. Comin' momma, comin."

"Very soon, your Eminence. I just want you to know."

"Archer, you have my deepest condolences."

"And, you will hold services for him at Saint Patrick's?"

"All is arranged. When you and Mrs. Nieves are ready just let me know."

Kip watched as scores of children tumbled out of the school doors. He stood across the street next to his car as instructed by Rebecca, waiting for her to complete her tasks and come out after all the children had been discharged.

Despite his nerves and her surprise there was no stumbling to their brief conversation in the hall. Natural, that's how it felt. Like the long interlude was only yesterday. "She's the one," he said aloud to the winter wind as he lifted the collar of his overcoat around his neck. Yet in the back of his mind it meant more than the overwhelming certainty that consumed him. How could it be that he had found her?

The keyboards were one with his hands, issuing the melody with his personal passion. She, by now, had had enough with the jostling partiers blocking her path and view. She pushed through, ignoring the occasional protest until she stood only a two feet from the edge of the stage. So close that she could lean in and touch the man's leg beneath the keyboard stand. She did.

He felt a charge run through his body. Samuel, in a coma, no longer controlled his fantasy. It went its own way, taking him with it. Suddenly, his lungs fought for breath. Dale heard the change and saw his friend's chest begin heaving with much more difficulty than before. He quickly went inside to alert Edna.

"Ellis, he's on the verge. Edna thinks it will happen at any moment." Archer T. Zane had few close friends. None who might understand the plunging sadness that gripped him at that moment. If asked, he would be unable to explain why he chose to call Ellis Dorman at Blossom Records. Maybe it was because Dorman also knew Samuel Jones.

"I'm sorry, Archer. Bad break, but better that his suffering will be over."

"Yes, I think so. I sat with him a few hours ago and worked out the details on his estate. Since the bulk of his assets are under your purview it would be best if we got together as soon as it's convenient after his death."

"I'll clear my calendar."

"Thanks, Ellis."

"Archer? Are you all right?"

"Yes, I'm fine. I just feel sorry for him, that's all."

"I can be in the city in an hour. Let's have dinner together."

"I think I'd like that."

"Good. I'll pick you up."

Zane hung up the phone, rose from behind his desk and quietly closed the door to his office. He went to his small bar in the corner, found a glass and poured a large amount of scotch. As he moved from the bar he took a heavy swig. Then he sat down on the couch and stared at nothing.

Edna hurried to the porch. She saw Samuel slumped in his chair, bundled tight, but laboring for breath. She came around to face him then lifted each eyelid seeking confirmation that his coma was deep. He did not rouse.

"Can you lift him and take him to his room?"

"Is he gone?"

"No, but very soon."

"Is he sleeping?"

"Coma."

Messenger bent down and effortlessly lifted his dying friend into his arms. Edna held the door. "Lay him on his bed," she ordered.

They conversed over coffee in a small restaurant around the corner from PS 0875.

"I've wondered about you ever since we met. I wanted to see you again."

"How did you find me?" she asked.

He watched her eyes as he spoke, each bright blue, beautiful. He swam in their brillance, wanting with his whole being to take her hands in his.

"I was recruited into a law firm here in the city right after graduating from NYU. Been there ever since as a protégé to Archer T. Zane, the founder. He'll be retiring in a couple of months. I'm taking over his clients."

She nodded, looking down at her hands. "You told me you wanted to be a lawyer."

"I left you in front of your sorority house, but I have to admit I didn't want to go."

There was a brief silence. She lifted her face to his. "I was sorry you did."

His heart leapt, but he couldn't bring himself to confess his years of longing. "There's a curious situation concerning one of the firm's clients, a musician and songwriter dying of brain cancer. For some reason my boss is determined to help a hospice nurse learn more about him. I've been chasing down some information and passing on what I find to both of them. Archer had some high school yearbooks. I browsed through them and saw your picture. When I searched your name on the internet PS 0875 came up. What about you? You found your way back to New York."

"I taught for two years in San Jose. Then I went to work in D.C. at the Department of Education. I earned my Masters Degree nights. While at ED I designed a curriculum for children with special needs. The Assistant Secretary liked it and twisted some arms to get money for a test run. New York's congressional delegation got behind it and paved the way to host it here in Queens. It was my chance to come home."

"Going well?" He wasn't really interested. Merely making conversation while his mind raced and his heart pounded.

"Seems to be. Evaluations will be completed in a month. Then we'll see if it can be expanded to other schools."

He mustered his courage. "Did you ever think of me?"

She blushed and looked away briefly before turning back. "Yes."

"I've never been able to get you out of my mind."

"I'm glad you found me."

"What now?"

"I don't know. Maybe we can get to know each other."

His cellphone rang. He pulled it from his coat and looked at the caller ID. Zane's secretary.

"Kip. Archer wants to talk."

Zane came on the line. "Samuel is very close. Just letting you know."

"I'm sorry, Archer. Anything you want me to do?"

"Ellis is coming into the city. We're having dinner. You're welcome to join us."

"If you don't mind I'll beg off. I'm with an old friend I haven't seen for a long time."

"Roberta said you might have found something in one of the yearbooks."

"Yes, but it has nothing to do with Samuel. She's the girl I met at San Jose State just before I came east for law school. It just so happens she graduated from that Catholic high school. I spotted her picture in one of the yearbooks, did a search online and found her teaching at an elementary school in Queens."

Zane stirred, caught by the coincidences and remembering Sister Genevieve's comment, *'I have a feeling. God works in mysterious ways'.*

"What elementary school? Where in Queens?"

"Jamaica. PS 0875."

Zane's hand tightened on the phone. "Are you saying you know a girl who went to college in San Jose? That she graduated from a high school in Queens and now she teaches at the same school Samuel mentions on his recording?"

"Yes, come to think of it. It's the same elementary school." Kip lifted his eyes and stared at Rebecca, so caught up in the excitement he realized he'd set the odd coincidences aside.

Zane spoke again. "Listen, do me a favor. Tell her what you know about Samuel. Then call me back. Maybe it's nothing, but we can't let it go without being sure."

"All right, Archer. I'll let you know."

Mid-song, he couldn't just stop playing, rise from behind the keyboard and search for the person whose touch sent electricity through his body. Yet he knew it was her, as close as a few feet away.

Edna tucked Samuel under the covers. She lifted his eyelids again satisfied that his coma was deep and painless. Nevertheless, she rolled the morphine drip to the bedside just in case. Then she turned to a weeping Dale Messenger. She approached and briefly wrapped her arms around the big man in consolation.

"He said something about his mom and dad. I know I heard it. Then he started breathing heavy. Edna, what can I do?"

"Wait." She released him and pointed to a chair. "Sit. Pray for him if you like. Talk to him. Or, just quiet your heart and mind. You're his friend. That you can be together at the end is all that matters."

"Will you stay with us?"

She moved to the doorway. "Call for me when you think I'm needed."

Kip told her everything he knew about Samuel Jones. He paraphrased some of the dying man's words from the recordings. "Ellis Dorman, who runs Blossom Records over in New Jersey, says he is, I guess was, extremely talented both as a piano player and a songwriter. Mute except for those recordings from his deathbed. He appears to have total recall, a photographic memory. Keeps speaking to this girl he seemed to know when he was a teenager. He talks about kissing her, going out to San Jose to find her."

She sat up. "When?"

"All this supposedly happened over the past ten or twelve years. You've heard of the group Rick and the Riders?"

"Sure."

"According to Ellis as well as what Samuel says on the recorder, he wrote the songs for the group's breakthrough first album. He played the piano on their maiden tour that ended when, the leader, Rick, was killed in a motorcycle accident. There was some controversy about Rick taking credit for writing the songs. That's when my boss became involved. He sorted out who wanted what and got all the stakeholders to reach an agreement. Samuel remained his client off and on after that."

"The kiss, where, when? What do you know?"

Kip looked at her, taken aback by the intensity in her voice. "Here in Queens. He lived in a residence for abandoned children before he turned eighteen. We think the girl in question went to a school in the area. She read to the children in the afternoons. He says he recited some of Ralph Waldo Emerson's writings and poems to her. There's a coincidence, my ancestor showing up in this mystery. Anyway, that's the connection. Calls her Dollface on the recordings."

Her hand shot up to her mouth.

Edna knew she should be with Samuel and Dale. Her grief forced her away. It was her lost son, of course, about the same age as Samuel. Missing in action, but she knew he was dead. She didn't understand why Samuel made her think so much about her beloved Eduardo, but from the moment he arrived at the hospice house her grief had steadily flooded back. Her emotional frailty was her secret, however. She was determined not to show it to anyone.

"Archer," Kip was on his cellphone, driving as Rebecca fidgeted nervously next to him. "It's her. We're on our way to the house."

"The girl? You're certain?"

"Yes. I told her what we know and she filled in the blanks. Tell me, Archer, how does someone I met nine years ago turn out to be the very person Samuel talks about?"

"Does Edna know you're coming?"

"No. I'll call her next. We should be there in ten minutes."

"You drive. I'll call ahead and let her know. You're sure it's her?"

"Yes. I'll explain later."

"Edna, Kip thinks he's found the young woman. They're on their way and should be there any minute."

"Archer, it's too late."

"What? He passed?"

"Barely breathing. His heart rate has slowed."

"But not dead. Is he conscious?"

"In a deep coma. Even if they arrive in time, which is doubtful, Samuel won't be aware."

"Is there anything you can do?"

"I'm praying. But no, it's his time."

"Edna, I'm sorry. We did the best we could."

Last song. Once again a melody, enchantingly beautiful and the perfect conclusion to a memorable night. At first, she simply listened, letting the music inside. She turned briefly, seeing that the crowd had quieted. Something in the music signaled peace, replacing the former exuberance with attentive calm. Hands were held. Arms wrapped around shoulders, pulling bodies close to one another. Even the distant chatter from the back edges of the crowded space was silenced. She moved. This time to her left one soft step at a time. Any in her way made room for her unlike before. She didn't need to weave and jostle. It was pre-ordained.

TWENTY

K ip idled at the curb as Rebecca opened her door and hurried from the car. "I'll find a place to park and be right in," he said. She didn't hear him.

Edna held the door, looking into the face of the young woman as she came inside. The recognition was instant, the teacher she saw with the orderly classroom as she was leaving PS 0875 a few weeks earlier. Rebecca, too, recognized the woman she saw in the hallway that day.

Dale Messenger could no longer sit. Instead, he stood at the bedside and took his friend's hand in his, staring down at his face. He didn't know if he was dead or alive, but his hand was warm. Then Samuel opened his eyes ever so slightly. Messenger felt a weak squeeze before the eyes slipped to half mast.

"Sam?" he pleaded, starting to cry again.

"I've seen you before," Edna said as she ushered Rebecca to Samuel's room.

"Yes, I remember you. In the hall outside my classroom."

Ellis Dorman pulled away from the curb just after Zane climbed into the car. Traffic was heavy on Avenue of the Americas.

"Waldorf?" Dorman asked. "We can have a drink before dinner."

"Sounds good. I just had a call from Kip. He thinks he's found the girl. They should be at the house by now."

"We can head over to Queens if you prefer."

"No, I'm not good at this kind of thing. Besides, Edna says he may already be gone."

The car inched through an intersection. "Tough break. So talented. Just brilliant."

"*Was* brilliant." Zane emphasized with a shake of his head. "A while ago I was sad. Now I'm mad. He deserved better from life."

"How's Edna taking it?"

"Well, I think. His friend, that auto mechanic fellow who dropped him at the hospital, is also at the house. It's good that there are people around. Better for Edna."

They came around to the Waldorf Astoria's entrance. Ellis handed the keys to a valet then followed Zane inside. They settled on seats at the lobby bar.

"Ellis, I'm not hungry. I think I'd just like to get drunk."

"Sure, Archer. Let's do that."

As the final song echoed sweetly into the night a stillness settled over the college students. Samuel no longer controlled his fantasy as his physical presence hovered between dwindling life and oncoming death. His last conscious awareness was of his friend, Dale, opening his eyes to see his face and squeezing his hand. Then his spirit returned to that other place, more real to him than the bed upon which he lay.

He could feel her presence. She was near and he felt as if he could rise up and touch her. He was warm, content. He let his fingers dance over the keys, bringing his brilliant melody toward the end. The fantasy would not reveal the song's message to him, but he knew it was a declaration to her. He could not see or feel beyond the vision of her, touching her hand, being close. After that moment there was a void. And, as he played these final chords, the space around him grew brighter.

Kip parked two blocks away, turned off the motor, but stayed seated, staring at nothing. Everything was changed. Changed forever. He was in love. He accepted it. Gloried in it. And, he was determined to win her heart.

"How is this possible?" He asked in a whisper.

"May I speak, Archer?"

Kip stood and pushed his chair back from the table. He stepped away and began to pace, seeming to organize his thoughts. He looked down at the floor for a moment then raised his eyes to the people at the table, meeting their stares individually until he came to Rebecca and stopped.

"I like to think I am driven by facts. The plain truth, which I use to guide my speech and actions." He began to pace again, looking up at the ceiling and wall paintings, trying to form the right words. "If I encounter something that is hard to explain I dig deeper until the facts come together to make sense. I'm doing that now, but I'm having difficulty making sense of these chance connections, coincidences would be the right word, surrounding Samuel Jones. Ever since Archer asked me to help him uncover some of the mysteries of Samuel's life I have been in a state of intellectual upheaval. I suppose that upheaval is emotional as well since it led me... that is, Samuel led me to Rebecca.

"My rational mind cannot reconcile the discoveries and events that have taken place since the moment I became aware of him. How is it that Mr. Brown, Cletus," he looked at Cletus, "with no records to support it, selected the name Jones? How is it possible that it could be Samuel's real name as later proven by me? And, while I speak to you of names let me tell you about me." He paused, drawing a breath. "You all know my family name is Emerson, but do you know I am a direct descendant of Ralph Waldo Emerson?" He looked at the others, letting it sink in as some smiled and others displayed surprise, recognizing the philosopher often mentioned on Samuel's recording. "I've never paid much attention to my ancestor, nor studied his writings. I'm doing it now.

"Then there are other oddities. My undergraduate alma mater is San Jose State University in California." He came around and put his hands on Rebecca's shoulders. She reached up and warmly placed her hands on his. "That's where I met Rebecca for the first and only time before we met again these nine years later. How can it be that she is the very same girl Samuel is speaking to on his recording? That *my attempt to learn more about him led me to the woman that I, like him, longed to see again? How can it be that the principal of her high school, Sister Genevieve, was so convinced that the answer was in one those yearbooks that she insisted Archer take them? And, how can it be that I chose to page through those yearbooks, recognized Rebecca, and found her just in time?*

"These coincidences, as I call them, seem to be random. Yet, my intellect is telling me there are too many. If one or even two of these occurred I could rationalize them as my mind wants to do. But, one after another? Jones, Emerson, San Jose, Rebecca, these cannot be random like true coincidences. It has to be something more, doesn't it?

"I have never been much on religion. I attended a few services when I was very young. That's all the exposure I've had." He looked at Edna. *"In recent weeks words like 'destiny' and phrases like 'meant to be' and even 'divine intervention' have whirled around in my mind. It seems to me that something bigger surrounds Samuel Jones. That we are here in this room, describing his influence in our lives leaves me in an uncomfortable state of mind. Yet, I embrace my connection to him. How can I not when through his sudden appearance in my life,"* he squeezed gently on Rebecca's shoulders, *"everything is better."*

Edna entered the room ahead of Rebecca. Dale Messenger stepped away from the bed to make space for her examination. He nodded at the woman standing by the threshhold. She nodded back, seeing his glistening, wet cheeks.

The precise moment of death is never certain. Few professionals will admit to this because it is human nature to identify and record finality in all things. Friends and loved ones need it. It helps the mourning process. Despite sophisticated tools, including experience, a conclusion can never be absolute. There was no pulse and no breath. Edna looked at her watch and made note of the time for the report she would write later. She lifted each eyelid one last time then let them return to their half-mast position. She rose up, looked at Messenger and shook her head. He turned and stared out the window. Then Edna went over to the night stand and retrieved the recorder. She held it up for Rebecca to see.

The sorority lawn was filled to capacity when he brought his final song to an end. Applause broke out as he rose from his seat. His eyes studied every face from the back of the audience to the sides and front. As his bandmates began to pull plugs from amplifiers, he grew anxious. The partygoers ended their tribute and began to turn away. Still, he felt her presence.

Rebecca came to the bedside. He looked peaceful and despite the physical torment of the cancer, much the same as the boy she had known twelve years earlier. She took his hand.

He decided to step from the stage. She was somewhere near. He'd find her. As he turned he felt the touch of her hand. Instant recognition.

She leaned down, staring into his deathly, peaceful face.

He raised his eyes to her as all sound and movement ceased. The scene of his fantasy changed from stage, music, warm night, people all around to exquisite whiteness, peace and joy.

Rebecca brought her lips to his.

"Dollface," he whispered.

Edna and Dale heard it and came to the bedside. It had not been too late.

"He called me Dollface." She began, rising from her chair after Kip sat down. Zane recalled how she looked, just as described by Samuel in his recording. *"He would whisper it sometimes when we were alone after I'd finished reading to the children. The whisper was not a declaration of love or intimacy. It was friendship.*

Mr. Brown came looking for him one day. He ordered him to the kitchen. Then I heard myself say, 'Let him stay.' I would never be so bold and it seemed like someone else was issuing that demand, not me. Yet, it was very important to me. There was something special about Samuel. He recited Emerson to me, poems mostly and excerpts from Conduct of Life and Natural History of Intellect. I was enthralled. It's all there in his recordings. You understand what I'm saying.

"I had never encountered anyone like him, a boy my age who never spoke to anyone except secretly to me. I was flattered, but even more I was awed. In retrospect, I now recognize he was my teacher, introducing me to a philosopher he admired as a gateway to opening my mind to the deeper meanings of life. Despite our similar ages I received far more than I could ever give. He mentions our souls talking. I share that sentiment. The instant I became aware of him in that house I was drawn to him.

"He had a gentle naivete that matched my own. On that last afternoon he kissed me on the cheek. I kissed him back and then fled in a state of confusion, a seventeen year-old girl who's mind had been opened for the first time, struggling to control my adolescent thoughts. My heart, too, I think, and my soul. Until I heard his words I never realized how much that kiss meant to him. I only knew what it meant to me. Everything.

"Recently, corresponding to the weeks Samuel was under Edna's care, I had visions that entered my consciousness abruptly. I saw a musician playing music at my sorority house when I was at school in San Jose. I could hear it as clearly as I hear my voice now. I could feel him near, but I could never get close enough to see him. Once before I had this same feeling when I was a student. An unknown man was taken away by the police a short distance from the entrance to our sorority house. That was the same night I met Kip for the first time. The recordings reveal that it was Samuel. These dreams and visions, though powerful, never frightened me. The opposite is true. They made me happy. It seemed like they had a deeper importance that I couldn't quite understand, but a meaning that would bring fulfillment to my life. So, I let them come, patiently waiting. Then Kip was there, standing outside my classroom door.

"Too late, I feared. Samuel was dying and I couldn't get to him in time. There are two others in this room who heard him speak after I took his hand in mine. And, when I kissed him I understood that it was Samuel playing that music in my visions.

"Kip wants facts. I am content with the mystery. It's what Samuel means to me that matters. Before he came into my life I knew the love of two people, my mother and my father. Now, call it destiny or purpose, call it fulfillment, call contentment, call it happiness, my life is filled with the love of two more, Lacey and Kip. Samuel made that possible. Not once does he say the word love in his recording. Yet love is what he means to me."

TWENTY ONE

T he movements of a Cardinal are well-chronicled. The daily schedule of such a prominent leader is almost always an open book for the press and all those who follow his spiritual guidance. Saint Patrick's Cathedral, too, as a magnet for tourists and the faithful, is always monitored for its schedule of masses and other sacred events. Yet, at this mid-morning hour, three days following the death of Samuel Jones, only a small few knew that his Eminence, Cardinal John Wolfkawitz, was donning his vestments in the vestibule nearest the high altar.

Tourists packed the famous church, walking about from front to back, examining sculptures and marveling at Biblical art. Pews hosted the prayerful on knees or sitting in meditation, soaking up spiritual solace. No one took notice of the casket on a wheeled platform tucked discretely to the left of the altar.

Just before ten a.m. two limousines pulled up to the sidewalk in front of the stately cathedral. Their passengers, dressed in dark formal attire, emerged from each vehicle en masse, men holding doors for the women in the brilliance of a sunny January morning. Kip guided a pretty teenaged girl of particular notice because she navigated confidently with the aid of a white cane, signifying her lack of sight. Rebecca held tight to his other arm as all three mounted the steps. Archer T. Zane, his secretary, Ellis Dorman, Dale Messenger and Edna Nieves followed.

Tourists on the steps made way for the group as did the many mingling just inside. Zane led the way down the center aisle to the first pew, which had been roped off since sunrise, awaiting their arrival. At his behest, his secretary entered first followed by Rebecca, holding Lacey's hand, then Kip, Dale Messenger, Dorman, and Edna who immediately kneeled in prayer. Finally, Zane entered, but stood for a moment, watching the side of the altar where a dozen priests, wearing the vestments of their rank, formed an avenue through which Cardinal Wolfkawitz would be ushered to center stage. Satisfied that all was at the ready, he sat.

The bright red colors worn by the most powerful man of the Catholic Church in the United States, could not go unnoticed by the hundreds scattered throughout the Cathedral. Most turned to watch as he solemnly climbed the steps to the altar followed by his minions who took pre-determined positions on either side of his august presence.

Dozens of nuns, some in habits of varying shades of black, white, beige and blue denoting their orders, touring the cathedral, praying singly or in groups and suddenly recognizing their Cardinal, made the first move. They hurried to the front, taking places in pews several rows back from the mourners. Wolfkawitz raised his arms in the traditional Catholic welcome. The Funeral Mass began with the herald of the organ, summoning the attention of any who had not noticed before.

While some, who merely came to the cathedral as tourists, continued to walk about, others recognized a rare opportunity to observe and even partake of a Mass celebrated by a famous church leader. It was a once in a lifetime event for those who just happened to be present at that moment and might never see or hear a Catholic Cardinal again. They, too, began to fill the pews.

Opening prayers, repeated chants, all the trappings of a High Catholic Mass preceded the three readings and, at the conclusion of the Gospel According to Saint Mark, it was time to be seated to await the homily.

Archer T. Zane rarely attended church. Its rituals were foreign to him. He'd come to Saint Patrick's Cathedral many times, mostly escorting out-of-town clients who marked a visit to the famous edifice on their tourist 'to do' lists. During those visits he'd rarely looked up at the artwork ringing the cavernous holy space. No, as a workaholic his mind spun with legal concerns while he studied only the faces and mannerisms of his client guests, seeking an edge, a better understanding of how to serve their interests. Now, however, as he waited on the words soon to be spoken by his friend, Cardinal Wolfkawitz, he raised his eyes to all that surrounded him, including a glance over his shoulder where he was stunned to see people filling the pews. A cough here, rustling there, but even the buzz of movement and talk at the far rear had ceased. He settled back, looking briefly at Edna. Samuel Jones would be remembered. If only because a lucky few happened to be inside Saint Patrick's Cathedral when a Cardinal celebrated his Funeral Mass.

Kip held tightly to Rebecca's hand. He, like his mentor, was not a religious man, but the eerie mystery of Samuel Jones haunted him. Nine years he'd thought about the woman seated by his side, longed to see her again. From the very beginning he'd known it was love. Now she knew it, too. He'd confessed.

"I have a daughter," she told him over dinner following Samuel's death. They had stayed with Edna and Dale for several hours, watching as Edna washed her patient's body, dressed him and prepared him for transport to a nearby funeral home. "Adopted. She's seventeen and will be entering Columbia after she finishes high school this spring, straight As.

"Her name is Lacey. It took a while to fight through the red tape and obtain the approvals to adopt her. Being single and never married, the bar to adoption is much higher than for traditional couples. I met her when she was five, abandoned like Samuel, and living in the same foster house. She's a beautiful girl, blind from birth. She knew Samuel. He was good to her. It will break her heart when I tell her he's passed away."

"And you?" He remembered asking as the shock of finding her subsided to loving curiosity. "How are you feeling?"

"Confused and sad, but grateful I was able to see him in time. He made a permanent impression on me and I never forgot him. For weeks I've been having strange dreams about him. Even while I was awake my thoughts were sometimes interrupted by visions of him. It's hard to explain, but I had a feeling he was near, that he was reaching out to me somehow. That's the confusion. I need time to sort it out."

An otherwordly connection through a now deceased man brought Rebecca back into Kip's life. That was the odd happenstance of one Samuel Jones in Kip's mind. He lowered his eyes to her hand in his. How?

Edna prayed. Samuel was dead, but she would not let her sorrow interfere with this, his glorious sendoff to the afterlife. Death was the central feature of her job. Each time a patient inevitably passed on she felt a touch of sadness, but it always abated quickly as the practicalities of her calling reasserted. Not with Samuel. She knew why, of course. There was little about him, other than his similar age that reminded Edna of her son, but from the moment he came under her care she felt a connection, a maternal obligation to do right by him as she would have done for her son if only she'd had the chance. Today, Saint Patrick's Cathedral was part of that obligation, making certain that this young man was delivered into the arms of her God.

To any who had heard the Cardinal preach it was well known that he was verbose. He had a vast knowledge of his faith and its teachings, knew scripture word for word and could summon exact quotes that supported the premise of any message he sought to convey. Hence, the knowledgeable settled in for a lengthy one-way discourse curious about what he would orate and seeking insight into why he celebrated an unannounced Funeral Mass in the nation's most famous Catholic Church. The Cardinal, however, had mulled his words for days, deciding in the end to keep them brief, departing from the expected as he prayed for divine aid. "Guide me, Lord Jesus, let my words do justice to this young man I do not know and to those who have assembled to remember him that do."

"We are here to celebrate a life," Wolfkawitz began. "It is not the death of Samuel Jones that we commemorate for we know his spirit, his soul, lives on forever as promised by our heavenly Father through His Son. And, it lives on in all those who have known him whether directly or, in my case, indirectly through others. I did not meet Samuel Jones, but a man I trust and admire knew this young man, respected him and I believe cared for him in his heart in the way that Jesus, our savior, taught us.

"By all accounts Samuel Jones was extraordinary, capable of reading, understanding and remembering the contents of hundreds of volumes on any subject from philosophy to engineering and fiction to poetic verse. He was a self-taught musician, songwriter and performer. His music can be heard on records and radio played and sung by well-known artists. He traveled the oceans, visited the world's greatest cities, partook of a myriad of cultures. And yet, I am told he kept himself mute, inscrutable to everyone except when his unusual manner of speech was heard by one who cared for him in his final weeks of life.

"That we are all assembled here in this beautiful edifice is testament to the influence of his existence. Jesus teaches that we are our brother's keeper. In preparing for this homily, I sought insights from those who knew him. I was told that Samuel sacrificed for them, giving money when needed, offering patience and fortitude in their darkest hours, lifting spirits, offering solace. Although there is no official Catholic record of Samuel Jones there is an indelible spiritual record written by his Christian deeds. That is why we celebrate his life. The foundation of our faith is enriched by the memory of those who befriend others in a time of need. It transcends the boundaries of rules and archaic tradition that might otherwise trap our faith and lead it away from the core values Jesus preached. Do unto others as ye would have them do unto you. Love thy neighbor.

"We *are* all connected. We *are* our brother's keeper. Let us each remember Samuel Jones for the goodness he bestowed upon others. Let us do the same for everyone we meet. That is why I stand before you to celebrate his life, to remember him. It is my duty to my Catholic faith and it is my honor as his fellow man."

The Cardinal's elegant brevity stunned those who'd heard him speak before. An off-duty *New York Times* reporter easily wrote down the sermon word for word.

After a brief minute during which those on the altar sat in silence, looking out at the parishioners, the remainder of the Mass was celebrated. Hundreds took communion with the longest line arrayed in front of the Cardinal who whispered his blessing as he raised the host and administered this most sacred sacrament of the Catholic faith. Edna was among the first to come before him. She smiled through misty eyes as she thanked His Eminence in a low whisper only he could hear.

At the conclusion four men, Archer T. Zane, Ellis Dorman, Kip Emerson and Dale Messenger rose as the Cardinal circled the casket with raised Aspergillum and sprinkled holy water. Two priests met the men and together the six hoisted the casket and carried it through a side exit for placement into a waiting hearse. The several hundred who spontaneously entered pews to participate in the Mass stared at Cardinal Wolfkawitz as he walked the length of the aisle to the front of Saint Patrick's Cathedral. There he waited with his entourage of remaining priests as Edna and the others followed, kissed the prelate's ring and exited to the limousines.

A sidebar headline on page one of the next day's *New York Times* urged readers to turn to page eight where a description of the Funeral Mass for Samuel Jones was detailed. The article was careful not to speculate upon the unannounced rarity of such an occasion nor the surprising celebrant, the Cardinal. The article did, however, include the complete word for word homily voiced by Wolfkawitz. Two days later letters poured into the offices of both the *Times* and the Cardinal universally praising his sermon. A small few also asked for details about Samuel Jones. The Cardinal's office referred all questions to the Law Firm of Archer T. Zane & Partners. A brief biography of Samuel Jones was hastily prepared, focusing primarily upon his career in music from Rick and the Riders to session playing for classical artists such as Australian violinist, Reina Das-Whitehurst. Celebrity followed as parts of the biography appeared in the obituaries of newspapers across the country over the next several weeks.

Saint Mary's Cemetery is most peaceful in winter. Little landscaping is done during the frigid months in Flushing, Queens. The exclusive golf course nearby is closed. In the distance the sound of traffic can be heard, but it is unintrusive to those who gather for an internment. All was at the ready, the grave opened with clean tarps covering the mounds of freshly dug dirt on either side. The casket had been lowered gently into the grave and flowers of varied colors were already in the hands of the small group gathered close together. They chatted with one another as they awaited Monsignor Michael Deignan, Cardinal Wolfkawitz's chief administrator, who was designated to officiate at the graveside. The Monsignor was a serious, efficient man who entered the group solely focused on his duty. The traditional words were spoken quickly, but gracefully and then Zane walked Deignan to his car.

The others remained behind, each approaching the grave and dropping a flower onto the casket. When Zane returned Edna held a flower out to him and nodded toward the grave for him to do the same. He approached, whispered a prayer for the first time in many years, dropped the flower and returned to her side. After a few moments of silence, Edna spoke without taking her eyes off the open grave.

"My son."

Zane turned to her, confused. "Your son?"

"You wanted to know why this means so much to me."

"What about your son? Where is he?"

"The official Army notice states that he is Missing in Action in Afghanistan. That was four years ago. We waited for more information, but nothing ever came. My husband died not knowing. He was never able to say good-bye."

"What does Samuel have to do with your son?"

"Nothing really. I mean he was about the same age. Closure I guess… I don't know. I suppose his coming into my life was God's way of telling me that I must put the pain behind me. Ministering to Samuel, listening to his recordings allowed me to let Eduardo, that's my son, go."

Dale Messenger, standing nearby, involuntarily shook.

"You believe your son is dead?" Zane asked.

"Yes."

Messenger came to her side and touched her shoulder. "Private Eduardo F. Nieves?" he asked. "Eddie Nieves?"

Edna whirled to face him. "You know my Eduardo?"

Zane took a step back, listening, sensing he should not intrude.

"Afghanistan? Kandahar?"

She grabbed Messenger's arm, pulling him close and staring wide eyed into his face. "Yes! Dale, what do you know? Please, please tell me!"

"Edna, I didn't know your last name was Nieves. Eddie and me, we served together."

"I didn't plan to say anything today." Dale Messenger remained seated at his place next to Edna. *"Truth is, me and Sam, and I never knew he didn't like to be called Sam until I heard his recording, the way I feel about him is personal. I can't even form the words to get it right in my head. We worked and lived together in the same place, him helping me stay clean and making it possible for me to build my business. Why did he do that? I don't know. He just did. Just like he did those songs for Ms. Singleton and that guy Rick. That's Sam, never saying a word, but showing the way just the same.*

"I have a coincidence... I don't know, a connection through Sam that makes no sense like Kip says. I did two tours in Afghanistan. Made sergeant the second time that got cut short when my Dad got sick and I got to come home. The connection I'm talking about is with Edna." He nodded at her. *"See, she had a son named Eddie. We served together over there and he was my best friend. The army told Edna that Eddie went missing in action. Look, as far as the army sees it that's the truth under the regulations. If they don't have a body it's MIA. End of story unless a body turns up later or some high-up officer signs off on a witness report. Maybe Eddie's body will turn up, but I doubt it. I was there and I know what happened to him and the other guys in my squad. No officer is going sign off on my witness report.*

"Eddie was doing his first tour and he came into my unit ready to go. Not like some of those guys who come in green off basic training, expecting a real fight. Eddie knew the score right from the start. The Taliban? They don't stand and fight. They put a little girl on the side of the road and wait for us, hiding somewhere until we

come along on patrol and make the mistake of slowing down. Then they blow up the little girl and us, too.

"There's no honor in war. Our lieutenant colonel was just going through the motions, killing time while he earned another ribbon on his way to making full bird. The way he killed time was gambling. He played cards, threw dice and even bet on body counts with other officers at other stations. Everybody knew it. He made some money and he lost a lot of money. Sometimes, he'd call his captains in and make a game out of which of them had to cough up a unit for patrol duty. That's what he did on a Sunday morning after he'd lost a thousand bucks the night before.

"Three captains were forced to draw a card. Loser calls in his lieutenants and they draw a card. Loser gets patrol duty and picks one of his units. And, by the way, our colonel bet on the those card draws, too. This Sunday my lieutenant was the loser and he picked me and my guys to make the patrol. Thing about this is nobody needed to go out that morning. There'd been a sweep overnight. The real purpose of that run from Kandahar was delivering money to pay off the gambling debt for our colonel.

"I had a small unit, six guys. Two were green, just assigned out of basic training. The other two were transfers from non-combat units. Eddie and me were the ones who knew the score. I put one of the green guys behind the wheel and the other next to him up front. The transfers took the second row left and right and I took the rear, watching our backs. Eddie had the topside gun. Brave guy and he liked being able to see in all directions.

"An hour out and we hit the mountain road, nothing but rocks and ruts all the way up. We all knew the overnight sweep found nothing so I guess maybe we let our guard down. We came over a ridge and down around a blind corner and there she was sitting on some kind of box, maybe five or six years old, left side of the road, driver's side. Now, the M1044 we were in, you've probably heard it called a HUMVEE, but it's a lot more than that. It's got some decent armor and can handle an IED as long as we keep moving fast. But the green kid behind the wheel slows way down. I feel it, Eddie sees the girl and we both start yelling at the wheel, "MOVE! MOVE! MOVE!"

Maybe it's the confusion. Maybe it's seeing the little girl, but the kid stops right next to her. I already know what's going to happen and I duck down as much as I can just as the box she's sitting on blows up. Driver and the one in the second row directly behind - dead on the spot. The two others are hurt bad. I was praying Eddie was OK because I knew what was coming next. The M1044 was out of commission. We were sitting ducks.

"I sniffed the air to make sure we weren't leaking fuel. Otherwise, I would have had to bail out, which I didn't want to do. Dangerous to be out in the open.

"EDDIE?" I shouted, hoping he was with me.

"HERE, SARGE!" He shouts back.

"GUN?"

"WORKIN' ON IT!"

I climbed over the rows and checked my guys. Shrapnel nailed the two dead, concussion and neck contusions on the other two. I worked on'em best I could, but the bleeding was hard to stop. Both of'em had some blood coming out of their ears, too. Real bad sign, which is probably what killed'em later. I called in our position, making sure HQ knew we were immobile with casualties. Then I hunkered down in the back with as much ammo as I could gather around me. I could hear Eddie fiddling with the 50C gun topside. Then I heard it whirling around 360 degrees and I knew he had it going. Eddie Nieves was the guy you wanted on your side when a fight's coming.

They came at us in two trucks; one approaching from the rear, the other from the front. Eddie opened fire right away, which was smart because he took out the truck in front and everybody in it before they could open fire on him. I started firing at the one coming from the back, but I knew it was no good because it was out of range.

"EDDIE?" I shouted again.

"GOT IT!" He put a burst into the second truck.

I told you the M1044 had pretty good armor, but the topside gun shield is vulnerable to one thing the Taliban like to use, rocket propelled grenades. I don't know where it was fired from, but it was a direct hit on Eddie and the gun. He didn't have a chance. I called out *to him over and over, but I knew he was either dead or hurt so bad he couldn't answer. I started praying for air cover.*

"It came a couple minutes later as I watched another truck coming at me from the rear. I knew they'd target me in the back with another grenade so I climbed forward, opened the blindside doors and rolled out. A Blackhawk roared in low just as I hauled my two guys who were still alive onto the road. Four bursts and the Taliban scattered. I crawled under the M1044 and pulled the two guys in after me. One was dead. The other losing too much blood. The copter came around for another run. I heard it come in, guns bursting along the mountainside. Then it roared off and everything went quiet.

"The radio in the M1044 crackled and I could just hear HQ calling me about our situation. Then the radio went dead. I crawled out and climbed inside to respond, but I couldn't get it to work. I didn't know if the enemy was coming back, but these were my guys and I had to see about Eddie. I climbed up on a fender. Gun gone. Just a smoking, black hunk of twisted metal. All I'll say is Eddie didn't make it.

"I took a bullet...well no, my right shoulder got grazed.. Three Taliban on foot were running at me. I could barely lift my arm, but I could run and that's what I did just as the Blackhawk came in again and covered my retreat. I got away, but the Blackhawk took some hits and took off past me. I put it in my report. Why didn't the pilot stay on station? That's his mission in that situation.

"I kept running up the ridge for as long as I could until I found cover behind some rocks up high. I figured the Blackhawk would come for me, but it didn't come right away. I could see the road and the M1044 and I heard trucks coming. The first truck pushed the one Eddie had immobilized out of the way. Then four Taliban jumped out and took all the bodies including my guys and threw them in the back of a second truck and drove back up the mountain. Another bigger truck hitched up the M1044 and pulled it up behind. Everyone and everything was gone in twenty minutes. I stayed put for another half hour until I heard the Blackhawk coming. I stood and waved with my good arm, back in Kandahar getting treatment for my arm in an

hour.

"Everything I'm telling you went into my report, especially the bit about the colonel's gambling debt. It never saw the light of day. A month later I got the word about my dad being sick. I put in for a hardship discharge, which was approved in lightening speed for the Army. The day before I left I got called into the Brigadier's office. It was a one way conversation. 'Your colonel has been reassigned. No Purple Heart for your wound. I granted your discharge, but this episode never happened. Is that understood, soldier?' That was it.

"I'm telling this to all of you because I owe it to Edna and because I need to make amends. Eddie probably saved my life. He deserved to be recognized with a medal, but the Army couldn't do that without an inquiry that would have shown the colonel's dereliction of duty. Same with me getting a purple heart. I don't care about that. I do care about the unnecessary pain I caused Edna and her husband by not finding them and telling them what happened as soon as I came back to New York. Oh, I've got lots of excuses; taking care of my dad, the general's order, PTSD. None of'em pass the red face test. Edna already knows, but I'll say it again." He turned to her, tears rolling down her cheeks. "I'm sorry.

"Kip talks about coincidences. Now it's my turn. How could my knowing Sam bring me to Edna so she could get the answers about Eddie...so I could to do what I should have done before? I never thought much about fate, divine intervention, what Kip said. I think about it all the time, now. I'll never stop wondering.

"As for Sam, he helped me get my business going. He used his own money to pay for things I needed. Without him I'd be hauling bricks and doing drugs instead of sitting here with all of you. I owe him a lot and I'm going to pay him back. I listened to his recording and I wondered about what he'd want. Mr. Zane got it right with Sam's will. So, I'm going to give back every penny Sam gave to me and more. It's the least I can do for the friend he was to me."

Zane thought about the moment when Messenger finished. He recalled that the room went silent, most looking down, mulling the story and reluctant to look at Dale or Edna seated by his side. He recalled the uncomfortable awkwardness and his sidelong glance at the Cardinal.

'Help.' Zane's eyes silently communicated to his friend.

Wolfkawitz met the unspoken plea by standing and clearing his throat.

"*I believe you have all taken the opportunity to reveal how you feel about Samuel, what he did for you and what he meant to you. Perhaps I have no right to comment but we priests,*" he smiled then chuckled, "*all think we have something profound to say.*" The somber mood was broken as the others laughed with the Cardinal.

"*I don't share the special first person influence that Samuel brought into your lives. Indirectly, however, I am touched by him through your wonder at his positive presence and his good deeds. Being here today, not in an official capacity, but simply as an observer, soaking up your reminisces, is a privilege. Thank you.*"

Zane remembered that his friend's words seemed to signal an end. He recalled rising from his chair, prepared to close the luncheon, but Wolfkawitz remained standing, looking toward the windows at nothing in particular. Sensing there was more, Zane lowered to his seat again and waited with the others. The Cardinal continued to stare as he spoke.

"*I empathize with the uncertainty and confusion some of you have described. Like Kip, I wonder at the inexplicable coincidences surrounding Samuel.* The Cardinal turned and looked directly at Kip, then Dale and Edna, finally bringing his eyes to Zane. "*Fundamental to spiritual belief is faith. For some, like myself, it is trust in a benevolent spirit that guides us and aids us on our journey through life. In time of need someone or something, through the hand of God, shows the way. Inherent in faith is the suspension of logic or incontrovertible explanation. I can understand why in these times of ever increasing knowledge, acceptance of anything on mere faith is met with resistance. And, words like coincidence simply cannot fill the void.*

"*The unusual events surrounding Samuel do raise questions. In the absence of faith I'm not sure there can ever be a satisfactory explanation and to seek one may simply be fraught with frustration.*

Still, are not his good deeds fact? Is not the inspiration, happiness and fulfillment he fostered in your lives plainly visible? I think understanding might better be found over time by dwelling on the answers to these questions and remembering him as you have done today. When you face uncertainty think of him. Let his positive influence upon you be your positive influence upon others."

TWENTY TWO

"Working, Archer?" Edna stood in the doorway, jolting Zane back to the present. "On Kip's wedding day?"

"No, no." He rose slowly, taking in her dress, shoes, white gloves and smile. Then he hastened forward to greet her as she stepped inside. "You look lovely." He kissed her cheek.

"What are you doing?"

"I was listening to Samuel's recordings again." He returned to his computer and closed the program. "It's been a while since I've heard them. What time is it?"

"Bill has the car waiting. We should go." He shut down the computer and retrieved his suit coat from the closet. Edna took it from him and held it as he slid his arms into the sleeves. "Do you have your speech ready?"

He took her hand as they moved toward the door. "Yes, in my head. No worries. Really, Edna, you're beautiful."

She leaned in close with a smile. "And, you are a very handsome man."

Bride and groom beamed as they navigated gently thrown rice and rose petals to the waiting limousine. There would be an hour's interlude for picture taking before everyone would reassemble for the reception.

"Let's take a walk." Archer said as he and Edna waved the newlyweds on their way.

"Where?" Edna asked, taking his arm.

"We have some time. It's a beautiful day."

"A happy day for a stroll?"

"Yes."

They walked casually among the typically smaller August crowds of New York City. Conversation came easily with much to share about the ventures they partnered on together, especially Edna's hospice care program, which was already approved by the State of New York. A building had been leased with renovations underway per Edna's instructions. Zane secured the financing. No shortfall in sight.

"I'm interviewing consulting physicians."

"Going well?" Archer inquired.

"No issues except compassion. They're all knowledgeable, skilled and experienced. They ought to devote a year of medical school to bedside manner. The right ones will come along at some point, I hope."

Zane chuckled. "Glad I'm not a doctor under your microscope."

"What's the latest with Cletus and Sheena in Chicago?"

"Step one was to get them on a sound footing with their personal finances. Kip has that squared away. They're buying a house of their own and plan on starting their own family. Like us, they secured a larger location for the foster care facility in a nicer part of the city, which is good. The Board formed a committee to search for several more locations. Abandoned children, orphans, poverty stricken...these conditions, when brought to their attention, bring out the charity in the wealthy. Money's pouring in.

"Rebecca's project is different, what with the U.S. Department of Education's involvement. Lots of red tape. I see some legal issues, but she's working her way through them. If she hits a wall I'll make some calls and see if I can break the logjam, but she's so capable. I just don't want to interfere. If she gets these schools going ten years from now she'll be one of the most influential educators in the country. Then she'll be able to accomplish almost anything."

They entered a small park. A dozen identical white tents formed a village of crafts and trinkets for sale. They wandered through, glancing here and there without stopping. Two more blocks passed in silence. Edna raised her eyes to look at him from time to time. He had something to say. When he's ready, she decided.

Zane spoke again. "Dale is running into some resistence, too. All he wants is qualified referrals. The military still tries to sweep PTSD under a rug. He's fired up though. He'll get his way, I think."

"I like him very much," Edna answered. "He calls or stops by once a week. We talk about Eduardo and Samuel."

"All your questions answered?"

"I have my answers, yes. I'm proud of my son. I know what happened. He was brave to the end. I'll always mourn his loss and my husband's heartbreak and death, but, I feel content, knowing my son and his father are together, now."

"In heaven?"

"Yes, that's what I believe."

Another period of quiet as they traversed past Rockefeller Center and on to Madison and Fifth. "Would you care to stop into Saint Patrick's?" he asked.

Edna looked across the intersection. "That would be nice." She slipped her arm from his and took his hand as they crossed.

"The wedding today, Kip is very happy. Rebecca, too. She looks utterly radiant." Edna let him continue, squeezing his hand in agreement. "You and I, we enjoy each other's company wouldn't you say?"

"Yes, Archer, very much." This is what he wants to say.

"I wonder," he hesitated, "I mean it feels so special."

"Pleasant?"

"Yes, but I care deeply for you, Edna. I don't want to relegate what I feel to a word as simple as pleasant. It's more than that to me. I hope it's the same for you."

She didn't hesitate. "It is, Archer."

They came to the steps of Saint Patrick's. He stopped and turned to look at her. "I want to be with you everyday and every night."

She knew what he meant, but needed a moment to collect herself. "What are you trying to say to me?"

He turned away and spoke without looking at her. "I'm afraid, Edna. I wasn't a very good husband or father. I don't know how to make up for that."

She heard his vulnerability. Archer, with whom she had grown deeply attached, feared her response. She reached up with her white gloved hand and turned his face to her. She looked into his eyes. "My sweet, Archer. I want to be with you for the rest of my life."

A heave of air burst from his lungs as his body relaxed and his eyes brightened. He released her hand and put is arm around her shoulders, pulling her close. In a more private setting it would have been a passionate kiss, the truth between them settled, their future together sealed. "Let's go inside."

Stands of votive candles in red or white are everywhere in Saint Patrick's, a few fronted by padded kneelers where the faithful offer up personal petitions. Most of the arrays are anonymously sponsored, but a few carry plaques identifying the people or institutions that made them possible. They approached two newer, ornate banks of candles that had recently been added, each with a small bronze plaque bearing a name and a few words of explanation. Zane took two twenty dollar bills from his pocket and inserted one in each of the offering slots. He selected two delicate wooden sticks from a tiny sand filled metal box, handed one to Edna and together they gently lit them from the flame of one of the candles. Edna moved off and held her stick to a fresh candle in the array on the left. When lit, she gently pressed the stick back into the sand, snuffing the lit end. She knelt down and folded her hands together, pausing to look up at the plaque before saying her prayer:

Eduardo Luis Nieves
Private First Class, United States Army
In loving Memory

Archer T. Zane also lit a fresh candle, kneeled and read the plaque above the array in front of him:

In Memory of Samuel Jones

The name was followed by an excerpt from the sermon delivered by Cardinal John Wolfkawitz. Zane read the words that meant the most to him:

We are all connected. We are our brother's keeper.

ABOUT THE AUTHOR

D. P. Macbeth

D. P. Macbeth is the author of four novels: The Silent Savant, AT 29: When Saturn Returns (Book One and Book Two), and the soon to be released titles, That 1970 Summer and BUCKMAN
He is currently researching the 18th and 19th century lives of his ancestors in South Carolina in anticipation of a non-fiction title.